Wiser Guys

D.R. Perry

Wiser Guys

By D.R. Perry

Cover Design by: James Ruggiero

Historical Consultant: Jared Leitzel

First Edition

The Tower. The Hanged Man. The Fool.

Bill and Millie Chiavo are at a crossroads. Just coming into their magic, the twins must choose their fate. Do they take the easy path? Or protect their friends and loved ones?

Wisdom comes at a cost; its magical power changes everything.

It's 1929 at the height of Prohibition in Plymouth, Massachussets. The stock market crashes, leaving the Chiavos in the poor house. Uncle Finn's Sight tipped him off but he kept it all to himself.

Finn's got money, powers, and connections with Boston to cement his victory. However, the Italian-run Speakeasy draws new players from the deck to oppose him. Magic, monsters, and mobsters will clash in this small town but the outcome is unclear.

How will Bill and Millie defy a man who sees the future?

Read Wiser Guys to find out.

A rattle, a bang, and a thud came from the kitchen. Bill and Millie Chiavo slapped their rummy hands face-down on the table almost in unison. They jumped up at the same time too, but Millie made it to the door before Bill even though he was closer. She was faster than Bill at everything. He knew it was to make up for the fact that he'd arrived on this earth two and a half minutes before she did.

Their mother sat with her back against the icebox on the floor with an open mouth and wider eyes, clutching the Boston Globe's morning edition to her chest. Millie stepped over the puddle of hot water and the pot it had sloshed out of to shut off the stove. Bill winced as her toe made contact with the puddle. She didn't flinch even though he knew she was already getting a blister.

"Mom, get up." Bill held his hand out to the woman on the floor. She looked up at him and blinked, leaking tears from the corners of her eyes. Mom didn't take his hand, but stood and stepped away from the stove.

"What happened?" Millie had already refilled the pot with water from the tap. She started picking vegetables up off the floor. "These potatoes are probably still edible, but the peas not so much. Mama?" Bill usually got annoyed when Millie called their mother that, but he was worried enough to brush it off. "Mom. What is it?"

"Bad news." Mom spread the paper out on the table with fluttering hands. "Bad for us, and so many more. It's going to change this town. America, too. Harder times are here again."

Bill glanced at Millie, trying to get a look at her face. She was blocking him, and he wanted to know if she thought this was something Mom had Seen or just a case of the vapors. His twin was occupied chasing peas and carrots around the floor with a broom and dustpan. He peered at the headline instead of helping. All the same, Bill would insist he was as good a brother as the day was long.

"Margin Account Dumping Brings Stock Crash," Bill read aloud. He glanced at his mother again. Her gaze rested on the paper's date, October 24th, but remained unfocused. She might have gotten one of the visions her partial Wisdom hit her with sometimes. The brush-tap of sweeping stopped and the dustpan clattered against the rim of the bin.

"But they don't mean our stocks, right Mom?" Millie put her free hand on one of their mother's shoulders.

"Your father would know for certain," said Mom. "We were in trouble already, hadn't lost everything earlier this week, but now—" Their mother sighed, one hand dropping to the table beside the paper. "Who knows?"

This time, Millie locked eyes with Bill. Neither of them had come into any Mind Wisdom yet, so they couldn't do any of the things Dad had taught Bill about.

Still, they'd always had more of a sense of each other than mundane twins. Bill and Millie didn't need to hop minds or send words at each other to agree that their mother had Seen something other people without some kind of Wisdom could not.

"Here comes my brother," said Mom. "Go to the front door and let your Uncle Finn in, William." She patted her hair, then tucked a stray strand behind one ear. "Please."

"Yes, Mom." Bill walked out of the kitchen and down the hall past the parlor, even though there'd been no knock at the door.

Uncle Finn was Sight Wise, having come into the full set of his abilities when he was seventeen. He used to tell stories, back before he'd become a shut-in, about the things his Sight showed him. He also used to smile like a person instead of a shark.

It wasn't until they were six that his Sight eroded his morals enough for the twins and all the other Wise children to fear him. He'd Seen the soldier at the door a week before he came with the Army's letter of condolence. He'd smiled while telling her that their baby brother Tim had died at the Battle of Sambres in the Great War.

Bill knew Uncle Finn made Millie just as nervous as him. She stood at the stove, adding stock and seasonings to the pot of future soup with a stiff back and rigid arms. Easy for her. She wouldn't have to answer the door for their Uncle. Finn could choose to See a future thread leading from any person who spoke the wrong way to him.

"Millicent." Mother stood and smoothed her skirt. "Put some tea on, please."

Bill heard his sister start filling the teakettle as he left the kitchen. Millie would have to be around Finn after all, a thought that made Bill uneasy. Mother's brief flashes of Sight came from objects and only when she wasn't trying to look at the future. She couldn't direct them either, for some convoluted reason Bill didn't understand.

That was the way partial Wisdom worked. Its limitations were all in the scope of power, not backlashes like the fully Wise had to deal with. Uncle Finn's arrival could come any time in the next five minutes or five hours.

A floorboard creaked out on the front porch. Someone stood on the porch, but it wasn't Uncle Finn. That floorboard noise was a signal. There was only one person besides his sister who used that squeaky old board to communicate. He opened the door.

"Gil." Bill smiled at his best friend.

"Hey-o, Billy-o." Gilbert grinned back. Bill loved that grin.

"Much as I'm happy to see you, this is a bad time." Bill wrinkled his nose. "We're expecting someone else."

"I know it's not the best of times." Gilbert cracked a grin at his own joke. "But is it the worst of times?"

"Maybe." Bill wanted to hold the door open and let his best friend in, but didn't want Gil's wit and natural chattiness to get him into trouble. "Mother Saw something bad and then something worse. Uncle Finn's on his way over here."

Gilbert was from a Wise family too, so he'd learned to hear all those capital letters. With his sister and Gil, it always felt like a cool secret code instead of a way to keep separate from the mundanes.

"Jeepers Creepers. What'd she touch?" They didn't have Sight in Gilbert's family, but he knew the basics, just like every kid in this generation of Plymouth's Wise.

"The Boston Globe."

"Ouch. I read it earlier. That market crash is something to take seriously then? Dad's back home laughing with Mom about it, making paper boats out of the front page and calling them the SS Chicken Little." Gilbert and his whole family tended to take most things lightly. It came with the territory for Wood Wise, whose talents let them nurture, grow, and get information from any type of flora.

The backlash from using their Wisdom to revive dead plants was a dizzy sort of forgetfulness. They tried to make as many good memories as possible because they'd have no control over which ones they lost.

"Go home and tell him to re-name those boats Titanic and Lusitania. Mom dropped a boiling soup pot just because she touched the front page."

"Wow. Must be a doozie, then." Gil turned to leave, then stopped and glanced back over his shoulder. "Put the left curtain down when you want me to come back."

"Will do." Bill watched Gilbert go down the walk. His friend raised a hand in a gesture of farewell without looking back again, then crossed the street to his house without looking both ways. Typical. Bill waited at the door until Gilbert went inside. He thought again about declaring his feelings, but pushed the idea from his mind. Too much was going on to think much about something like that, let alone act on it.

Bill stepped back from the door so he could swing it shut. Before he did, a shiny bottle-green roadster he'd never seen before came slowly up the street, coming to a stop right in front of the house. The driver carried a wiry strength on his medium frame and wore a tan suit punctuated by black accents. The man nobody wanted to see approached the house.

"Hey, little shaver." He tipped the brim of the tan trilby perched atop his head of salt-and-pepper hair. "I already knew my sister and her dago family would be expecting me. Bet your piggy bank there's tea on. Let me in, little pal."

Bill stepped aside without speaking and of course, his uncle dropped him a wink. All he could think about was the story of how wolf blew all those houses down. As if on cue, the kettle screamed out in a protest Bill couldn't give voice to. The whole morning had unwound like a reel of good news for people who like bad news. The fact of Uncle Finn's happy camper demeanor might just be the worst of the lot.

Millie wished she could be invisible and serve tea from the tray. She thought maybe she'd better wish for inaudibility also, under the circumstances. Uncle Finn got more dangerous the more someone talked to him. Millie had gotten herself in trouble with him before by running her mouth.

Dad took a serious risk even letting their uncle into the house, which was why she'd agreed to stay and play tea hostess. One way to avoid Finn's Sight was by answering all of his questions as though speaking to someone else. Mom was still reeling from the morning's visions and Bill had run interference the last time Finn paid a visit. Millie was up but felt like Casey at the bat after he'd struck out.

"Ownership of this house reverts to me if you can't pay the taxes on all of the property," said Finn. He leaned forward menacingly in his heat, chest puffing out like one of Rachel's roosters.

"Possession is nine-tenths of the law, Millicent, did you know that?" Dad put his hand over his mouth as though stifling a yawn. Even though his frail frame rested in a nest of blankets, she still thought him more powerful than Uncle Finn. All the Wise families in town knew it, too.

"The will is in my possession and you you're walking a thin line with the finances after today, Giuseppe. Still, I'm willing to let my sister stay here after I move in. I've got deals in the works with people from Boston. People who, by rights, would have had their way back in 1922 if you hadn't interfered." Finn puffed his cigar. "You know my terms."

"It's unfortunate, Millie, that your Uncle does not recall the reasons I can't agree to them." Dad took the cup of hot tea Millie held out to him, wrinkled hands curled around it like a pair of crispy brown autumn leaves. She was glad she'd only filled it half way as she watched the surface of the liquid ripple with the tremors that plagued him.

"You've spent sixteen years teaching your boy, time you could have spent avoiding this situation instead," said Finn.

"Your Uncle knew precisely how and why I wouldn't avoid it. He's known every move I'd make since the night we met but never why." A grin stretched across Father's face. He closed his mouth over a cough, then sipped the tea. "And I've managed to help others surprise him because of it."

"Enlighten me then," said Uncle Finn. His tea cup had remained on the tray since Millie poured it, but he picked it up now and took a sip. He never drank or ate anything until someone else tasted it first. Over the years, her uncle had collected irrational fears like other men collected stamps or coins. His obsessions had grown harsh and inhumane, making him expect the worst from everyone else in the process. Only objects he desired were immune from his judgment. Such was the cost of his Sight.

Dad didn't speak, just shook his head and grinned again. A draft from somewhere stirred the fine wisps of white hair that still sparsely graced his skull. She'd known her whole life that rapid aging was the cost of altering memories with Mind Wisdom, but it still seemed more harsh a penalty than any other family's. Anyone meeting Father for the first time today might guess his age at over seventy. He had turned thirty-five this past September.

"The tea is especially soothing today, Millicent. Thank you." Millie heard a squeaking sound as Uncle Finn ground his teeth. Father's grin turned into a smile. Millie gasped a moment before her Uncle's teacup shattered in his grip.

"The winds of change are whipping up a storm here in Plymouth. You're directly in its path." Uncle Finn brushed shards of china from his hands casually, as though crushing other peoples' dinnerware was an everyday thing for him. The sharp bits had barely scuffed his callused hands. "My Sight advises you to get out of town and my way as soon as possible. You waste time, Giuseppe."

"One man's waste is another man's want. The grass is always greener. Having is overrated. The best things in life are free, but freedom isn't." Another way around Finn's Sight was to use quotes or adages. Father's stubborn optimism beamed through the room like a sunrise. Millie couldn't help it. She chuckled, then covered her mouth with both hands.

"What's so funny?" Uncle Finn punctuated his words with the three steps he took to stand in her face. This time, Millie didn't think of a rooster. Finn snarled like a cornered badger. A sort of miasma clung around her Uncle that reminded her of a smell, though it nothing so physical. That not-scent got stronger just as his hand closed around her wrist.

"Mr. Chiavo, please pardon me." A familiar feminine voice came from the hallway just over her left shoulder. Rachel Howe, Millie's closest female friend. "I've brought the vegetables and would like Miss Millie's help bringing them in."

"Go, Miss Millie," mocked Uncle Finn. "Go and help your farm girl friend. You'll need that kind of work experience soon enough when I own and run your house and this town. The Italians have controlled it long enough." His lips twisted into a cruel smile, and he let go of her wrist.

Millie frowned down at the reddening imprint his fingers had left on her skin. She wanted desperately to get away from her uncle, but didn't want to leave Father alone with him. She couldn't think and hesitated instead of leaving with Rachel.

"Don't worry, Millicent. Your Uncle will show himself out, I'm sure. It's been a lovely tea, but for now this weary old man needs a nap."

Uncle Finn lingered, looming between Millie and her father until Bill's footsteps sounded on the stairs. "This isn't over, Giuseppe. I'll be back with my friends and you won't like the kind of meeting they'll want to have with you."

"That sounds lovely, my old friend." Father gently placed his tea cup on the tray, masterfully deflecting both Finn's threats and his Sight. He'd replied in the third possible evasive manner, by fashioning his words in response to something Finn hadn't actually said. "Until then."

Millie was almost to the kitchen when the door slammed behind her uncle. She jumped, then choked out a floodgate-opening sob. Rachel put her arm around Millie's shoulder, making concerned and comforting noises. Millie wondered why she got the impression that Rachel was confused but just as frightened as she was herself. That only ever happened with Bill before.

"There's a dead teacup all over the floor in there. What happened?" asked Bill. He followed the girls into the kitchen.

Millie waited until the door shut to answer him. "He's trying to get Father to agree to whatever it is he keeps asking for again. He's got friends now, from Boston even, and we apparently don't. According to him, we've got no money, either. Father fended him off as usual, but he took it much harder than the last time."

"I'll say," said Rachel. "Last time he didn't dare lay a finger on you."

"Rachel!" Millie couldn't believe her friend would spilled the beans like that. Usually Rachel kept secrets like dragons hoarded gold.

"He did what?" The outrage in Bill's voice sounded so similar to Uncle Finn's that Millie went weak in the knees. She managed to get to one of the chairs before ending up on the floor like Mom had this morning, sans visions.

"He had her by the wrist," said Rachel. Millie's trust in her was running out like the sand in the egg timer they kept on the shelf above the stove. Rachel blushed, too. Good. She should be embarrassed while ratting someone out. "Look, there's even a bruise."

Millie glanced down and sure enough there was a thumb-shaped purple mark on the inside of her left wrist.

"Oh please." She rolled her eyes. "I've had worse falling out of trees a few years ago. We should go and clean up that cup before Dad tries to and has a fall."

"Let me see it." Bill leaned over to get a better look at the most unimpressive bruise in New England. While he did, his arm brushed in passing against Rachel's bosom. The blush deepened until her skin was a shade that made her barely remembered Algonquian ancestry unmistakable. Millie immediately understood that Rachel's blushing had been from an embarrassment unrelated to ratting out a friend.

Bill didn't even notice what had happened, or Rachel's reaction. He never noticed Rachel the way almost all the other boys their age did. A tap came from behind her on one of the glass panes in the side door. Bill glanced up and his face blossomed in a sunrise smile the way Father's did. Rachel made a small gasp and started to smile back. Then she followed Bill's gaze and cast her eyes toward the floor.

A rush of cold air came in the door with a male voice chiming a greeting they'd used since they were old enough to cross the street together.

"*Ciao bella,*" said Gilbert.

Bill had smiled at Gil Elmwood. Of course. Bill must have been upstairs closing the curtain to let their friend know Uncle Finn had left the building.

"Nice try but ugh, your accent." Bill responded with their old childhood countersign, a gleam in her brother's eye. He gazed at Gilbert the way young men did at her sometimes.

"I'll go and look in on your father." Rachel took the broom and dustpan off their hook next to the pantry. "Do some sweeping, too."

"Thanks, Rachel," said Millie.

Bill barely acknowledged she'd left the room, too occupied with filling Gilbert in on the Uncle Finn report. She got up to snag and carry bushels of turnips, potatoes, and onions down to the root cellar while they talked. When she finished, Millie went back toward the table to sit down.

"Go help Rachel finish up in there and bring her back," said Gilbert. "She should hear this. I should probably go down the street for Theo or Sarah, too. This is big, not to mention secret."

"If it's so hush hush, we should probably talk about it at Theo's," Millie said. "I'm not trying to be difficult, but if Dad's awake, nothing's hidden in this house."

"Oops, forgot." Gilbert tapped his temple. He was more absent-minded than he used to be before his Wisdom had come in. "Thanks for pointing that out."

Rachel came back in with a rattling paper bag as well as the broom and dust pan.

"It's all swept up. Your father said he'd like to spend some time reading in the parlor, so I also fetched his book." She peered at the empty space by the door. "Where'd the vegetables go?"

"I put them downstairs," Millie took her coat off the hook by the door. "We're going to Theo's. Come along, okay?"

Rachel and Bill got their coats, and they headed out into the chilly morning air.

Theodore and Sarah Webster lived in a house almost as old as the Chiavo's, but smaller and shabbier. Fire Wise had talents and temperament that tended to lose money rather than gain it in this day and age. Sight could help predict future events. Mind-reading could help negotiate sales and contracts. Fire just burned things. Only smithing was a viable profession for them and that had gone by the wayside since the rise of industrialization and the automobile. Bill felt sorry for them.

Theo's younger sister Sarah came around the side of the house before they knocked on the door. She wore her typically distracted expression and a faded mustard-colored woolen dress a size too big for her. Sarah avoided paying much attention to people in general. Her preference was for graphs, equations, and numbers.

Sarah Webster should have been a grade behind the others but her brains had earned her early advancement. The only reason Sarah hadn't graduated already was that they had to mail her arithmetic work out to a Professor at Radcliffe. The Primary School teachers in Plymouth weren't up to the challenge of reading her papers on Gaussian curves or imaginary numbers.

"Oh, hello," said Sarah. "Mama can't have any guests inside the house. Pop said it's better if she cools off before seeing anyone else today. Theo and I have been back in the old smithy since dawn if you want to join us." She turned and went back the way she'd come. Bill followed her, knowing the rest would go where he went.

The old smithy sat to the west of the house and slightly behind it. Mr. Webster talked every winter about converting it into more living space, but never got around to it. The floor was dirt, no weeds or plants grew around it thanks to the Elmwoods. Its walls were brick and the chimney fieldstone. Though no fire burned in the furnace it seemed warm when they went inside. Whatever upset Mrs. Webster had also angered Theo. He was the first of them to gain his full Wisdom.

Theo leaned on the anvil in front of the furnace with his back to the door and sighed. "Go away, Sarah."

"Everyone came over, though. I think you should talk to them about it." Sarah turned her back, beginning to head past the others and out the door. "Anyway, I'll see you later."

"If I'm staying, so are you, Sarah. And what do you mean by everyone?" Theo turned around. He scanned Bill's and Gilbert's faces with an expression that would have seemed at home on a sleepy lion, but that stopped when he saw Millie and Rachel. Both sides of his mouth still turned slightly downward in a moody pout, but his eyes crinkled at the corners. He stood up straight to give the full effect of his stature and broad-shouldered physique. "I'd say good morning, ladies, but it's been no such thing."

Bill was used to watching his sister and just about any other woman simper around Theo Webster. You could tell by looking at him that he came from a line of blacksmiths, but since that wasn't the family business anymore, he had none of the burns or scars that usually came with that profession. He'd also gotten his mother's pale skin and full lips, but those had gone to Sarah instead, freckles and all.

Theo's hair was almost black with hints of red when he was in direct sunlight. The man could have posed for a classical painting, but Bill always wondered why he felt like the only person put off by Theo's broody persona. Sarah had the same taciturn disposition and nothing like the same popularity. The most important thing he'd learned from the Websters was the remarkable advantage of beauty on opinion.

"So, which did you get from Finn Mullins this morning? A visit or just a letter?" Gilbert kept his tone casual and more light-hearted than usual, but the air warmed all the same.

"If you came to mock our troubles with that bottom-feeder—" All hints of friendliness fled from Theo's voice.

"Commiserate, is more like it," said Bill. "He was at our house just now, threatening us with my grandfather's will and his Boston friends. Gilbert had something to tell us, but wanted to wait until we were all together."

"Fine, Gil," said Theo. "Do what Elmwoods do best. Talk."

"Well, like Billy-o said, Mullins went to his house this morning. Drove up in a mint new roadster, had on his

Sunday Best. Got in a property rights argument with Mr. C, then scared our Millie half out of her gourd by doing this." Gilbert pointed at Millie's left arm until she rolled her eyes and held her hand palm up. Then she winced, eyes wide.

"That seedy, yellow-bellied, son of a—" The air got hotter, chokingly so, as Theo moved to get a closer look at Millie's wrist. The mark had swelled up and darkened until it resembled a purple robin's egg. And she'd tried to brush it off as nothing, of course. Typical.

"She needs cold, not heat," said Sarah. She stepped between her brother and Millie, looking Theo in the eyes. Sarah was a mousy slip of a girl, timid most of the time except where her temperamental brother was concerned. Up until now, Bill had always thought it was because she knew Theo could never hurt his own sister, but he understood better now. It was the other way around. He saw what she must have always known, that Theo needed protecting from his own temper, especially with full Wisdom. "Make the temperature go the other way, Theo, like Mother taught you."

"You're right, Sare." Theo closed his eyes, then took a deep breath. As he exhaled, he counted to ten. The heat in the smithy went back to something more sensible on a late October morning. "Let me see that bruise, Millie."

"Okay," said Millie. Her shoulders tightened and hunched the way they always did when she got nervous, but she held her arm out toward him anyway. He put one hand under it and held the other one just above the bruise. They both smiled down at her arm and her hands. "Oh! Cold!" She laughed.

"Better?" Theo asked. He looked up from her hands as he spoke, and their eyes met. Millie nodded, dark brown curls bouncing around her sparkling blue eyes. Blotchy patches of crimson bloomed on Theo's neck and he pulled his hands away from Millie's arm. Bill knew what that kind of attraction looked like, but up until now he hadn't seen it directed at his own sister. He suddenly needed to divert attention away from that little exchange. He wasn't sure why it made him uncomfortable.

"Now that everyone's a little bit cooler, let's finish talking about my uncle," said Bill. "Gilbert?"

"Right." Gilbert nodded. "Finn Mullins didn't grace my house with a visit. We'd had a letter. Some of you know and some of you don't. The houses on this street are owned by the families that live in them. But the land is on the deed that goes with the Chiavo place. Technically, everyone on this street leases the land, even though Giuseppe set the rent at zero dollars. So if Mullins gets his hooks into that Chiavo property, he can price all of us out by increasing the rent. We'll be over a barrel. And if his friends from Boston horn in here, Finn will have us working for them and paying for the privilege."

"We're not on your street," said Rachel. "How does this affect us?"

"Your family's farm isn't part of the parcel," said Gilbert. "But you know how my mother's your oldest sister? She's got her heart set on moving back in there now that she might have to pay rent."

Rachel's mouth dropped open in outrage. "But we're

all doubled up in there as it is! No one even has a bed to themselves!"

Gilbert nodded sympathetically. "At least my Pa could help with lumber for additions to your house. But wasn't there a problem last year when they were going to do that? Couldn't get a permit to build an addition or outbuilding, if I remember correctly. Well, Pa told Ma this morning that Mullins has a mundane buddy from that Gentleman's Club working in the town planning office. Said the buddy likes games of chance more than dock workers like their hooch."

"It looks like he's been planning all this for a long time." Bill decided to share his worries with the group. "We don't know what kinds of things he's Seen. Considering he's gotten more paranoid over the last few years, we should assume he's been going behind our parents' backs for at least that long. There might be more nasty surprises coming. We know he's watching our parents. Probably you and Gilbert too, Theo, since you got your Wisdom. He might think they'll try and foil him somehow. But he pretty much ignores the rest of us kids." Bill didn't mention Millie's arm again. "We can find things out so our parents won't be flying blind."

"It keeps on coming back to a problem of money." asked Rachel. "He said Mr. Chiavo didn't have any on the same morning all the papers are full of headlines about the stock market. If part of his planning's based on that, we could make things harder for him by making our own wages."

"If it were summer," said Gilbert, "that would be a good point. I could start throwing my Wisdom around down on the farm and get you a bumper crop. But it's almost November. Not much I can do until spring."

"Some of us have to start heading to school, anyway," said Millie. "We can think more during the day and talk about it later. Sarah, go and get your books. We'll walk together."

"We can meet back here after supper," said Theo. "I can go down to Town Hall to look up some deeds and property records. Maybe there's an old loophole or something Finn forgot about."

"I'll go to Pilgrim Hall," said Gilbert. "I know it's a boring museum we've all seen the exhibits in, but they have archives. If there's a discrepancy between those and the ones in Town Hall, we'll want to know."

"We're canning at home all day," said Rachel, "but that means I'll be with Gran and she loves spinning yarns. I'll ask her everything she knows about the past generations of Mullinses. Maybe she knows something useful about countering Sight Wise."

Bill wished he could do more than sit in a classroom all day, but that was just part of his life for the rest of the year, family feuds or no. He'd check the library if he got the chance.

Salvatore Tucci didn't make mistakes, he just had learning experiences. After last time, he went out of his way to make an appointment with Esmerelda Cavalcante. He sat at a table near the swinging double doors to the kitchen, waiting.

The Plymouth Supper Club practically stood at attention with a crisp kind of class. White starched tablecloths and little gilded vases with a red and a white carnation adorned each table. Gleaming polished brass railings marked out the boundaries between seating sections. Wood paneling practically blushed with deep stain, polished to the point where murky reflections lingered on each wall. Pine hardwood graced the floors except for the area directly in front of the upright piano where bi-color parquet lay in wait for future dancing feet.

This place wasn't half so nice seven years ago. That was back before Raul Cavalcante got himself clipped over some bootlegging dispute with the Irish and nearly lost Giacomo Bianco his foothold here. Raul used to drink as much as his patrons did, and didn't put much of his own take back into the place. His widow ended up making a supply agreement with the Boss of Fall River, who also happened to be her cousin.

Everyone assumed Giacomo Bianco must be giving Esmerelda business advice, but Sal Tucci suspected otherwise. He'd watched the place for a month and had never seen Bianco himself. The only one of the Fall River guys he'd seen was the rumrunner, and he wasn't even a made man. Then again, Sal had his own shortcomings, secret for now.

"Thanks, doll." Even through the kitchen doors, that term of endearment sounded fresh and new in a woman's voice. "When will I see your gorgeous mug again?"

The doors swung open, revealing a handsome bronze-skinned man in his mid twenties. Now that Sal saw him close up his half Italian blood was unmistakable, which finally explained why he was no wise guy. Pomaded slicked back his black hair and strong cologne shunted every other scent out of Sal's nostrils.

"Just call when you're running low, smartie," said the man. He glanced at Sal. If he was surprised to see another fellow here his face didn't show it. "Your cousin will send me back with more supplies."

"You'll have me calling every night if you aren't careful, Jimmy!" Esmerelda's gaze stayed below Jimmy's belt. There was confirmation of one rumor at least. Esmerelda liked banter with the gigolos. His hope for a good outcome for this meeting decreased.

"Homely" was the kindest way to describe Sal Tucci's borrowed looks. The face had a Roman schnoz plus a physique indicating a lifelong love of baked ziti. He'd have to hope good manners and charm would be enough to sway Ms. Cavalcante Sal couldn't change his appearance at this point without hopping a boat to Providence or Boston for a prettier full-blood Italian. The time for that had come and gone.

At least he'd invested in some snazzy suits in this body's size. Seven of them hung from a pipe at the room Sal rented, each a different shade of purple, his signature color. It wasn't red or blue, but something else entirely. A color between two primary ones suited a man like Sal Tucci, who had hands and feet in different worlds.

Ms. Cavalcante probably wouldn't win any beauty contests either. That had more to do with her audacity in running this business and her taste in clothes than anything else. Bobbed ash brown hair brushed her chin on either side like wings of a mourning dove, lustrous and thick and healthy with just a touch of gray at the temples. An aquiline nose divided bloodshot eyes with honey-brown irises. These sparkled with more intelligence than most men generally liked. Sal was different from most men.

An of-the-moment drop-waisted dress that skimmed Esmeralda's physique, but it was made of garish fabric in fuchsia and green paisley print. The colors tried to compensate for her own naturally muted coloring. Sal could relate. He spent much of his time thinking about what else he could be beyond what nature intended.

Sal waited until Jimmy had left the building. Esmeralda turned back toward the double doors and began walking toward the kitchen without even acknowledging his presence. Instead of tolerating her dismissal, he stood up, smiled, and gave her a slight bow.

"Ms. Cavalcante. My name is Salvatore Tucci, here for our nine o'clock appointment." He tried to suck in his too-large gut and hoped his brow hadn't perspired too much.

"Hmm." She tilted her head to the left, then the right, like an antiques appraiser. "Call me Esmeralda for now. That may change depending on what you have to say. Mr. Tucci." He waited for her to either sit at his table or invite him into her office. She did neither. Her expression reminded him of his mother's while considering discounted produce at the market; unimpressed. "Well? You've got five minutes of my time. Use them wisely."

"You might not remember the name Tucci, Esmeralda, but your late husband would have. My father was Louie Tucci and he worked with Raul for a long time, before the two of you took over this operation."

"Louie? Sure, I remember Raul's old pal Louie. The man taught my husband almost everything I ended up learning about this business. But he died seven years ago, if I remember correctly."

"You do, Esmeralda." Sal tried not to wring his hands or rub them on his jacket as usual when his nerves got to him. "My dad was supposed to continue working for Raul and you once this place got established, but he never got the chance."

"Yeah, okay. But you didn't make an appointment just to gab about your old man. You came here for a reason and I'll have it out of you. Spill it, already." She looked at her watch. "You've got two minutes now."

"You still don't have an enforcer. I learned everything I know about this business from my dad. You considered him an asset and wouldn't you like another? I have the money to buy my way in."

"Well." Esmeralda smiled. "That wasn't what I expected to hear. Your proposition is interesting and I'd like to say I'll think about it because I remember old Louie so fondly. But one important ingredient is missing from your pitch. Why now?"

"Excuse me?" Sal almost heard a little echoing sound as the other shoe dropped.

"If you were so hot to work in this Supper Club seven years ago, why'd you only come here now? You were old enough to step up and fill his shoes then if I'm any judge of a man's age. God knows I could have used the help all this time. So, where have you been?"

Sal couldn't tell her about his borrowed body. He knew she must think it had something to do with the police, maybe even J. Edgar Hoover. She'd be wrong. But it didn't change the fact that the reason he hadn't come to Plymouth directly after his father's death was that he'd been too young. How did you tell a prospective employer that the only reason you looked older than her is because you borrowed a body? The answer was, you didn't. She'd have to either accept that and him, or turn down his offer.

"I can't say, but I can promise you I wasn't with any law enforcement agency." At least he hadn't lied.

"Sorry, Mr. Tucci, but that's not enough. You'll need

to find someone to vouch for you, a person I can trust. You can come back to see me once you have that kind of good word. No hard feelings?" She held out one hand.

"Of course not, Ms. Cavalcante." Sal clasped her hand firmly in one of his, and pumped three times, exactly as he'd do if she were a man.

She blinked. Esmeralda must have been used to most guys going overboard to make her feel girlish. But Sal took Ms. Cavalcante for what she was; a shrewd business owner. It's how he'd want to be treated if he were a woman in her position, after all. Thank God he had the power not to be one.

"No hard feelings." Now that right there was a lie to shame the Devil himself. And his feelings? Those were like diamonds, hard and precious, too.

Sal would regroup his efforts, recruit an ally or few. He'd fully expected Esmeralda to play like a man and the challenge that presented only urged Sal to meet it with relish. He'd mastered that game, after all, and looked forward to pitting his skill against a formidable opponent like Ms. Cavalcante.

Sal headed back toward the rooming house he'd been staying in. Plymouth was picturesque, even in late October when most of the foliage was gone. As he turned the corner, he could see the service entrance to the Supper Club. A couple of strapping young men hung around the back, loitering and laughing over the funny pages from the newspaper. That's what Esmeralda Cavalcante wanted working for her. Young bucks she could train up into loyal enforcers and book-cookers.

It was too late for him. With seven unaccountable years, no one would vouch for him. The days of Louie Tucci were too long past for anyone outside the Supper Club's camp to remember him, a double edged sword. He couldn't anyone about his Wisdom or the particular challenges of using his abilities.

Walking up the street, Sal passed by the High School. Two girls and a boy, clearly late, ran up the steps with toast in their hands and coats flapping along in their wake. The boy looked like exactly the kind of kid Esmeralda would hire. He ought to get some employees himself, as soon as possible.

If Sal used a bit of his buy-in money, he could set himself up with a loyal mole. All he really needed to find out was the kind of information a smart kid might notice while nobody paid much attention to him. Intel like that could at least lead to a way to prove himself. It'd be risky, but not too much.

Because Esmeralda was a woman in business, she wouldn't want to call in help and risk some wise guy trying to cut in on her operation. She'd probably never suspect a kid waiting tables or running dishes.

Sal didn't go back to his room at the warehouse. Instead, he headed to Town Hall. Squeezing into one of the phone booths, he pressed as much of his bulk as he could against the stool in the corner. Maybe the indignity would pay off. Sal only had to look through the town telephone directory.

Tucci had just started skimming the A names for vowels when he saw a brawny young man with dark hair sitting at the far end of a long table, a stack of old records in front of him. There was plenty of room out there and the chairs looked more comfortable than the puny stool in the cramped booth.

He squeezed out of the dinky excuse for a closet with the phone book, then gave the burly fellow a friendly nod and smile before taking a seat. The guy nodded back, sans smile but he didn't seem the type to have an easy one anyway.

This town was a tough nut, but he'd come here to crack it and carve out a place for himself in the only business he ever wanted to do. If Ms. Cavalcante could run a successful operation, Sal Tucci could find a way into it.

He scanned the book sure enough he got rewarded with a name. Chiavo. He hadn't expected to find anything in the front of the hefty directory, so there was nothing to mark the page. Sal looked around. The middle of the table had a box with a stack of small slips of paper next to a tin can full of little pencils. Sal reached over and took one of each, then jotted down the name, number, and address for G. Chiavo.

He thought the name sounded familiar but couldn't place it no matter how hard he tried. Maybe it would come to him later. Important memories had a way of surfacing eventually. Sal went back to searching the book.

He added information for E. Cavalcante when he saw it, but only found six other names of the Italian persuasion. A couple of those were Anglicized. Even families here since before the Civil War got their names mauled by the bear of Immigration. Tucci liked to entertain the possibility that some families might welcome change like he did. There was always a reason to leave home. Having something or someone to to hide from was a common one.

Tucci considered his own secret, discovered a few years before the death of the man who's name he carried with the aspiration to be worthy of it. Sal wasn't anything like his father, not even after all the body swaps. But now wasn't the time to think about that. The young fellow from the other end of the table loomed beside him, peering over his shoulder at the phone book.

"Good morning," said Sal. He stood up and extended his hand. "I'm Salvatore Tucci, nice to meet you."

"Theo Webster." The young man took his hand and shook it like a world-class wet blanket. "I've had better and worse mornings than this. Is that the phone book? You look like you could use some help from a local. Are you trying to find someone?"

"You're absolutely right. My father was from Providence and used to work here a while back. I'm looking for people he might have known." Sal plastered a genial smile on his face. Webster was six feet tall and built like a truck, but probably not much over eighteen. A kid his age wouldn't remember Louie Tucci or Raul Cavalcante.

"So you need information?"

"Exactly. What I'd really like is to hire someone, a person who could go around town and find things out.

Are you interested in some work?" This kid probably wasn't Italian. Sal's luck was never that good.

"I don't have the gift of gab," said Theo, "but I've got a friend who might be able to help you. William Chiavo. He's still in school, but they're out later this afternoon."

And there was that name again. Chiavo, Chiavo. Where had Sal heard that before and why did the deja vu give him the heebie jeebies? Was it a wise guy from Boston or Providence?

"Sounds perfect." Sal leaned over and grabbed another piece of paper. He wrote the address of the Pilgrim Diner on it. "That's where I'll be later."

"I'll let him know. It was nice meeting you, Mr. Tucci." Theodore waved.

"Likewise, Mr. Webster."

Sal sat back down to scan the book one more time, even though he'd probably found the most useful information possible in this little building. Out of the corner of his eye, he noticed Theo Webster shelve the records he'd been looking through. Theodore opened the door out of Town Hall, late-morning light transforming the young man into a shadow in the doorway before it closed behind him. The light around him reminded Sal of fire.

"As long as Jacky runs things in Fall River, this supper club's doing all its business with him and his guys." Esmeralda Cavalcante's hand tightened on the handset the same way it used to strangle chickens in Aunt Lena's Fall River backyard.

"You know you've got me between a rock and a hard place, Esme." The old lilt that used to lift Liam O'Connell's voice had been dragged down and drowned by the thick South Boston slur of his new neighborhood. "I can't do nothing about the big boys no more."

"I know." Esmeralda sighed. "While you're reminding me how different the new times are from the old, stop calling me that. It's either Esmeralda or Ms. Cavalcante now."

"There ain't no right and proper way to name any woman in business, so I'll call you what I please." Liam's chuckle muffled a glassine clink but not enough to hide the fact of his continuing whiskey habit from as old a friend as Esmeralda.

"Fair enough, Lee." Esmeralda tapped the front on the desk drawer where she kept mementos of her youth and childhood in Fall River.

The old nicknames gripped her like that time machine

in the Wells story, dragging her backward through decades until she could almost feel the itch of woolen knee socks and pinch of patent shoes.

"All the same, childhood pals or not, I have no real choice. Your current position might be smack in the middle of two immovable objects but mine's the Horse Latitudes. Woman in business, as you said."

"Yeah, yeah. I *capisce* but can't capitulate." Ice definitely clicked against glass on Liam's end of the connection. "Sooner or later something will shake loose. Word on the street is there's a boyo with a toehold down your way. And good old Giacomo's operation has a few new policies I'm not sure you're privy to. But you never heard this from me."

"Thank you, Lee."

"I never did nothing for you, Esme." Liam snorted. "Irish don't help Italians in this business without a selfish reason, no matter how far back they go."

"I suppose this means you'll come calling someday, asking for favors."

"You always were the sharpest pencil in the case, Esme. Shame you've got all the wrong, um, attributes."

"Yes." Esmeralda hung her head. Family business hadn't extinguished the flame she carried for Liam. Now that they'd spoken again she found that time had not diminished it either. "Good afternoon, Lee."

"Thanks for the chat."

They raced to hang up. Esmeralda won.

She slid the drawer open, reaching in. Her hand bumped the lockbox containing Cousin Jacky's stolen book. Esmeralda brushed aside memories of nights spent scaring each other with monster stories, including that one night they may have actually seen one. Pushing past papers and pencil stubs, she found it; the envelope taped to the back of the drawer.

Esmeralda held the yellowing packet at eye level, sighing. Was she really going to do this again? Would reading Liam's letter truly help lay her misguided affections to rest? If only she were back in Fall River, just a few blocks from Saint Anne's and Father Francis's confessional. Father John over at Saint Peter's just wasn't the same.

Weariness didn't begin to describe Esmeralda Cavalcante's usual mood. She'd been greener than Liam's Ireland when she'd married the wiseguy Cousin Giacomo had chosen for her. Being the mover and shaker behind Raul Cavalcante's throne hadn't been easy but she'd managed to get him to take her advice. As a woman operating openly in a man's world in the seven years since his death, she'd heard almost everything and seen even more. If only she could get back behind the scenes where she did her best work, perhaps she'd manage to rest.

She pressed Liam O'Connell's envelope to her chest, on the left, over her heart. With eyes closed, Esmeralda remembered the first time she read that letter. He never should have written those things to her, about how he felt. But she understood why. The War to end all wars was on, Lee's brother had died in it, and no one knew how long it'd last.

Esmeralda shook off all of the should haves. They never helped and neither did brooding over what might have been if Jacky hadn't been tapped as a Boss. She hadn't lied to Liam when she'd described being stuck. What she had feigned was surprise about the state of her cousin's operation down in Fall River. Giacomo Bianco was in over his head and she had a fairly good idea of why.

Her cousin hid an illness, something he probably wouldn't even admit in in the Reconciliation booth. They used to be able to tell each other almost everything; more like siblings than cousins, everyone said.

That all ended the first time Raul clenched bruises into her shoulders during a day-long binge. They'd fought a confidant's war of attrition ever since, truths falling away from their conversations like front-liners. A no-man's land widened between them even with her husband seven years in the ground.

"Dammit, Jacky." Esmeralda let the letter drop to the desktop. "What's eating you?" She reached for the phone but stopped. "I can't call him like this."

Esmeralda Cavalcante pulled the drawer open as far as it would go. Then, she took the little key from the chain around her neck and unlocked the box. Liam's feelings were as true as that moldy old book about monsters in the Crusades. She tucked that letter away under the tome, closed the box, and locked it again but not before a shiver of guilt chilled her.

She should have marched that book back down to Fall River and into Saint Anne's Cathedral years ago. But Esmeralda was as stuck with it as she was using Giacomo's rumrunner to supply her speakeasy. If she didn't answer to her cousin, accept him as Boss in all things including stolen Church property, she wasn't sure what he'd do. Cutting off the hooch might not even be the worst possible consequence.

As Esmeralda closed the drawer, she resigned herself to the fact that she'd have to phone Jacky and tell him about Liam's call. If he found out from someone else, she wouldn't be in hot water with him; she'd be in molten lava.

Lifting the earpiece off the receiver, Esmeralda mouthed a brief prayer of thanks that she could afford direct dial and a private line. A straightforward and pragmatic woman, she disliked all of the organization's typical dodgy euphemisms though she understood the need for their use. The line clicked through connections and then she waited through three rings before Giacomo answered.

"Hello?"

"Hi, Jacky. It's Esmeralda."

"You're not due to call for another couple of days, Essie. What happened?"

Esmeralda explained her conversation with Liam, leaving out the banter. Jacky didn't need to know that she and Lee still engaged in mild flirtation, mostly because the last thing she wanted was her cousin casting kittens. When she finished, Jacky laid out a long silence on the line.

"So? What do you think, Jacky?"

"I think you can wait this out, Essie."

"Really." Esmeralda's voice fell flatter than a penny on a railroad track. "Because from where I sit, the situation passed dire about a hundred miles ago."

"I've got something in the works."

"It'd help if you told me what that was."

"You know I can't, not yet."

"Won't, Jacky." Esmeralda pushed the button on the cut-glass lighter that sat next to her ink blotter and lit her cigarette. "I know you, remember?"

"You know me but the element I'm working with isn't a sure bet."

"So you don't want to jinx it is what you're saying."

"Maybe." A crackle came from Giacomo Bianco's end of the line, a jittery, twitchy sound.

"Fine." Esmeralda took a deep drag on the tightly-wrapped tobacco, held her breath for a moment, exhaled. "You can have your secrets. But if someone else comes along and opens this cage, I ain't waiting on you anymore."

"You'll wait, Esmeralda." Something squeaked on Giacomo's end. Esmeralda recognized his teeth grinding. "You'll do as I say or you won't be in business or anything else for much longer."

"I said fine, Jacky," Esmeralda said. "Go take a walk in the park or something. Relaxation clears the head."

She waited through another long silence. Those had been more frequent recently and Esmeralda wasn't sure why. Something to do with the mystery illness, she supposed.

"Maybe I'll do that, Essie." Giacomo's use of the nickname signaled that whatever fit of anger gripped him had loosened its grasp. "For now, I've got to go. More business to attend to, you understand."

"Yeah, Jacky." Esmeralda took another drag on her

cigarette. "I understand."

"Good. We should have these talks more often."

"I agree." She didn't. "Until next time, Giacomo."

"Next time." Giacomo Bianco hung up the phone.

Esmeralda Cavalcante sat waiting again, almost done with that tactic. She had plenty to lose if she moved too soon. But the promise to her cousin had been a ruse. She wasn't in the doldrums, adrift in a becalmed sea. Instead, Esmeralda imagined herself at a remote train station. She'd grab her things and hop the first engine that rattled through.

She'd survived being married to Raul Cavalcante, after all. Everything after felt like that walk in the park she hoped her cousin would take.

Sal knew he shouldn't order another piece of apple pie a la mode. Hell, he probably shouldn't have ordered the first one, but it had been a full-pie kind of day and this body craved all kinds of food. Sal wasn't in a situation where he could afford to be picky about the body's habits. He was lucky to have one that was full-blood Italian.

The one slice was all he'd have. Maybe two, he still hadn't made anything final. If he ordered extra, he promised himself to hold the ice cream. Apples were supposed to be healthy and all, what with their purported doctor-banishing properties. The waitress, Helen, was still in the kitchen, so he'd have to wait on her. Ha.

The bell above the door jingled as a kid and a girl came in. Here were two of the teenagers he'd seen running up the school steps that morning. They stopped and stared almost in unison, the girl's soft brown ringlets bobbing as she moved her head. She was a looker but daintier than Sal himself liked. The boy wasn't the brawny type either, just average build with a wiry strength about him.

More similarities became plain. Their eyes were the

same shade of blue and both had an olive tone in the skin which told him they were at least part Italian. Good. They didn't hold hands. In fact, the boy rolled his eyes at the girl while she openly stared at the specials on the chalkboard. He swatted her shoulder, then jerked his chin in Sal's direction. Sal understood that sibling rivalry fueled the tension between them, not young love.

"Good afternoon. I'm Bill Chiavo here to meet Mr. Tucci. Is that you, sir?"

"One and the same," said Sal. He smiled and nodded toward the chairs opposite him without standing up. "Mr. Webster didn't say you had a sister." He grinned at the girl too.

"My name is Millie." She walked over bold as brass and took the seat next to the wall. She had a smile to shame a spotlight. "Our friend Theo Webster sent us a note that you have odd jobs around town, but didn't say what. We could both use some work."

The Chiavo girl stuck out her hand, and kept smiling. Sal shook with her. What a shame if the girl was the only one of the pair with the temperament for this job. Sal knew for sure that a woman, no matter how pretty, wouldn't help him horn in on the Italian operation in Plymouth.

"It's good to meet you." Bill managed to sneak up and sit himself down while his sister did the distraction act. Neither of the kids showed the least hint of calculation, either. Good on them. He thought he had it worked out now.

"You two are twins." This time, Bill returned Sal's smile. "Great. Either or both of you can do this work.

What I need help with is getting information. I'm not from around here, but if I want to do business in this town, I need to know about the way things work here." Sal slapped a piece of paper on the table, tapping it three times before he pushed it across the table for the kids to look at. He read along with them.

1. How many and what kinds of boats come in and out of the harbor and who the dockmaster is.

2. What kinds of food and entertainment are the most popular, including as much about the proprietors of those establishments as possible.

3. How hard the labor is and the hours they keep at the docks and the Cordage Company.

"This sounds almost too easy." The girl turned her head, peering at Sal with one eye like a crow might eye a shiny but unknown object. "What's the catch?"

She was sharp. He'd been expecting a question about his business or the pay and here she was asking him something he wasn't prepared to answer without establishing either trust or leverage. Her brother gave her the good old eye roll again.

"You're right, this work is the opposite of challenging. No catch. I know too little about Plymouth to even decide whether I fit in here."

"How much does it pay?" Bill had a decent poker face, but Tucci found his tell right where he'd expected. Greed. The kid's eyes might have looked this bright a couple years ago if he'd been standing in front of a candy store.

"That all depends on the quality and quantity of the information you bring me," Sal said. "But I realize you'll want an idea. If you get me the name of the dockmaster, you'll get two bits. Get me his name and one way to contact him, you'll get a dollar. Get me all that and how he spends his time on Saturday evenings, you get a deuce. And so on. What do you say?"

"I'll have something for you tomorrow," the kid said. "Same time, same place all right?"

"Sure shooting, Billy the Kid."

Bill stood up, holding out his hand for a shake, but Millie didn't follow his lead. She stared Sal down, unsettling him. The girl's eyes got all watery at the corners and her cheeks blossomed with spots of color. A hot tingle itched and burned on the right side of his forehead next to his temple. The girl stared there instead of looking him in the eye. Her hands gripped the edge of the table so hard, he couldn't make out the half-moons in her fingernails.

"Hey, Mil. Come on or we'll be late for supper."

She whispered in a *voce* so *sotto* he barely saw her lips move. "I want no part of your business or your money, Mr. Tucci. But I will give you a warning. You hurt my brother in any way, shape, or form, you won't even remember to regret it." Her fingers released the table.

Sal's forehead felt cool and usual again and the roses in her cheeks went dun. The moisture vanished from her eyes in one blink. She smiled with her lips while her eyes blazed fury, then turned on her heel to stalk out the door ahead. Sal Tucci hadn't been this terrified of anyone female before, not even Esmeralda Cavalcante.

"See you tomorrow, Mr. Tucci." Bill smiled and gave a friendly wave, a wise choice considering Sal had essentially ignored his offer to shake.

If Billy the Kid had heard his sister's threat, he was a regular Sarah Bernhardt. That was good. Faking good cheer like that would only help the kid get plenty of intel.

"Thanks, kid." The bell jingled as Bill exited the diner. Sal's knees felt weak and his bowels watery. He was glad to know the kid would work out, but the sister with her wits and that *malocchio* had him worried. It reminded him of how his Wisdom felt every time he used it.

Except the girl couldn't possibly be Wise. He hadn't heard about them existing in this town. Then again, the Tuccis hadn't lived in Plymouth for long. *Madonn'*. He should get down to Church and could go say a novena or something, thank the Virgin that Millie was the tough customer instead of her brother.

"More pie, hon?" The waitress was back.

"No thanks," he said. "Just the check please, miss." After that bit of unpleasantness with Millie Chiavo, Sal didn't want any pie. A serious case of *agita* threatened on his guts' horizons and too much pie would only lure it in faster.

"You can't be serious about helping this guy, Bill." Millie pitched her voice low enough to shame the Devil. She would have shouted at him, but not in the middle of town on their way home. She had to settle for mimicking Mom's quiet angry.

"It's no big deal," said Bill, "and we don't know much either. The information he wants might help us, too, even if he wasn't paying."

"Don't you get it? Are you so *calabrese* that you don't see what kind of business he wants to bring here? Crime. Illegal stuff. He must think we're the biggest bunch of bumpkins he's ever seen." Frustration paced Millie's brain like a caged tiger.

"You think I'm some kind of babe in the woods? Of course it's not legal but drinking alcohol wasn't that way forever and it shouldn't be. I'm two and a half minutes older than you. I know what I'm doing." The last rays of the sunset lit streaks of fire in Bill's dark hair. His anger indicated that he hadn't expected her to challenge him on this.

"That's right. I think you don't know what you're doing." Millie tried leashing her anger but it slipped her grasp. "With a name like Tucci, what do you think he's going to do? Open a nice quiet drinking library? We'll have booze here, but also guns and hookers everywhere. Or don't you care about bringing that kind of element here?"

"I can't believe you just said that." He paused his diatribe as they passed old Mrs. Lumley hobbling out of the library. "That was like the exam review version of the Uncle Finn Opinion Society," Bill said. "We're half Italian, in case you forgot. For all we know, his bias against people from our country is half our problem. Maybe Tucci could help us by being a distraction."

"Oh yes. Tucci's distracting, all right. He's distracting you." A red rubber ball flew over a fence and landed at Millie's feet. She picked it up and sent it sailing back the way it had come. After a brisk walk past the yard of happily squealing children, she continued. "You want to keep our uncle from owning the town. What do you think this Sal Tucci character is trying to do, run a charity? The Plymouth Supper Club already serves illegal booze but at least it's run by a lady who's been here since we were babies. That pot's already on simmer. Why make it boil over?"

"Oh, so now that I called you for parroting Finn, you play the Townie card?" Bill shook his head. "Change happens whether we like it or not. I'd rather have Tucci in charge than Finn. He'd keep things copacetic and not much would change on our side of the slate. Finn's going to bring the Irish Mob down here from Boston, maybe in exchange for a place in their ranks. Do you really want a war between crime organizations? That's a whole Hell of a lot more dangerous."

Bill blushed a little, realizing that he should have watched his language as they passed Saint Peter's. Father John spotted them and stopped sweeping leaves off the church's front step to wave. Millie returned the greeting, then linked her other arm in Bill's so she could lean closer and speak more softly.

"Uncle Finn's paranoid. It's the consequence for his Wisdom, just like aging is for Dad. He can See into the future if you're stupid enough to actually tell him anything, but he's ruthless because he thinks everyone's out to get him. Do you want to bet Tucci's motives are any better? Aren't you worried it'll bring back all the old trouble, start taking lives like Aunt Cloris and that Mr. Cavalcante? What if our friends are casualties?"

The absence of expression on his face kindled a fire of rage in Millie's belly. She lashed out with the name that'd hurt him most without thinking how she knew it would. "What if it kills Gilbert?"

"You leave him out of this discussion." He shook her hand off his arm like it was a spider. "I'm the one selling information to Mr. Tucci, so you don't have to. You should be grateful since you hate Italians so much."

"You dimwit." Millie pressed her lips into a thin line. "There's more to this than who came from which country in the Old World. It's about bringing more conflict here than we need to. Look at Dad. That's what happens when Wise get mixed up in crime or any other group with their own agenda. Mind Wise are mayflies. We get used up and men like Finn and Tucci don't care." She caught Bill's eye then glanced at the monoliths and mausoleums in Saint Peter's graveyard as they passed.

Her brother followed her gaze, his expression sobering.

"God, Millie. We're talking about giving Tucci a list of names and places here, not joining the Mob."

"Aren't we? You ask Father what happened in 1922, what it cost us. He won't say because he's got this mad idea that battle equals glory. But Rachel's Gram tells it differently." She pointed with her little finger at a corner of the graveyard where the paupers' graves were. The men she'd mentioned were buried there. "I've heard that story every time I stayed over at the Howe farm the last seven years. That Raul Cavalcante put us all in danger because his eyes got bigger than his Supper Club. Add that to your list of things Tucci needs to know about Plymouth. The Mafia tried expanding here before."

"I bet he does know. It's probably why he wants so much information, to avoid repeating history." Bill kept his tone even but Millie still knew she'd shaken him. "I still think he's better for this town than our uncle, so I decided he's going to get our help."

"You decided?" Millie's temper flared almost to the level Tucci-threatening level from back in the diner. "Who died and made you king? You can't decide something like that for all of us when you haven't even got your Wisdom yet. Why shouldn't I decide, then? Is it that I'm younger or that I'm a girl?"

They finally reached their street, turned down it. Her brother left those questions hanging between them like the guy in the Roman parable's sword. Millie tried not to blame him but the idea of letting his biases stand rankled, making her own feel more justified.

"Millie, this isn't about suffrage." Bill didn't roll his

eyes, at least. His face reminded her of Dad's when he played peacekeeper. "Stop with that line, okay?"

Millie refused to be baited or placated. She wasn't wrong about the assumptions their local community of Wise families made. Even though she'd be able to vote when she turned eighteen, Millie knew that her sex limited all of her other her options. If she turned out to be Wise, she could have more control of her destiny than the average young woman but not by much. Her life would never be what she wanted, mind powers or not.

Bill had all the chances in the world and she could do nothing but watch him squander them. His shoulders relaxed, softening his physical stance. Maybe the rest would follow. But Millie didn't want to risk her brother brushing this protest under the rug.

"I'll stop when I'm done, Bill. Wisdom is unpredictable about who it chooses and how. Maybe neither of us will get it. You think you're smarter about what's right and wrong because you get better grades at school? Fine. Go ahead and set up Little Capone in Plymouth. You'll do it without your sister. There's got to be another way through Finn's mess."

Millie kept walking, but didn't notice Bill still standing on the sidewalk until she'd put one foot on their front stoop. He stared up at the curtains in the window of Gilbert's upstairs hall. Both stood closed with the philodendron on the outside, signaling some kind of big family news.

"Come on, Bill," said Millie. "Whatever music we're facing in there, we'd best get it over with."

By the time she opened the door, Bill's heavy tread

creaked on the steps behind her.

Giuseppe Chiavo had shambled from the parlor to the dining room after he'd made all the phone calls. He'd wanted the extra space. Giuseppe met with the other Wise parents and Gram Howe two hours after school started for the day. They all came to an agreement based on his discussion with his wife, Katherine about the visions she'd shared with him mind to mind.

Giuseppe got more information than what she'd been able to put into words. Mind Wise started out with reading verbal surface thoughts and emotions, which remained as a latent part of their abilities. Giuseppe knew how to change the focus of this "third ear" to read the bigger picture between the lines of his wife's thoughts. That either took years of practice or raw talent. The former applied to him.

He hadn't been able to ask his peers everything, but that was no obstacle for Giuseppe. It had been harder to hide the danger Katie saw coming and still negotiate the arrangements they needed. The Edgewoods were especially resistant, which made sense considering how badly fire and plants mixed. Without their cooperation, the Wise community in Plymouth would be doomed to shackles he'd left Italy to escape.

Directly warning the other families wasn't an option and Giuseppe couldn't use his Wisdom to nudge them to the best course. Finn's visit had all but wiped him out.

All the same, Giuseppe got through the second meeting without consequences more severe than needing a long nap. Katie had offered to help set him up in his favorite brown leather chaise in the den and he took her up on it. The rest had done him half a world of good.

The twins made themselves known in Giuseppe's mind's ear before they came inside. Of course the Elmwood boy had alerted them to the fact of big news at hand. Their puzzled fear and speculation confused him far more than the remnants of their earlier argument. They should be able to guess at what was in store for them, all things considered.

Every generation of adolescent Wise and their siblings went through the same thing at this age. He and Katie were a rare exception, but the Great War had changed circumstances for arranged marriages back then. At the turn of a new decade, the pendulum swung back to the center. At least, that's how it looked to the rest of the families. Affinity with temperature, plants, the earth and its creatures were useful ages ago, but insight and power into events and the hearts and minds of men meant more in this modern era. Such powers also gave people with them a more complete and ultimately disturbing perspective to the world.

Giuseppe considered his own Wisdom more curse than blessing. Knowing the unfiltered hearts and minds of most other people was like viewing the world through mud-colored glasses. The first thing he'd learned was how to block them out. With agitation or fatigue, however, the strongest feelings and thoughts around him bled through his defenses like a leaky ink pen in a white breast pocket.

He sensed that both his son and daughter fumed with anger even though they had just turned down their street. Giuseppe knew already that both their hearts would break in this next chapter of their lives. He wished the twins weren't currently at odds. They'd probably wish they hadn't argued today at any rate.

"Katie," said Giuseppe, "they're almost here."

"I know, dear." His wife of eighteen years set the tea tray on the table in front of him. Only three cups stood sentry beside the teapot.

"Aren't you joining us *mi amore*?" He looked up into the blue eyes both their children had inherited. Katie's mouth had smile lines at the corners, but her cheeks and brow still smooth. He'd always insist that she marry after he died but she wouldn't let him talk at length with her about it. He couldn't imagine being widowed twice himself. Giuseppe prayed often for his wife, that she wouldn't fall into despair after he passed on. If she'd Seen her fate she never shared it.

"I think it's better if I don't because we simply can't risk it. It's impossible to keep my mind off everything I Saw while part of it's being discussed." She poured for him, adding exactly the amount of milk he liked.

Tea was his favorite drink and the culinary prop of his premature old age. Back in the Old Country, coffee had been Giuseppe's beverage of choice. How different would his life have been if he'd stayed in Italy, joined the Camorra as they'd insisted? He couldn't have found this much happiness there and didn't regret its brevity. Life without Katherine or the twins was impossible to imagine. Now here he was, preparing to harm them for their own protection.

Giuseppe felt the draft when the front door opened. Two sets of footsteps paused at the door to the parlor, then continued on down the hall toward the dining room. Katherine left through the door to the kitchen, glancing once over her shoulder before closing the door.

Only one set, soon. Katie's words went unspoken, though Giuseppe read them in her mind. The pain he felt was his and hers, like the monogrammed towels she'd unpacked from her Hope Chest for the second time. He held the cup of tea under his nose and inhaled. He would not weep.

"Father. This must be important." Millicent busied herself with the tea, fixing the remaining two cups the way she and her brother liked them. She curled her hands around her drink and sat down at his right, leaving her brother's beverage on the tea tray.

Giuseppe knew she was still shaken by the scene with Finn earlier, but it showed nowhere except in her own head. He'd always sensed something in her, a center pillar of her personality with a springy strength, flexible enough to bend without breaking.

"Good afternoon, Father." Bill's formal address told Giuseppe that his son expected a grave conversation. Picking up his tea, the young man sat in the chair to his father's left. "What do you want to talk to us about?"

"The two of you are almost at the age of consent. It's time to discuss what grown children in Wise families always do at this time. Marriage."

"But Father." Millie followed her brother's formality,

a hint that this topic had caught her off guard. "Neither of us has shown evidence of Wisdom yet. How can any marriage be arranged when you don't know which one of us has it?"

"We do know, Millicent. Your mother's vision this morning included that detail. William will be Wise." Neither of them had anything to say about that. He savored the peace for the moment, knowing it would soon be broken. "You will be married this spring, Millie. To Theodore Webster."

"Not Gilbert?" His son's heart gushed over with outrage, though it didn't soak his composure. "But why? The three of us have been best friends since we started crawling."

"Gilbert is to wed Sarah Webster. Besides, your sister can't very well marry your future bride's nephew. Your wife will be Rachel Howe, William."

Neither of his children protested further. They'd grown up knowing this decision would be out of their hands, as well as why. All the same, even with the strongest wall he could build around his heart, Giuseppe experienced starry-eyed excitement with his daughter and numb despair with his son. Ten years ago, his head would have spun. As it was, Giuseppe held each of their feelings in, balancing them on the fulcrum of his own heart. He weighed, scrutinized, analyzed.

He'd always suspected, but tonight he finally knew for certain. William had been in love with Gilbert Elmwood for most of his life. There was nothing at all he could do to ease his son's heartache. He couldn't even acknowledge that he knew. If Giuseppe said too much, neither of his twins would survive the next year.

Bill shuffled out of the house, numb. Millie went beside him like the ground beneath her was made of a springy substance. He knew the lot of them had agreed to discuss whatever they'd found out about Uncle Finn, but they'd surely talk about wedding plans instead. Bill wanted no such chat, friendly or otherwise.

He'd been so afraid that his father would find out that he was in love with Gilbert. Dad had given no indication that he knew any such thing. Maybe he was tired, or had other things on his mind. Maybe the mind's ear sound of his heart breaking got swept away and drowned in Millie's excitement like a kitten in a river. He knew he might be wrong but Bill felt betrayed by the possibility anyway.

He thought Millie loved Gilbert as much as he did, and he'd gotten himself used to the idea of them getting married over the last few years. If Bill couldn't be with the man he loved, he wanted Gil with someone who'd stick up for him. It would have softened the blow for Millie had been even a little bit disappointed.

The area around the Webster's smithy was pleasantly warm even during the late October twilight. He wasn't surprised to find Theo inside but didn't expect the look in Theo's eyes when Millie walked through the door. His sister blushed and smiled.

Sarah carried in a jar of jam and a loaf of bread. Theo must have found something important out then, if they'd need a snack. She dusted off the workbench with an old handkerchief, then set the bread things down on a tea towel. She leaned against the wall nearby, staring at her feet. Theo and Millie didn't even notice she was there.

Sarah was usually quiet and detached. Somehow, the tilt of her head and shoulders made Bill imagine ill-will. Could she be devastated about her engagement like Bill was? At first he was surprised that he considered her feelings at all. Most of the time, he ignored Sarah because she seemed to like going unnoticed. Tonight, he didn't have that impression.

Perhaps she'd be reluctant about marrying Gilbert. That idea turned the back of his throat sour with anger. He couldn't muster any sympathy for her and it was all his fault. Bill would have to slay his green-eyed monster before he could consider Sarah a friend again. He'd have to work on treating her with civility until then.

Rachel arrived, carrying the Howe family's old Bible. He had no romantic feelings for her whatsoever, but he loved her like a sister and recognized her cleverness. One of the things they wanted to know was a reason for Uncle Finn to turn his Sight against the other Wise families. They all set so much importance on their ties, which meant they'd factor in somehow. The Howes kept all of the birth, death, and marriage records, recorded through war, peace, and religious turmoil since before the American Revolution.

That information lived on the flyleaves of the farmsteading family's Bible, transcribed every time a new copy replaced it. The Howes were Protestant until just after the Civil War when the only other Wise around were Catholic. Preserving Wisdom by marrying into other families with magic trumped religious freedom. Rachel's Gran was one of those converts. She had probably been happy to help the younger generation sift through their collective past.

No one looked anyone else directly in the eyes except Millie and Theo. The subject of nuptials loomed like an elephant in the room. Those two seemed more interested in physical conjoining than the actual joining of two lives in matrimony, anyway.

Bill wondered why his parents hadn't appointed a chaperon for Millie, but they'd be sixteen in January. It wouldn't matter if he got her with child, another assurance of the arrangements' finality. He found basking in the glow of abject lust more uncomfortable by the minute, though no one else seemed as affected by it. Maybe Bill's Wisdom was rearing its head. The five of them shuffled their feet, waiting for Gilbert.

"Where was Gil supposed to go, anyway?" Rachel asked. "He said something about going through records, but not where."

"Pilgrim Hall." Sarah spoke without looking up. "It's closed by now."

"I wonder what's keeping him, then." Rachel leaned against a wall, tapping her foot.

Maybe Gil was stuck arguing with his folks about being engaged to Sarah. He'd never liked her much, barely tolerated her presence. He embraced unruliness more than the rest of them. It made sense; his folks were more likely to cave to his demands since his older brother died in The Great War.

"You don't think he ran off, do you?" Sarah's question shook Millie and Theo loose from their longing gaze duel.

He blinked then swallowed the unease rising in his gut. That was a possibility, a course of action Bill hadn't even entertained the idea himself. He'd stay in Plymouth married to Rachel if it meant he could still be near Gilbert. Bill knew Gil was queer for sure. He'd mentioned it before, asked to keep it a secret, but Bill had chickened out of confessing his own feelings. Did Gil hate Sarah that much or was there a man he loved in another town?

"It's getting too dark to read anything in here anyway." Sarah waved one hand at Rachel's bible. "Maybe we should call this thing off." She fidgeted her fingers like she did during any test at school that wasn't mathematics. Sarah's nervousness reminded Bill of a bad smell, like milk just gone over. He usually got that impression when Millie lied. Was Sarah hiding something?

"Don't worry about the light, I've got these." Theo rattled a pencil box. He opened the lid to reveal a rainbow jumble of crayons. He went around the smithy setting them into holes in molds, clamping them in vises, and sticking them inside dusty old lanterns meant for candles.

"How will crayons help?" asked Millie.

Theo didn't answer, he only furrowed his brow and glared at a crayon in one of the vises. Its tip flared up and a flame as bright as a regular candle's began burning steadily. He repeated that glare until each crayon was lit, providing the smithy with more than adequate illumination.

"Aces!" Millie was impressed and Bill wasn't exactly sure how he knew his sister's feelings. "Where'd you get that idea?"

"One of the fishing boat Captains ran out of candles in the middle of the ocean. His first mate made drawings of the horizon to pass time on the way out, so they tried burning the crayons. They last longer than you'd expect. We'll get at least a half hour out of these."

"Well, I know we probably want to wait for Gil," said Rachel, "but I can't stay as long as the rest of you. I found some things out and want to make sure you know them before I have to go."

Rachel put her Bible on the anvil in the middle of the room where they could all crowd around and get a look. She opened it to the end pages, where there names and dates sprawled in a spindly copperplate hand. Some of the names, including Rachel Howe had the letter "b." with a month, day and year. Other names also had a "d." and another date. There were names beside other names with a "m." and a date in between them. This Bible was newer than Bill had expected and the handwritten part was no exception. In places, names were crossed out with a single line through them.

"Gran's sister transcribed these names just three years ago, the spring before she died. I remember when she did it and Gran wanted her to leave out the crossed off names. She insisted on keeping them because she said they're part of history even if nothing came of them." Rachel pointed at a pair of names. The one that was crossed out was Rachel's oldest brother George Howe. It was linked to another name with an "m." in between. Katherine Mullins. The date was about a year before Mom and Dad's wedding day.

"But the only Katherine Mullins back then was our Mom," said Millie.

"Well obviously she'd been married to Rachel's brother George at some point." Sarah's whole demeanor perked up in the face of a puzzle. "But look, George's name up here has a death date. Looks like he died just about two weeks after getting married. That's why he's crossed off."

"Oh." Bill had just seen something he could barely believe. "This can't be right. There's a William Howe with a b. and a d. on the same day. And that's a few months before Mom and Dad got hitched. Your great-aunt must have made a mistake in her copying."

"That's what I thought too," said Rachel, "but I went to the cemetery earlier. There's a marker for William Howe there, away from the family plots with that same date two times."

"We had a half-brother. And Mom never told us." Bill didn't know how he should feel about that, but surely it shouldn't be waking-limb tingle.

"She wouldn't want to discuss something that painful. I can see why agreed to marry a Mind Wise from out of town, though," said Millie, "it makes perfect sense. He'd be the only person to understand how she felt, losing her husband and then her son in less than a year."

"That's not all I found out at the cemetery." Rachel's voice lowered, her words as reluctant as the feeling Bill sensed wafting from her. "There's more graves in that corner. Two died in July fifteen years ago. Two more passed seven years ago, on December 31, 1922. They're Italian names, but none of them is Chiavo."

"Hmm," said Bill, "well don't leave us hanging Rachel, who were they?" He felt certain of her answer before she gave it. Was that his Wisdom was coming in?

"The oldest two graves were Federico Bianco and John Houlihan. The newer ones are Louie Tucci and Raul Cavalcante. On the way out, I passed our family mausoleum and saw that July date from fifteen years ago on one of the plaques. Guess whose name was on it?"

"Dunno." Sarah was fidgeting again and looking at her feet.

"I do." Theo looked over at Sarah, then put a comforting hand on her shoulder. "Our mother's sister, Cloris. She was married to Finn Mullins. I saw that at Town Hall today and I bet it's in Rachel's Bible, too."

Rachel ran one finger down the page, then stopped and nodded.

"But what happened in 1922 on December 31st to get two guys from someplace else killed? Why would two other out of towners be buried here in the same plot as a stillborn from a Wise family? And what do they have to do with Aunt Cloris? I thought she died of influenza." Sarah still fidgeted, but she'd gotten a scrap of paper from somewhere and scribbled names and dates on it with a crayon from the box. "I have to go and look this up."

"Why you?" Millie grumbled. "It's not as though you're the only one of us with a brain."

"Because it reminds me of something I saw over at the Dockworkers Union office on Friday." Sarah gripped the paper scrap, hands trembling. She squared stiff shoulders and stopped her shakes. "You remember I've been getting bookkeeping lessons after school on Fridays? Well, last week was at the union office. I'm supposed to go to the Cordage Company tomorrow, but I can try and convince Mrs. Pickering I need to repeat the dues archive study."

"Sounds like you're our best chance to get that information." Bill wondered how much Tucci would pay for whatever Sarah could find out. "But Cavalcante? That's the same name as the widow running the Supper Club. I bet that grave was for her late husband." Bill wondered of Louie Tucci was related to Sal, and if so, how. He hadn't bothered asking Rachel for the birthdates on those graves, and wasn't about to now. Millie glared at him. Why couldn't she undress Theo with her eyes again instead of judging him for wanting to make a few bucks?

"Bill and Millie already know this, but I met a man at Town Hall today." Theo took a couple of scraps of paper from his pocket and shuffled them. "His name was Tucci and he had questions about this town. He said his family lived here years ago. Bill, did you meet with him?"

"He did." Millie spoke with a reporter's neutral tone,

sounding less angry than Bill expected."I don't like him. He offered money in exchange for information about businesses in town. The docks, Plymouth Cordage, the Supper Club. He says he wants to do business here, whatever that means. I don't like him."

"You said that twice." Sarah raised an eyebrow.

"I know. Take that as you will." Millie rolled her eyes.

"Okay." Theo frowned down at his pieces of paper. "The Supper Club was something I found at Town Hall. I looked at records for all the property that Finn Mullins doesn't already own. Did you know that the Supper Club, Plymouth Cordage, and the Old Colony Club are the only places he doesn't have a stake in? Most of the property he's bought over the last seven years, but some of the titles changed hands just in the last two weeks. Funny thing, he only just bought the property our houses are on in 1923. Any time someone died with no will, there was Finn Mullins, trying to buy their buildings. There were plenty during the Great War. If I didn't know he was Wise, I'd think it uncanny."

"The sun's all the way down now," said Rachel. "This interesting and all, but I have to go. If I see Gilbert on the way, I'll tell him to high-tail it over here."

"We'd better all go," said Bill. "Sounds like we've got plenty to think about before figuring out what to do next. How about meeting again this weekend?"

"Sunday after church would be good." Rachel looked at the floor. "We'll all be in the same place, and our parents will expect us to talk over recent...um, announcements."

"Sunday, then." Bill gazed at one of the burning

crayons as Rachel left. Sarah went out the door after her, but turned toward the back of her house mumbling something about payments from 1922. He left too, thinking Millie had followed him.

She hadn't. Bill turned back to see her standing inside the smithy, holding hands with Theo in the improvised candlelight. He didn't see her again until after he washed his face before bed. Her hair was mussed but she wore a big dopey smile and hummed some melody or other quite contentedly.

So much for chaperons.

Finn Mullins stood in the doorway of the Records Room at Pilgrim House, sneering at the sight of Gilbert Edgewood's head bent over a ledger.

Everyone loved the Elmwoods. After all, why wouldn't they?

If your trees held back their apples that year, an Elmwood had the power to coax fruiting blossoms from their branches. If your corn sprouted puny ears, there was an Elmwood, ready to convince them to fatten up before harvest. If your lawn got overcome by flat-leaved invaders dropping fuzzy spores in perpetuity, who might rally your grass and clover to resist the dandelion occupation. An Elmwood, of course.

Everyone forgot that Wood Wisdom let them see and hear just about anything people did around a plant they'd bonded with. If they put their minds to it, Elmwoods could learn most anything. Ironic, considering their Wisdom's drawback.

The Wood Wise family didn't get ornery or psychologically disturbed by doing it, either. The cost of that kind of Wisdom was a dippy and sickeningly good-natured absentmindedness that reminded Finn of the works of Dunsany. He'd never met an Elmwood that he actually liked.

But young Gilbert was the worst Finn had ever heard of. Pompous, used to getting his way, and more flamboyant than any self-respecting man should be, the kid practically exemplified entitlement. His brother Andrew died in his first battle after being conscripted in the Great War. The elder Elmwood had a woodenly stoic demeanor that Finn had understood even if he didn't admire it. The last warning he'd given to the Wise families was that Andrew should not enlist. Of course they hadn't heeded him.

If it wasn't bad enough that Gilbert played at European dandification, Finn had Seen how weak a link the kid would be. Like him or not, Finn needed to convince the kid to talk to him. He needed to get one over on these kids because each one of them would kill him if given the chance.

Finn almost stopped himself. He hadn't actually Seen any murder staining the kids' hands. Was this the paranoia talking? Maybe Gil Elmwood was only looking something up. It might have nothing to do with him.

His sister Katherine had phoned earlier, chattering about the next generation's arranged marriages. What if the Elmwood kid was only trying to find a genealogical way out of his engagement? What if he'd been sent by his parents to verify their choice? Finn would have done the same if he'd been told to marry anyone other than Cloris.

But Finn couldn't afford to assume good intentions, not when his plans for the Irish takeover were approaching the point of no return. The last time he'd made a blind assumption was fifteen years ago and Cloris had paid for his carelessness with her life. He'd loved his wife, but even more importantly, she'd belonged to him.

Cloris wasn't the only thing that dago Giuseppe Chiavo had taken from him, but her death had been the last straw. The bits of sanity Finn chipped off his own block by using his Sight were a fair price for total control over Plymouth in general. His own specific circumstances felt like a fringe benefit, including power over the rest of the Wise, like the increase in his net worth.

Finn Mullins approached the most annoying kid in the world.

"Need help, kid?" A yes or no question was too vague to let Finn See anything, but he had to start somewhere.

The little twit shook his head without even looking up.

"You're not going to find the original record here, you know." Finn let that idea sink in before he continued. "These are only copies of the ones on file over at the Old Colony Club."

"The Old Colony Club requires all prospective members to have a sponsor." The kid had quoted Club rules at him, ruining Finn's chances of using his Sight.

Gilbert was dodgier than he'd expected, but all he had to do was keep talking and wait. Elmwoods just weren't that crafty. They made living plants do anything they wanted but people were another story. Eventually, everybody talked.

"I'm a member. The new decor is really something,

especially the new dining room. I'm headed over there next."

"Throw off the bowlines. Sail away from the safe harbor." Gilbert's use of Twain's words foiled Finn again.

"It would be even better with company. The Club's no fun alone."

"Hear no evil, speak no evil and you'll never be invited to a party."

"Is that Oscar Wilde? I can't stand that fop. Where's the Twain?" Finn shook his head when Gilbert didn't answer. "Say, I have an idea. The museum's closing soon. I want company and you'd like a look at those passenger manifests. Why not head over to the Club with me? I'm not sponsoring anyone right now so I can bring an interested guest." The kid kept looking over the page of names and dates, and Finn thought he'd failed to get his attention. He stood waiting anyway. It took almost five full minutes before his patience paid off.

"It's wiser to find out than to suppose." The kid sure did love his literary quotes. Gilbert put the pages back into the file folder and gave them to the curator. Finn waited as the kid took his coat from the stand, then led him out into the fading light and down the street to the Old Colony Club.

The Old Colony Club smelled like Old English Oil and Velvet Pipe Tobacco. Gilbert had expected bland coastal New England food. He ran a long-fingered hand through the shock of wavy ash locks at his crown. This building housed no plants. Even other Wise didn't understand how much plants could add to his perceptive.

A vein of information lived in plants from which Gil could extract information like precious gems about a place and its people. Gardeners, farmers, and florists talked to plants to help them grow. That idea led to the right track but the wrong train. Plants absorbed light, water, minerals, and human energy.

If there'd been a philodendron in this place Finn Mullins frequented, Gilbert would have known his typical mood. He'd sense how frequent Finn vented his anger here, or whether he ever laughed. He could count political allies and business partners, might even discover the identity of an opponent or two. Without a plant here, Gil sailed blind. He'd have to bring one over tomorrow as a gift. Everyone would think he wanted a membership. Everyone but Finn, anyway. But if he presented the plant in front of a dozen or so members, they'd have to accept it.

Following Finn down a hallway, Gilbert dragged his fingertips along a wood panel. He blinked and got the layout of the first floor, then forgot whether he'd brushed his teeth that morning. No more using Wisdom on dead things, he couldn't afford to forget not to ask Finn questions, or worse fail to remember that the man was his enemy.

They went into a room to the left off the hallway. Every wall except the one with a window wore shelves of books like armor, patched together with plates of all shapes and sizes. A large card catalog stood in the center of the room like a baby elephant. This library skipped utilitarian tables and hard chairs. Instead, the seating was plush, with little side tables tagging along beside velvety wingback chairs.

Gilbert headed straight for the card catalog. He had to avoid speaking directly to Finn about himself, his friends, or anything they investigated. Sight Wise could only See if you gave them something to look at. Finn Mullins needed to be directly told about a person, place, or thing and he'd be able to See the unfortunate noun. He'd need to hold himself to a tight course.

He'd have to stick with quotes as he'd done at Pilgrim House. The empty library meant that Gilbert couldn't talk to a bystander to skirt the danger so mum would have to be his word. Bill's father had a knack for benign conversation with Finn. No one in his generation could match Mr. Chiavo at such diversion. Still, Gilbert would have to try and fake it.

He found the card with Dewey Decimal number for the Mayflower passenger manifests. Mr. Mullins stood at his shoulder holding a document box. He'd known exactly what Gilbert wanted. Jeepers creepers. Gil bit his lower lip. Was Mayflower research a popular pastime or something?

Or maybe Mullins had Seen this whole sequence of events years earlier. He might know exactly what would happen in the next ten minutes. Gilbert couldn't stop his body from displaying his fear. He had to push his spectacles up his nose to hide the tremor in his hands.

There was no point in estimating the risk now that he was here. The safest thing to do was turn around and exit stage right. But he'd promised to help, needed to see that manifest. Careful navigation of these waters was essential. Gilbert smirked and reached for the box. Mullins let him have it.

"Where do you want to sit?" asked Mullins. If he was just going to phrase everything as a question, Gilbert had more chances to run aground on a mistake. He kept his lips buttoned and let his imagination run with the idea of a ship at sea.

"Why so quiet, young fellow?" Gilbert shrugged and turned his prow toward some seats by the window without answering either question. He becalmed himself in a plush chair, and opened the records box.

"Oooh." He could already tell the manifest was different from the one at Pilgrim Hall. Names had older spellings, for one thing. He turned pages over, jotting down anything that caught his eye on a small notepad. His albatross landed in the nearest chair, watching him. Time rolled along like sea water beneath a ship's hull.

"It's different, isn't it? Helpful?" Gilbert's foot tingled where he'd crossed it over his knee. An elderly gentleman had battened down with whiskey and a copy of The Man in the Iron Mask near the radiator.

"Like a voyage in uncharted waters." There. He'd said something, but kept his mind firmly on imagining the Pilgrims during their time on the Mayflower. He couldn't justify blatant rudeness in front of another Club member. It wasn't a direct quote but Gilbert doubted a simile about an historical document could let Finn See present day concerns. He'd have to work harder at steering any conversation away from obvious rocks.

"Speaking to me now, I see. Good." Finn leaned against the velvety back of his chair. "You wouldn't want to imagine how lonely it gets. Your parents and Theo's and me, we all grew up at the same time. Friends, like you and yours. We went everywhere together, just like the three girls do. None of them speak to me anymore, for reasons with which I'm sure you're familiar."

Gilbert's stomach turned, like that one time he'd gone out on an actual boat instead of an imaginary one. Finn had been shunned because of his Sight. Gilbert's overactive imagination told him how he'd feel if everyone he cared for cut him adrift and shunned him. He'd rather die.

Once Gilbert let the idea in, it perched and wouldn't leave, like Poe's raven. His imagination tread water in an alternate existence with no Saturday visits at the Howe farm. It got worse. No bridge games with Millie, Bill and Rachel. No tea with Theo and Sarah. No endless summer hours watching the docks with Bill.

Finn Mullins had just confessed that his every-day life was one of unwanted solitude. Finn lived stranded alone, with a picture-perfect outsider's view of everyone he ever loved. He carried the burden of his Sight around his neck like the Mariner in the poem had carried that decaying bird.

"What evil looks had I from old and young. Instead of the cross, the albatross about my neck was hung." Gilbert's heart unbuttoned his lips. A quote from the literary work currently plaguing his mind wouldn't give Finn anything to See.

"Yes, from the Coleridge poem. You're beginning to understand." Finn folded his hands in his lap. "I've been a member here since age eighteen. I'm well acquainted with everyone, but it's not the same. The Club is exclusive, but lacks the degree of Wisdom to which I am accustomed."

Of all possible dangers and obstacles he'd considered, Gilbert hadn't expected to run aground on empathy. He continued making notes until he'd gleaned everything interesting from the old record. It was full dark before he finished. He shut the box, handing it back to Finn.

"All through? I suppose you'll need to get home by now." Gilbert pressed his lips together, nodding. Mr. Mullins rose from his chair, so Gilbert followed him back to the front door. Finn stood in the doorway as Gilbert walked down the front steps. Just as his foot hit the sidewalk, he thought he heard a rattle like dice or bones, perhaps even bone dice. It was probably a tree branch tapping against a window but the sound gave him the chills all the same.

"Congratulations, by the way." Finn put his hands in his pockets. "I heard you're engaged now. Who's the lucky young woman?"

"Sarah Webster." The name tumbled from his lips like dice from a cup in a damned man's hand. He glanced back at Finn. Crap. Shoot. He'd just thrown Sarah overboard but that wasn't the worst thing. He didn't even feel bad about it for her sake, only his own.

"Oh." Finn's eyes sparkled like a snake's as he

chuckled. "I See."

Finn Mullins headed south on Main Street, away from his shiny new car. He needed to think, not drive, so he allowed his feet to carry them where they would without much effort on his part.

Tolerating the Elmwood kid hadn't yielded a big payoff but it gave him a place to start. Sarah Webster. Finn's brief flash of Sight showed him that she'd be a most satisfying ally if only he could isolate her from her peers. There was no love lost between Gilbert and his new fiancee. He'd known about the marriage arrangements for years. Asking the kid had merely been a ploy, of course.

The girl was bright, maybe even too much so. Her skill with anything numeric was uncannier than Prince Albert in a pipe. She'd displayed signs of partial Wisdom already, keeping them hidden from her peers and even her parents. Finn would have to be on his guard while dealing with little Miss Webster. That meant he'd need to leave it for later and move boldly to claim her when the right time came.

Music, its muffled tones and rhythms, met his ears and his feet stopped. Finn looked up, gazing at the sign that read Plymouth Supper Club. He chuckled, then approached the door.

Finn Mullins had been in two types of speakeasies. One had a bruiser at the door, asking for a card or a password. The other served their hooch only to those who knew the right names to order it by. Plymouth's only drinking establishment was one from column B. He pushed on the door and it yielded to him as easily in the physical sense as he hoped the proprietress would in a more lucrative way.

Inside, Finn sidled up to the brass railing between the upper and lower tables. A trio of fellows sat onstage. One plunked away at an upright piano while the other two plucked an upright bass and a banjo respectively. He took a seat at one of the many empty tables and waited until he heard the tap of women's shoes approach and stop beside him.

"I'll have the cold tea." Finn smiled down at the tablecloth. He didn't have to look up to identify the woman in the expensive paisley shoes.

"I'm not here to wait on you, Mr. Mullins."

"Of course not, Ms. Cavalcante." Finn tilted his eyes up without moving his head. "You're here to ask me to leave."

"I'm glad to hear that you understand the situation." She crossed her arms over her chest. "Now go."

"Not until I've had my cold tea and the benefit of your company." Finn smiled, turning the charm as high as it would go.

"You'll have no company," Esmeralda placed one hand on the table, leaning over him in a clear attempt at intimidation. "But if you insist on cold tea, I will stand by the usual practices at my establishment and have it served."

"I insist on both." Finn placed his left hand over

Esmeralda's right.

"I'll send one of my girls over." She slipped her hand out from under his, a move he hadn't anticipated even with his Sight. After that, she raised her left hand, snapping the fingers on it. A waitress high-tailed it through the kitchen doors. "They're better company than I'm likely to be for you at present."

"I'm afraid that just won't do." He reached for her wrist, caught it in his fingertips. "You control assets no other woman in this town has. I need you specifically, Esmeralda." Homely women like Esmeralda got caught off-guard by flirting in one of two ways. Either they simpered and fawned or went clammy and disturbed. Finn preferred the former but the latter didn't surprise him in this case. He decided to back off before she embarrassed him by making a scene. He couldn't abide people watching a woman with sub-standard looks reject him.

"You'll have to do without, Mr. Mullins." Esmeralda Cavalcante twisted her arm out of his grasp and turned her back.

"Even if I'm here with a strictly business proposition?" Finn lowered his voice to a warm purr.

"Business is another matter entirely." She turned around, facing Finn again. "But I never conduct business related discussions during the hours I'm open to the public."

"When can I see you again, then?" Finn leaned back, making room for the waitress to leave his tea on the table.

"Tomorrow, ten thirty."

"I'll count the moments." Finn stood, reaching for his wallet. "How much do I owe you?"

"On the house." Esmeralda stalked off toward the back, no doubt to call ant tattle to her cousin Bianco down Fall River way. The waitress stood, shaking her head and looking at Finn's wallet.

"Don't worry, doll." Finn pulled a bill from the wad of cash he carried and handed it to the waitress without looking at it. "I'll still tip you."

Finn Mullins sat back and sipped his tea, watching the waitress's legs as she trotted off with the ten-spot he'd slipped her. He already knew what Esmeralda Cavalcante would say to his proposition the next morning. All the same, he'd show up just to see the look on her face in person.

Finn looked forward to the end of Esmeralda and all the other Italians in town, like that dried up old prick, Giuseppe. If only he could See it as clearly as he'd dreamed it.

Jimmy Delaqua had a feeling. It wasn't anything more or less, just one of his hunches. But since his usefulness to Giacomo Bianco's operation had grown out of those, Jimmy heeded them. That's why he found himself back at the Supper Club later the same morning after he'd already made his delivery and gotten the boat ready to sail. He could barely believe that he'd walked in on Esmeralda rebuffing what appeared to be a second gentleman caller. Except this one was Irish and reminded him of a shark instead of a teddy bear.

"Mr. Mullins, what is this actually about?" Esmeralda leaned against one of the rails between dining sections. Jimmy knew from experience that her pose was like a cat's; sitting still with a flicking tail. The Boss's cousin was prepared to go on the warpath if the Irish fellow made the wrong move. And he did.

"It's about you and me joining forces, Esme. Seventy-Forty, in my favor of course." Mullins slid one hand along the brass railing, like a kid on a carousel reaching for a prize. He leaned, too, facing the dining room like she did. Jimmy imagined his face leering, which felt like the right assumption considering the guy's tone.

"Me and you, Mr. Mullins." Esmeralda wasn't asking

for clarification. This was a grammar lesson. Jimmy smirked, waiting to see the man get himself schooled by this woman in business.

"Yes, a match made someplace south of Heaven."

"I'm sure you're well aware that I think you're entirely unsuitable."

"Indubitably. But I don't care. I'd prefer to do this with the best of intentions on the highest road a man like me can manage, Esme."

"The road to Hell is paved with those, Finn Mullins."

"Says the woman running a barely-veiled illegal business." Finn's arms clasped around Esmeralda's waist like an iron vise. "I'll have what I want from you, one way or another."

Jimmy planted his feet, unbuttoned his jacket, and held his hand just an inch from the butt of his concealed piece. But Esmeralda Cavalcante didn't need his help. She pried her way out of Mullins's grasp like a doctor might shake off the grip of a disturbed patient.

"You'll have exactly the part in this business that I want to give you, Mr. Mullins. Nothing more." Esmeralda's eyes gazed daggers of steel. Jimmy froze even though that look wasn't for him.

"And what's that, Miss Esme?" Finn's voice carried a sort of ironic mirth, absent of tension that a man waiting for an answer usually had. Jimmy wondered why the Irishman bothered asking this question when he probably already knew the lady's response.

"Absolutely nothing." She put her hands on her hips. "Now leave this establishment, sir. And don't bother coming back for anything but dinner and a drink."

"I'm not sure who could possibly argue with a sentiment like that." Finn turned his back on the woman, meeting Jimmy head on.

Jimmy Delaqua's neck prickled with a chill straight out of the Arctic. Faced with an armed, dangerous, and ready-to-draw man, most people paled or got nervous or even staggered back. Not this Finn Mullins character. The man smiled, stepping around Jimmy as though the rumrunner was part of the decor. No. Mullins acted like he'd fully expected Jimmy to be there, gun and all, and that he knew for sure that Jimmy was no threat.

Jimmy's eyes traveled to Esmeralda. She shook her head, so he stood down. As far as he was concerned, Ms. Cavalcante's wishes would be respected inside her establishment as long as both of them worked for the same Boss.

He listened for Finn's exit, waited for hinges creaking and latch engaging before he spoke.

"Is everything copacetic, Ms. Cavalcante?" Jimmy dropped his gun arm to his side.

"As much as it can be just lately, Jimmy." Esmeralda smoothed the sides of her dress where Mullins had rumpled it. "What brings you back?"

"Dunno, just a hunch, I guess." Jimmy shrugged.

"You keep on following those." Esmeralda turned, took a glass of something brown with ice off the bar, then had a sip. He'd never seen her drink before noon.

"I don't always like where they lead, though, Ma'am." Jimmy buttoned his jacket.

"All the same, I stand by that sentiment." Esmeralda headed toward the door that led to the kitchen and her office. She stopped, turning her head to look at him over her shoulder. "Not a word of this, Jimmy. Not even to the Boss."

"What about that Tucci fellow?" Jimmy raised an eyebrow.

"You can mention him, sure." Esmeralda nodded.

"Is there any reason the Boss shouldn't hear about Mullins?" Jimmy stood still, not sure whether this request from the Boss's own cousin amounted to mutiny or not.

"Plenty of them, but only one I can tell you." Esmeralda turned her head away from Jimmy, took another sip of her drink.

"And that is?"

"You and I know what Mullins is really after. But my cousin will never believe I've had two apparent gentlemen callers in as many days at my age." Her shoulders drooped.

"Aww, Ms. Cavalcante. I'd believe ten times that." And Jimmy did. He knew plenty of guys attracted to power and Esmeralda Cavalcante had more than most women even if she didn't have stunning looks to match. Her stern wit was an asset, too.

"You flatter me too much, Jimmy." She sighed, shoulders drooping. "You ought to be more careful about that."

"I understand, Ma'am." Jimmy's half Puerto Rican heritage already made him an odd duck in Giacomo Bianco's organization. Closer association with Esmeralda would lower any full blood Italian's opinion of her, too.

"Do you really?" Her head tilted and one corner of

her mouth lifted. She had him pegged for sure. "You're a good kid, Jimmy. And that's why I want you to consider things closely when you get back to Fall River. Really take a good hard look at the situation there. Your situation."

"And what should I do after that?" Jimmy blinked.

"Nothing." It was Esmeralda's turn to shrug. She turned back to the bar and waved one hand. "I doubt you'll find anything you can do. But it's best not to be caught flat-footed, don't you agree?"

"Yes, Ms. Cavalcante." Jimmy nodded even though there was no way Esmeralda could see it. He couldn't have agreed with her more if she'd said that water was wet or the sky was blue.

Jimmy watched the door close on her paisley-clad back, wondering why he found it so much easier to agree with his Boss's cousin than the man himself just lately. Later on he'd realize that he didn't know the half of it.

"Yeah, what?" Giacomo's voice rasped like sandpaper.

"Jacky, It's me, Essie." Esmeralda Cavalcante hadn't wanted to make this call and now she thought it'd go worse than she could have imagined.

"What happened?"

"Nothing really." She stifled a sigh. "Just calling to let you know that your guy Delaqua's got a late start but he's on his way back."

"My guy?" Giacomo cleared his throat. "The amount of time he spends in Plymouth, everyone's gonna think he's your guy."

"You're the Boss, Jacky. What's mine is yours."

"Well don't go counting that particular egg. He's a half-and-halfer." Something stuttered against the phone over on her cousin's end of the line.

"Delaqua's also the most talented rumrunner in your operation, possibly even New England." Esmeralda could hardly believe what her cousin Giacomo implied. "Half PR or not, he's shipping hooch, not angling for Capo. You can't possibly think he's less than a valuable asset right where he is. Jimmy's blood makes him less suspicious."

"So he's Jimmy now to you." It wasn't a question. "What's the real reason he's late, Essie?"

"Dunno for sure, he didn't tell me." Esmeralda told the truth because her cousin always seemed to know when she lied. Omission was another matter entirely. Or at least, it always had been before.

"Don't lie to me." Giacomo's voice turned strange, high-pitched and strangled like the neck of a helium balloon. He let out a breath, hissing against the receiver like a snake.

"I'm not lying, Jacky. You know Jimmy gets weird hunches. Maybe he got the heebie jeebies about cops or something."

"So he was with you." Her cousin's flat tone revealed more of his anger than any rampant tirade.

"Yeah."

"You listen to me now, Esmeralda Cavalcante, and you listen good." Giacomo's voice dropped by an octave. "You don't carry on with that Spic. He's good for nothing and his days on this Earth are numbered."

"You're killing the Golden Goose, Jacky." The old folk tale's outcome had been a bone of contention between them practically their whole lives. Jacky always said that sometimes you had to kill the things you loved or life would be too easy. But he couldn't understand that just being female came with its own set of hardships that never died no matter how many times their heads got severed. "You lose your rumrunner, you're going to regret it on your bottom line."

"You don't tell me what to regret, Cousin Esme. I own your business and I own you. What I say goes. Delaqua either puts up or gets shut up and I'm gonna make sure he does one or the other the hour he gets back into town. Bad enough I gotta deal with a Mick, the last thing I need is the Spic thinking he can get a foothold by wooing my cousin. If word gets back to me that you and him are anything but importer and exporter, he's iced and your shop's closed down. *Capisce?*"

"Yes, sir." Esmeralda kept her voice level even though her eyes pricked with unshed tears.

"Don't expect a shipment for a while. What you got this time will have to do."

"But Giacomo, people are drinking like fishes with this stock crash."

"I'll send over a bootlegger if you got an emergency order, then. Guy with a truck, no one you know."

"Fine." It wasn't. Esmeralda froze. She couldn't even

blink.

"You'll hear from me when I feel like it. Don't call." Giacomo slammed something and then the connection cut. He'd hung up on her.

Esmeralda pressed one hand against her temple, then rubbed that hand down the side of her face and reached into the drawer on her left for a fresh pack of Lucky Strikes. Unwrapping, removing, and lighting one of the cigarettes came automatically.

She should have given Jimmy a sterner warning, maybe even told him to head all the way to Providence instead of returning to Fall River. The Club was more than busy, it'd been packed since the day everyone was calling Black Tuesday. Esmeralda needed help and she couldn't count on her cousin to give it. Maybe Sal Tucci's offer merited a second listen. She wasn't sure what had eaten Jacky or how to stop or mitigate the damage. He might decide not to help her even if Boston's Irish came calling. Esmeralda only knew one thing for sure.

Giacomo Bianco was a hazard, even to his own flesh and blood. She'd have to take a page out of Teddy Roosevelt's book; walk softly and carry the biggest stick she could find.

"It's the perfect cover, Theo, come on." Bill never understood Theodore Webster. He'd always been a hesitant sort of fellow, the opposite of what Bill expected for someone with Fire Wisdom. This bothered Bill, because personality was key for Wise families to predict which children developed full Wisdom.

Theo surprised everyone two years ago when he'd set his failing arithmetic homework ablaze with a glare. He just hadn't seemed the Fire Wise type, just like Millie didn't seem the Mind Wise type. Something wiggled behind the scenes of Bill's thoughts, like a loose tooth. He left it alone, sure that it'd fall out on its own when it was good and ready.

"I can't swim, and I like water less than a cat." Theo looked nervous. "I can't go over there and look for work on a boat."

"You don't have to actually swim." Bill tried to sound comforting, but worried that his apathy was showing. Gilbert would have been less boring to work with on this but Theo looked the part. "You're not really trying to get a job as a sailor. We're just there for information."

"You couldn't have brought Gilbert instead?" Theo sighed and rubbed his left temple. Had Bill somehow projected his thoughts?

"Are you crazy? They'd laugh the both of us right out of there. Gilbert's a good egg, but he looks more like a scholar than a trawler." He waggled his eyebrows like Groucho Marx in Cocoanuts. Theo blinked and wrinkled his brow, reminding Bill that he'd missed that movie as well as the joke.

"Maybe you and Gil should be looking for jobs." The side of Theo's mouth twisted up as he gave Bill a sidelong glance. "Honest on-the-books ones, I mean."

And there was the dig about Tucci. Bill expected it. Ever since the engagement announcements the week before, Theo and Millie spent most of their free time together. He walked with her to school, leaving Bill and Sarah in the dust. Theo was on the school steps every afternoon to walk her home, too. Millie insisted several times a day that she didn't hate Tucci, just his illegitimate business plans. She must be insisting all those same things to Theo as well.

"Well, say you're inquiring for a cousin from out of town or something." Bill shrugged because he didn't really care about Theodore Webster's hydrophobia. Unkind, but true. Still, if he wanted Theo to play along, he'd have to put on a good act. He tacked a smile to the end of his words. "Or tell him you want to work the docks. That's a job with no swimming required."

"I'll do that, then." Theo breathed his shoulders down from his earlobes. They continued on, heading for the dockmaster's office.

Pushing through the door, they blinked and rubbed their eyes, striding halfway across the room. Bill found the dim interior indecipherable at first. In moments, he made out dusty shelves, corners breeding dust bunnies, and a series of untidy paper stacked on a long counter.

"No soliciting." The man with the feathery mustaches didn't bother looking up at them.

"The sign says you need able bodied workers, though, sir" said Bill.

The dockmaster peered at them with beady walrus eyes, the skin around them crinkling at the two young men. His gaze went first to Bill, then up and to the left toward Theo.

"Ayup. You two look to be able bodied all right." He looked back at Bill again. "You look a tetch young though, son. We ain't hiring weekends only, so if you're still getting your book learning at the High School, you got no chance at working here."

"I am, sir. I'll leave it to Theo, then."

Backing away toward the door, Bill let Theo rattle off a list of handy and physical tasks he'd done around the houses on their street, inventing a cousin who'd gained similar experience by his side.

Bill nearly overturned a podium with his hip, rescuing it before it toppled. A log book lay at its apex, open like a flower gazing at the sun. The pages held the names of boats, their captains, and whether they were freight, fishing, or passenger vessels. Spaces splayed out in four separate sections, dates and times listed in columns down the page connected by rows to the boat identification.

Bill saw that the first column of dates was labeled "expected arrival." Most listed days in the past week, a few from that very day. The rest were in the future. All of the boats listed today or earlier had the second column for "arrival" filled in. All of them matched the expected date, but only one exactly matched the expected time.

Scanning up the column, he saw this was a trend. The other columns for departure listed "expected" and actual. These aligned much more frequently in both date and time, and again just one of them matched exactly. The same captain had the exact arrival match every time, except for today's. He was about forty-five minutes late.

Bill lifted the earlier pages in the log, searching for that captain's name. It was there once a week, always with an exact match for departure and arrival, though it seemed his boat had a different name every other time. Bill noticed another anomaly as well. The punctual captain had the only Italian name in the entire ledger.

"That log ain't for kids." The dockmaster had noticed Bill's presence at the podium. He turned to give the man a sheepish grin. While he apologized Bill heard clear as a bell, "leastaways, the young fella didn't flip any pages, see something he shouldn't have."

The dockmaster's lips still pressed together in a thin line. Bill had actually heard someone else's thoughts. His heart stopped with shock even though he'd been told to expect this for as long as he could remember. He inhaled slowly through his nose, feeling life beat out its rhythm in his chest again.

Bill knew that if he leaned a little, he'd get the rest of the weathered man's surface thoughts. But he was too boggled to actually try it while putting on the apology show. Besides, he wanted to hear what the man said to Theo.

"…earned a chance to prove you can do a dockworker's job. We'll give you a week's trial with half pay. You start tomorrow morning at oh five-thirty, that's five thirty since it's clear neither one of you's a Navy man." The dockmaster winked, then nodded at Bill. "If'n you're still interested when summer starts, son, come back then." Bill heard the afterthought about how soft the dockmaster thought his hands looked and knew the offer was less than genuine.

"Thank you so much, Boatswain Albermarle. I'll see you tomorrow at oh five-thirty." Theo's already sturdy chest seemed to practically double with pride. Bill did something that felt like leaning on his friend's thoughts and found his assumptions correct.

They both smiled and waved at the dockmaster, then headed out of the building with Theo in the lead.

As they reached the street, Bill asked, "he was in the Navy?"

"Yeah, veteran in the Great War. Wait, weren't you listening?"

"I was reading a log with loads of information written in it." Bill got an idea. "Hey, I don't want you to make waves or anything, but if it's not too much trouble do you think you could keep your eye out for something?"

"Sure, as long as I don't have to flip through that book or ask questions about it. Mr. Albermarle doesn't seem like he'd abide that."

"No, you won't have to do those things. Just look for a particular boat whenever it comes in. If you happen to see its captain, describe him to me."

"Sure. Which captain and which boat?"

"The Maria. Says the Captain's name is Jimmy Delaqua."

"Ok."Theo walked along in a silence Bill knew for sure was companionable. It wasn't until they got halfway to their street that Theo's mood changed. He expressed it by making a snort of disappointment.

"What is it?" Bill asked, although he already knew perfectly well the thing Theo hadn't thought of.

"I've got to work at five thirty," grumbled Theo. "That means I can't walk your sister to school anymore."

That suited Bill just fine. He'd been getting tired of feeling like a third wheel around his own twin anyway.

"It's still nice enough outside to visit Brewster Gardens, Rachel," said Millie. "And don't tell me all the canning still isn't done or I'll march down to your farm and help you myself."

"Please don't threaten our produce like that!" Rachel laughed, a rare occurrence the last two and a half weeks. Millie's disastrous attempts at putting up preserves was an old joke between them. Her failure at most cooking tasks except making soup hadn't bothered her since getting engaged to Theo. Cooking had been part of his Fire Wisdom education. Considering the passionate events of the past week, Millie thought she'd be happy with any amount of cleaning and dishes.

Happiness was a new state for Millie Chiavo. She imagined Theo and herself as unicorns; a singular pair, unique in contentment with their marriage arrangements. Rachel had seemed hopeful at first but that mood clouded over with Bill's disdain. If old cooking jokes and time spent in the park would help cheer Rachel up, Millie was game.

"Yeah, I'm Millie Chiavo; vanquisher of quality fruits and vegetables. All I need is a stove, no apron required." She stuck her tongue out and pulled down the corner of her left eye. Rachel's dying laugh revived for one more burst.

Millie waited it out, grinning. "So what do you say? I'm talking about the gardens now, not canning."

"Okay. I still don't know why you want to go there in the middle of November, Indian Summer or not." Rachel still smiled.

"Just to get out, walk and talk at the same time. Today's probably one of our last chances to loiter like teenage miscreants outside, even after it gets dark." Millie didn't bother mentioning her plan to spy on Tucci if she could.

They headed toward Brewster Gardens. The park had opened when they'd been little, back when Father looked his current age. He'd brought her and Bill to see the flowers and monuments every day during the summer it first opened. After that, it became one of their childhood meeting places with Gilbert, Theo and Rachel. Even Sarah stopped by on occasion, with a mathematics book and her prized slide-rule in tow every time, of course.

"People don't come to Brewster Gardens to discuss their Mob woes and parental finances. Well, except maybe Sarah. Finances have plenty of numbers." Rachel kicked a pebble. "Anyway, I'm not exactly sure what we have to talk about at this point. Everything's decided now."

Millie had been friends with Rachel for so long, they thought alike. Either that, or she had some sort of Wisdom coming in after all. But no. Her mother had Seen, and that was that. Maybe the girls would all end up with a Partial version, something like Mom's visions. She'd be content with that.

"Rachel, it's only been almost three weeks since everything changed for us and a whole lot of other people. There are still front page articles in the Globe about the market crash. And really, you can't convince me that we've talked out all of the other stuff."

"Those articles are scary, I'll give you that. All those suicides." She shuddered. "Most people aren't comfortable with change like you are, Millie."

They walked along in a strained silence until the pergola came into view. Crossing Leyden street, they walked down the path under it and stopped halfway.

"Remember when we were kids?" Rachel smiled up, the sun lighting her face. Millie wasn't sure what her friend meant; she felt like they were all still kids. "We used to pretend this marked an entrance into another world."

"Yeah, and I remember us arguing about where it went."

"I still think it's faerie." Rachel reached out, ran one finger down a weathered support beam, then turned her head. "And you?"

"I still think it's Tartarus." Millie leaned against the structure, trying to catch a glimpse of her old pal's face. A muffled sniffle told her all she needed to know. No Wisdom required. Millie waited, letting Rachel compose herself.

"It figures, with all those Classical myths you heard at bedtime." Rachel turned around with red-rimmed eyes but a dry face. "Remember the nightmares I'd have when your father told stories on the nights I stayed over?"

"Didn't your Gran say the name Howe came from a faerie legend?"

"Yes, and she reminds us of exactly that just about every day. She thinks that's where our Wisdom comes from, too. Since the engagements, she'd been threatening to make me write her stories down for my own children." Rachel's words were meant for Millie even though she delivered them to her shoes. The part where Rachel doubted she'd ever get with child went unsaid.

Millie couldn't figure out why all the parents couldn't see that marriage wasn't for everyone. Over the last week she'd been honest with herself, admitted that the broadness of Theo's shoulders excited her more than anything else about him. The new light that had taken up residence within her fell earthward at the prospect of spending years with such a predictable fellow. They didn't have much in common. Her good spirits eroded, threatening even the small measure of ground a girl like Millie Chiavo needed to thrive.

They walked past the Pilgrim Maiden and Rachel stopped for what had to be her hundred-thousandth look at the statue. Millie stopped with her even though she couldn't share her friend's fascination with the artist's idealized vision of a woman from the past.

The maiden's too serene round-cheeked face struck Millie as profoundly unrealistic. This image of an early explorer wasn't lean and hungry, nor haggard or troubled enough. After a long sea voyage and subsequent hardship, how could even a young lady

Pilgrim resemble a flapper from a Coca-Cola advertisement?

"I bet they all had to marry who their parents told them to back then, also." Tension in Rachel's shoulders that Millie hadn't noticed before eased.

Had Rachel been this upset every day these past weeks? If Millie didn't know before, she had the answer now. She'd been a bad friend, ignoring Rachel and everyone else in favor of stolen and definitively sinful moments with Theo.

"That was one of the only easier situations in the old colony days." Millie put her hands on her hips, as though defying the artist's vision. "Those girls hadn't gotten the idea that they could decide most everything for themselves. Back then, they didn't watch other girls heading to Boston for work, or planning an education at Radcliffe."

"No suffragette teachers telling them every day to run off and study advanced mathematics instead of bookkeeping, either," said a small, quivering voice.

Millie jumped and spun around, searching for the unexpected speaker. Rachel only made a shuffling half-turn.

"Sarah, you shouldn't sneak up on people like that, jeez, we're not eight anymore." Millie rolled her eyes. "How many times do I have to tell you that's not funny."

But Sarah Webster hadn't been joking. She wasn't smiling, either. Her face, pale except for splotches of red high on her cheeks, dropped its usual vacant mask. Underneath lived a turbulent anger.

"You know what, Millie?" Sarah put her hands on her

hips. "I'm sick of you telling the rest of us what we should and shouldn't do. You've been walking around oblivious to everything but my brother's body for weeks." Sarah stepped between Millie and Rachel. "This is your best friend here, looking like she's about to cry her eyes out. Guess what? She's been like that this whole time. My future's out like a baby with the bathwater because your dad decided I've got to get married now instead of in three years. And the best you've got to say to us is it's okay because the Pilgrims didn't have college or other dreams to aspire to? You can't be serious."

"Well, but we need to focus." Millie managed a reply without stammering but it was a near thing. "Uncle Finn's out there, trying to sell us all out to the Irish Mob."

"Don't pretend like that's what's distracting you, because we all know it isn't. You haven't been out getting dirt on Finn Mullins, I have." Sarah wadded her hands into fists, dropping her arms as though she wanted to turn the pavement beneath their feet into molten lava. Good thing she couldn't. "Millie Chiavo drew the straw she wanted in the marriage lottery, so no one else's happiness matters. Even I didn't think you were this conceited. You've done diddly squat about Finn Mullins and I can't figure out why. I know you're not stupid, Millicent Chiavo, so what is it? You hate your friends all of a sudden or just decided that you like what's in my brother's pants better than us?"

Sarah's head rocked to the side as Millie's left hand connected with her right cheek. The slap echoed off the Pilgrim Maiden statue, amplifying its sound. Sarah was even smaller than Millie and the force of the blow knocked her off balance. She would have tumbled face-first to the ground, but landed on her hands. Righting herself, Sarah straightened glasses knocked askew. Her hand left a crimson smear on the cheek that was already reddening from Millie's blow.

"You're bleeding. Let me see." Rachel stepped over to Sarah and took her hands, turning them over. Millie looked down at them, barely believing she had just struck one of her friends. Something shiny on the ground caught her eye, so she looked at it. Bits of broken glass shone in the gravel like lost diamonds. One of the eyepieces in Sarah's frames was missing its lens.

"I have to get her to the doctor, Millie." Rachel was pressing Sarah's hand with her handkerchief. "She's got a pretty deep cut here, but I don't know how it happened."

Millie just pointed at the glass on the ground. She didn't trust herself to say anything. Her hand stung and throbbed, her head spinning as if she'd been the one slapped. She glanced at Sarah, who looked the way Millie felt. There was something she'd forgotten to do. What was it?

"Bye. I'm bringing her now," said Rachel. "See you tomorrow."

Her friends moved out of earshot before Millie's head cleared enough to remember what was wrong. She should have apologized. "I'm sorry," she said too late to the empty park. The Pilgrim Maiden gazed in her general direction. That serene expression felt like a mockery of her temper.

Millie watched them leave until Rachel and Sarah turned a corner near a row of warehouses. After that, her eyes caught a flicker of movement, like the obfuscated shadow behind a stage magician's hand during a card trick.

A man Sal Tucci's size shouldn't have been able to move that stealthily. Somehow he managed, giving Millie the impression that he was used to a smaller body. But where would she get an idea like that? She trotted toward the other side of the park, following him at a distance.

Before he headed into the warehouse on the end of the block, Millie watched him turn his head one way and then the other like he prepared to cross a street. She also noticed something wrong with his hair. Was it longer? Yes, almost to the point of being feminine.

Millie headed to the door after he'd gone in, pushed it open. But the hallway inside stood dark and empty. She couldn't follow without knowing which way the aspiring wiseguy had gone.

Turning away from her impromptu investigation, Millie remembered what she'd done to Sarah. She would have to head back, face some bitter music at the bottom of the reality her all too fleeting happiness had crashed and burned into.

Hanging her head, Millie Chiavo turned toward home.

Salvatore Tucci had shaken the Chiavo girl. She shouldn't have seen him in the first place after the slap sandwich she delivered to the poor little kitten with the glasses. He'd been focused on sneaking like he did every few days when he had to come back to the warehouse. Maybe the fact that he'd mastered stealth back in his old body explained why the girl saw him. He would need to be more careful next time.

Sal oiled the hinges before unlocking and opening the door. Out here by the ocean everything rusted and he couldn't risk a fight at this point. Inside, he threw the deadbolt, then made his preparations before approaching the sleeping figure on the cot. Sal took his coat and jacket off, hanging them on a nail. Then he rolled up his left sleeve past the elbow, leaving his forearm bare.

As he crossed the room, Sal felt an ache in his bones and an itch in his skin, sure signs that he should have come back here sooner. He wouldn't be able to keep this body if he dropped the swap even once. His captive would escape and he'd have to assume a new identity. Then again, his results with Esmeralda Cavalcante told him he'd have been better off finding someone easier on the eyes than Rico Fatone anyway.

Reaching down, he brushed a dark, wavy lock of hair off the olive-complected cheek that used to belong to him. The skin was smooth except for faint crinkles around the eyes, laugh-lines mostly. Sal took one of the slender, fine-boned hands in both of his and pressed, calling on his Wisdom.

Sal's body stabilized, putting an end to the aches and

itches as Rico's fat settled around his middle. His limbs stayed heavy, arms covered with hair like his chest. As soon as he finished exerting his will to keep the swap, Sal set the dainty hand back down on the old quilt covering the figure on the cot.

"It won't be much longer," he said, slipping a needle-tipped syringe from a box beside the cot. Sal flexed his bicep, then stuck himself and pulled back on the plunger until the chamber filled. After that, he jabbed his captive's arm with it and delivered the dose. Sal shared blood type with whoever he'd currently swapped with.

His captive's brow furrowed then eased. Sal pulled out his hankie, pressed it to his puncture. Gazing down at the sleeping face, Sal could hardly believe he'd been the one wearing it less than a month ago. It never seemed like his then and even less so now.

Opening his borrowed hand, Sal blocked the face from his field of vision and studied the palm. Long life-line, broken love-line. He shook off his mother's superstitions. Real magic wasn't anything like reading palms or séances in tapestried parlors. Wisdom had let him borrow this male body, something Sal had longed for since he was old enough to understand the concept and expectations of gender. But he didn't love this body.

"Male is as male does just ain't true," Sal said to his captive. "And I know you'd feel just as trapped in that body as I ever did so don't worry." He tucked the hankie away, unrolled his sleeve. "I won't make this permanent, Rico."

Sal felt like the kitten with the glass slippers and the Godmother's dress except he got more time than that poor soul. Without a renewal like this every three days, his Wisdom sent him back to his default state. If he paid the price to keep Rico Fatone's body it'd be the one he came back to every time. He wasn't sure he was ready to lose so much for a convenient form instead of one that felt like home. Sal put his jacket and his coat back on, dragging the sleeves up his arms.

The bit of bloodwork made it so Rico Fatone benefited from his activities; food and drink, restroom visits, fresh air. It also kept him in a coma so he wouldn't remember.

Sal took one last look over his shoulder at the sleeping female body he'd been born into. He shook his head, then shut the door and locked it behind him. He had a business to pursue.

The day before Thanksgiving, Bill finally had enough information to meet with Sal Tucci again. He wondered how to get the most money for what he had. He had information about Dockmaster Albermarle, Captain Delaqua's strange schedule, and the enormity of the Old Colony Club archives. After arriving home from school, Bill snuck right back out again, avoiding Mom before she could assign him a chore. With such a busy cooking holiday and Millie no good at anything culinary, his mother would have tagged him in for kitchen and cleaning activities given the chance.

Millie had gone directly to her room. She'd been moping since the day Sarah hurt her hand. Both girls stayed mum on the matter, not even speaking to each other. No matter how sweetly Bill asked, Rachel would only say there'd been an accident with some glass. There must have been a fight but he couldn't make any of them talk about it. For now he'd just take advantage of the solitude that came with his sister's mutual avoidance society.

Once outside, Bill headed toward the diner. As he passed the church, he spied Gilbert coming toward him down its steps. Bill waved. Even though he'd have to ditch Gil before he went into the diner, he couldn't just ignore someone he cared that much for.

"Church, huh? And it's not even Sunday. That's not like you, Gil."

"Confession. Like a visit to the toilet for your soul, only it smells better. I had to clear my conscience." They chuckled together at the old irreverent joke.

"Oh. Well, at least you weren't sitting in your own P.U." Bill wanted to know what weighed on Gilbert's mind, but wouldn't ask. Usually Gil would just spill whatever beans he happened to be holding at the time.

"And where are you off to this afternoon?" asked Gilbert.

"The diner. I'm looking for work." It wasn't technically a lie but felt all wrong, keeping things from Gil. None of the others thought associating with Tucci was a good idea except Sarah. Leave it to the Fire Wise's sister to believe in fighting fire with same. Millie had played up that incident when she threatened Sal Tucci, stoking their friends' worst fears.

"I was on the way to Cordage myself." Gil took off his glasses and started wiping them with his handkerchief. "I'd bring you along, but they don't hire part-timers. It'd just be a repeat of the dockmaster's office, except with me instead of Theo."

"That's a good idea." Bill watched his friend complete the glasses-cleaning ritual he always did when he was nervous. "But I thought you said regular earnings won't make a difference compared to what the less legal element brings in."

"Not as far as kicking sand in your uncle's eye right

now," said Gilbert. "Nothing in town pays well enough to stop a guy with enough bank to interest Boston Irish. But we're in this predicament because your Finn Mullins played a long game. Now it's my turn to think long-term. A job makes me an upstanding citizen instead of the eccentric spouting literary quotes. I'll be more credible speaking to the authorities if we manage to get some dirt on him."

"Good thinking." Bill tried to keep any trace of confusion off his face. When had Gil grown a work ethic? "But, um, isn't the library or the museum more up your alley than Cordage?"

"Indubitably. But I'm not going to appeal to the Plymouth everyman as a quiet librarian or a pompous curator." Gilbert put his glasses back on, then folded his handkerchief. "Or by using words like indubitably around anyone but you. But as a worker at a company that employs two thirds of the working population in Plymouth, I'll stand a better chance of being known and liked by the mundane community."

"What are you, thinking of running for office?" Bill watched Gilbert's deft hands make the cloth square into a neat triangle, then tuck it away in his pocket.

"Exactly. I could gum up plenty for your uncle that way." Gilbert's voice took on the sort of rushed and breathless enthusiasm Bill hadn't heard from his friend all month. "The Wise never had a vote on the board of selectmen. I'm not as convincing as someone from your family would be, but if I play my philodendrons right, I could say the right things to get them voting our way. What do you think?"

"Go for it. You're a likable guy, Gil. If any of us could pull it off legit, it's you." Bill kept his pragmatism to himself. He thought it would be too little, too late, but had to let that light in Gilbert's eyes stay. It felt like the least he could do, under the circumstances.

They got to the intersection and parted ways, Gilbert leaning forward slightly to shake Bill's hand. As they traded grips, Bill felt his face redden. His mind had read an unexpected foreign emotion. Gilbert turned his head slightly, eliminating the glare on his spectacles that usually obscured his eyes.

"You have no idea how much your confidence means to me, Bill." The light in Gilbert's eyes had gotten a little watery. "No idea at all."

"But I do, Gil." Bill had to tilt his head up just a hair to look his friend full in the face. He'd been about to tell Gilbert that he might have just read his mind by accident, but stopped himself. What if he considered it an invasion, a violation of trust? He erred on the side of caution. "We've been friends our entire lives. That's how much it means. Our entire lives."

Gilbert looked away first, then broke their handshake, clearing his throat. Bill decided to block his mind from Gilbert's for now. He understood that everything between them would be revealed in time, for good or ill.

Bill hoped for good.

His knuckles ached as they tapped on the door, but

Giuseppe knew Millie wouldn't come out of her room if someone didn't fetch her. Invoking a small pain in his body was worth easing hers. He already felt what bothered his daughter, even through his mental blockade. Her shame and guilt were like a siege engine against the fortress of his mind.

"Millicent, I'm coming in." He counted to ten slowly in his head before opening the door. She lay across her bed the wrong way, with her head by its foot. She wore all her school clothes except shoes, which jumbled together with her books beside the footboard. Giuseppe tried to pick his feet up to reduce wear on his shuffling slippers as he made his way carefully past the books to the reading chair by the window.

"Are you here to punish me, Father?" Millie sounded wearier than Giuseppe felt. He turned his back to the reading chair, reaching to grip its left armrest with his left hand.

"If getting past this whole fight with your friends can be considered punishment," he lowered his creaky old bones into the chair while he spoke, "then yes. I am here to punish you."

"I don't want to talk about it. It's just some stupid thing. Girl stuff." She wasn't whining, or being obstinate, just holding her hand over her eyes like she had a headache. She sounded like a woman preparing to attend a funeral.

"Stupid girl stuff was when you and Rachel gave Sarah a haircut the night before her first day of school. This new thing is wearing you out, feeding on you like a leech or the *Biscione*. This new thing is just like that old serpent from Italy. It doesn't want you to talk or even think about it. It knows that if you expose its true nature, the thing causing all of this," he gestured at the little heap of damp handkerchiefs beside the bed, "dies."

"Daddy, I know you're bringing the Visconti's snake up to make me feel better. But this is only kid stuff, just like that old bedtime story." Millie removed her hand from her eyes. "Any fight we have is supposed to be no big deal. Rachel and Sarah and me, we're just girls."

Giuseppe knew better. This wasn't a small problem, something to ignore. Katie's vision had taught him better. If Millie didn't stop moping, she wouldn't do what she was supposed to.

"There is no just when it hurts you this badly." Giuseppe leaned back in the chair. "And you're not girls all the time anymore. Sometimes one or two of you are girls. Other times, one or two of you are young women. You clash like hot and cold fronts because that is what all three of you are, stuck on the edge of two seasons in life. Isn't that part of the problem, Millicent?"

She didn't speak, just waved the freshest handkerchief vaguely like a flag of surrender. Her eyes rolled, looking everywhere around the room except at him. Finally, her eyes lit on a bundle of dried wildflowers on top of the bookcase. "None of us have been happy all month and I didn't even notice. What's worse, I didn't even care. Wish I still didn't."

"Part one of growing up is knowing how you feel about things. Part two and part three are realizing which things in your life you can change and which you can't." Giuseppe tucked his hands into the sleeves of his knobbly sweater, let them hunt for warmth. It seemed his fingers were always cold lately, despite the burning pain in their joints.

"You mean the way I know I can't go back to pretending we're happy?" Millie rubbed the handkerchief under her eyes. It was too damp to do more than smear tears around on her face.

"Yes. That's part one, how you feel." He closed his eyes, visualizing the barrier between her mind and his ability to sense it. He imagined it growing thicker. "On to part two now. What's a thing you can't change?"

"My whole life." She turned her face down so it pressed into the bed.

"You're a clever girl, and you know that's not true. There must be something more specific, Millicent. Narrow it down." She mumbled something. "Come again? These ears are too old to make that out through mattresses." She showed her face again, revealing fresh tears.

"School, I said." She rolled her eyes again and sighed like the world was ending. "I have to keep going to school, for starters."

"Do you?"

Her mouth dropped open. She stared at him as if he'd somehow transformed himself into the *Monaciello,* another of her childhood legends. He supposed he was trying to lead her to treasure, after a fashion.

"You have to keep going to school. You have gone to school since you were a child. Does that mean you must, or do you go because you see some benefit for yourself? Are you a child, whose only reason for any activity is that someone told her it must be done?" She shook her head. He asked her again, "what's a thing you cannot change?"

Millie closed her mouth. The handkerchief slipped through her fingers and dropped to the floor. She sat up, then stood, then smoothed her clothes and fluffed her curls. Leaning over, Millie scooped up the pile of damp hankies, immediately crossing the room to deposit them in her hamper. She set her shoes next to the door and stacked the books on her desk, neatly, by her standards.

She turned around to face him, putting her hands on her hips and cocking her head. Millie looked exactly like Giuseppe's own mother before she'd overused her Wisdom in the process of getting her family to America. He could have laughed uproariously if he didn't worry it would start him coughing. He still would have chuckled if he didn't know it would come out as crying instead. His mother had died at age twenty-nine, but looked a century old when she went.

"It's almost time for supper, Dad. Let me help you get downstairs."

He nodded, smiled, allowing her to support him even though he felt less creaky than usual today. He wanted to be able to enjoy his daughter's company while he still had the pleasure of it.

Sal Tucci was disappointed. They'd run out of apple pie, and he knew it was his own fault. Well, his and the Rico's because he always ate for two. Now that he knew the woman who baked the pies took Thursdays off, he'd be sure not to order more than one slice that night so there'd still be some on Friday.

"Sure, I'll try the pumpkin, Helen. Not a la mode, though, please." He smiled at the waitress, but his heart wasn't in it. He hoped she didn't think he that her service disappointed him.

Sal knew he was more polite to outsiders than the kinds of guys his dad had done business with. That would be an asset here in Plymouth. He knew he'd never blend into the crowd in a town with so few Italians. The less he acted like a wiseguy the more likely he was to succeed here when he eventually became one.

People stayed quiet when you kept a little garden-variety mystery. If you scared them or they learned too much, they'd turn into a mob with pitchforks. The balance between carrot and stick varied. Plymouth needed more carrot and less stick than cities like Providence, or even Fall River. He wondered if it was too late to change his dessert order to carrot cake, then recognized that impulse as his borrowed body talking. Rico Fatone loved anything with cinnamon.

The bell above the door jangled. It was Billy "the Kid" Chiavo, without his sister this time. Good on him. The sister was a tough customer, pure trouble. Sal had enough of his own to deal with.

"Mr. Tucci, I have some information for you." Bill didn't sit down. The kid used some of the most formal manners Sal had ever seen.

"Please, kid, call me Sal. Mr. Tucci was my dad." Sal nodded at the seat across from him.

"Of course, Sal." Bill sat down looking even more stiff and proper than he had when he'd been standing.

"Okay, fine. Call me whatever will help you relax."

The kid nodded and held an envelope out across the table. Sal took it, opened it, and looked at the words on the single page.

The dockmaster's name was Albermarle, and he'd been a Navy Boatswain in the Great War. He was a Sox fan and had two grown children who owned a cranberry bog out in Carver. Most of the boats were fishing rigs, with cargo coming in second and barely any passenger vessels. He had percentages on the paper and everything.

The kid had noticed Jimmy "The Hooch" Delaqua on his rumrunning trips from Fall River, even saw he used the same boat but changed the name. Sharp. Bill also wrote that Jimmy's cargo went to the Supper Club, but hadn't noted the little crate of communion wine that went from there to Saint Peter's Church. Bill's notes also revealed that he didn't know for sure what was in the shipment packaging. That was fine, since Sal did. Hooch, of course.

There was a note about the Old Colony Club. It was gentlemen only and the kind of place you needed a sponsor to join. Very much a WASP kind of establishment, in fact. Bill's paper said the place had a smoking room and a dining room, but no bar. The Old Colony boys supposedly had more historic records than the local museum. Sal made a mental note to himself about looking into expansion at Old Colony.

This kid had done good. In just under a month, he'd gotten all the information Sal needed about the docks. Sal thought he still needed to know more before he started really moving and shaking in this town.

"Not exactly what I asked for, but the extra things you thought to include will help." Sal put his right hand in his left inside pocket to get the billfold, letting Bill get a gander at his side arm. He peeled six two-dollar bills off from the rest of his cash. "Here's your pay."

The kid's eyes were like silver dollars as he put the money in his pocket.

"What else do you need to know," he asked. Carrot. Definitely, the vegetable-offering tactic worked specifically on good old Bill.

"The Supper Club. I need all the information you can get about it. I've met the gal who runs it, talked to her once but that went nowhere. I need someone to get a real good inside look at her operation. Someone who works in there, say as a waiter, would be able to tell me loads. What its strong points are, anything it might be missing, that kind of thing. I'll pay triple what you made tonight every week and you keep whatever she pays you, of course."

Bill nodded, stiffer than a starched collar. "I'll go over there tomorrow and get myself hired on, then."

"Smile when you talk to her. I heard she likes that kind of thing in her staff, a friendly-type attitude." Sal thought Bill needed a stiff drink or few to loosen up, or maybe to go park with one of his sister's friends. Nah, definitely the drinks. "And hey, go out tonight and have a good time. The Supper Club's busy shifts are all on the weekends. You might not get out except to wait on everyone else for a while."

"Good idea. Thanks again for the opportunity and the pay Mr. Tu…I mean Sal." Bill stood up.

"Don't mention it, kid. You earned it." Sal watched Bill head out the door, making way for Helen as he went. The door jangled as the pumpkin pie appeared in front of him. He thanked Helen, then took a bite. It was creamy, but had less cinnamon and more sugar than he expected. Pretty decent for pumpkin, but it didn't hold a candle to that apple pie. He'd remember next time. Sal had always been a fast learner, like his first employee was turning out to be. That was one reason he liked Billy the Kid even though he acted like a Mrs. Grundy. Sal himself was a grim bird for a few years at and around that age himself. Figuring out you were born in the wrong body did that to a person.

Whatever the reason was that this kid needed money, it must be bad news. Sal wondered what could have happened to bring a straight-laced cat like Bill Chiavo to a crooked business like this. It might even be as bad as some of the issues Sal had to handle back in the day.

He'd better stick to business with Bill Chiavo. He didn't want to tango with any of the kid's closet skeletons. Taking on more risk was bunko without good odds for profit.

D.R. Perry

Millie had knocked at the Webster's door for what seemed like forever, hoping she hadn't made a mistake. Maybe Sarah wasn't ready to hear an apology from her yet. She shifted her weight from one foot to the other, rubbing her arms in an attempt to keep warm. Rushing over here at the end of November in a light Fall jacket was another mistake. She'd been in a rush and hadn't gotten her winter coat from the attic. Now Millie felt like she stood in an ice box. She knocked again.

A tread too heavy to be Sarah's came from the other side of the door and the curtain over the side-light twitched. The door opened and a few seconds later, Theo walked out. He wasn't wearing a coat, didn't need one, of course. He shut the door behind him, his eyes grim and mouth flat.

Theo's face didn't even wear the usual moody pout she'd come to recognize as part of his resting expression. Millie couldn't blame him. She had slapped his kid sister, after all, and Sarah had only told Millie the truth. He went down the front steps until he got to the corner of the house then looked back at her before turning the corner to head toward the smithy. She followed him.

It was darker around the side of the house, especially

by the low stone building. Millie stumbled over something and fell without expecting Theo to catch her, all things considered. He did anyway. Once they got inside the little outbuilding, the room illuminated, by magic of course. Theo had lit up the crayons again. He opened a cupboard and pulled out a blanket, tossed it to her. Millie wrapped it around her shivering shoulders.

"Thanks. You know, I really came over to apologize to Sarah." She tried not to look at him too much as she spoke. Lack of common interests or not, Millie was still intensely attracted to him physically and she didn't want this visit to be about grappling with that.

"I think that's good, but she doesn't. You should have done it the day after. She's gotten over it, but Sarah might be on the other side of you now as well." His brow gathered like storm clouds, his hands down at his sides, arms tense. That made all of his muscles stand out. She looked away, a vague sick feeling in the pit of her stomach.

Several thoughts floated to the surface of her mind. How she hadn't hit Sarah all that hard, hadn't known glass was on the ground, had been defending Theodore's own honor as well as her own. None of them seemed like anything but excuses.

Millie knew that all she'd done was act without thinking as usual. But this time, her impulse resulted in bringing harm to a friend. Dad already said she couldn't change the past, only what she did in the present.

"Sarah's right to be angry. I just do things without thinking. But I was wrong this time. I can go off the handle all I want if it only hurts me. I should stop and think in the future."

The air got warmer. Theo clenched his fists and ground his teeth, turning his back to Millie and facing the furnace. Then, he threw a punch at the firepit, letting the motion carry his body forward until he touched the pile of dry and dusty wood inside. A rush of fire and heat flared from out of nowhere.

Millie's feet carried her backward until her back hit the wall. She sucked in a ragged breath, smelling burning dust and old soot. Her eyes watered from the smoke and heat. She heard a whine and wasn't sure whether it came from her or someplace outside. The fire invoked a fear in her so strong she almost fled the Webster's property.

"Do you get it now, Millicent?" Theo spoke without turning around. "Do you see what I go through every minute of the day? If I lose my cool, it always hurts people. That's just the way my Wisdom works. And the more I make excuses, the easier it is to slip next time. That has nothing to do with Wise magic, it's just the way self-control works. Every time we fly off the handle it affects other people. Each person's presence on this Earth pulls on everyone else, like the moon and tides. Do you understand?"

"Maybe." She understood but didn't want to believe it. How could a girl like her matter that much? Millie cleared her throat. Just being in the same room with someone who could start a fire with a touch had her jumpier than a cat in a room full of rocking chairs. "You're saying everything I do affects other people, even when I go home and knead dough or tenderize meat when I get angry."

"Someone bakes that dough or eats that meat, is what I'm saying, and baking your rage is better than bottling it under pressure. You do something with your anger, it gets to other people somehow eventually. Bread and meat don't do any harm. Our folks raised Sarah and me to understand this. They couldn't gamble on which of us got Wisdom because of its drawback. Controlling fire gets its hooks into you, makes you want to do it bigger every time. But you have to stop yourself. The damage we have the potential to do is nothing I can think about for long without wanting to go live at the North Pole or something."

Theo turned toward her, but the blaze in the furnace behind him made it hard for Millie to make out his features. She couldn't tell what kind of expression he wore.

"Even one of us with partial Wisdom can do serious harm."

Partial Wisdom. There was something she hadn't thought of, even though her own mother had it. Maybe all her recent mood swings came from some kind of limited Mind Wisdom. Her mother could See things only from items and never when trying to, unlike Uncle Finn who could do it any time in exchange for a slice of his sanity. Up until October 29th, Mom hadn't Seen anything since before Millie and her brother were born. What if Millie's crazy feelings actually belonged to other people? She'd been feisty all her life, but not this volatile.

The flames in the furnace banked down as Theo tended it. It was still warm in the smithy, but no longer uncomfortably so. Millie heard that whine again and recognized it as canine. It did come from outside. The fear she'd felt loosened its grip on her, and she felt a stab of empathy for whatever poor pup skulked around in the cold out there. But Theodore said nothing about it.

"Theo, there's something…" She waved one hand, unable to explain. "Look, I'm opening the door." Her distress must have been obvious, because the hard, caged anger in his eyes banked just like the fire. The door creaked open under her hand, and a dog scuttled through it.

It was a tall breed and so shaggy she couldn't guess at how lean it was. It shivered and she felt fear coming from it in waves as it gazed at the fire. Its tatty red-brown fur bulged out with thick mats like clumps of sod.

"It's all right, boy." Millie extended her hand so the dog could smell it. He acted a perfect gentleman despite his appearance, sniffing her hand exactly twice and then raising a paw toward it. She put one hand under the paw and the other one over it. The poor animal's foot felt like ice. "You're a charming fellow. How long have you been on your own?"

Visual impressions entered Millie's consciousness, first as places she hadn't seen before. She viewed a series of nights in the woods or on the outskirts of mountains. After that came farms along a rocky shoreline, which she recognized as the coast north of Plymouth. Her mouth dropped open. The pictures of those things hadn't come out of her own mind.

"Millie, what's going on?" Theo's voice sounded over her shoulder. She noticed that the dog's paw had warmed in her hand. It yawned, then looked up at her and panted, tilting its floppy ears back and glancing apprehensively at Theo. She got a feeling of fear and a memory of fire, being chased by men with torches.

"He's afraid of fire, Theo. I think he came from somewhere near mountains west of here. People chased him away."

"Are...are you hearing a dog?" Theo hit her with a barrage of questions she wasn't sure how to answer. "You're not supposed to be Wise or we can't get married, right? You can hear animals? Does that happen with partial Mind Wisdom? What does he want?"

Millie got a picture of some paper-wrapped packages falling off the back of a meat truck. Her stomach growled even though she'd had supper just before coming over here.

"He's hungry." She pulled one hand away from the dog's paw and raised it to a spot behind her ear, then realized the itch wasn't her own. She let go of the foot and scratched the animal behind both ears. One of its rear legs twitched comically. Millie laughed.

Theo threw back his head and laughed with her and the dog belled. He wasn't just imitating the noise, either. Millie could tell the shaggy fellow shared their amusement, though whether that had to do with his own intelligence or her window into its mind, she didn't know. The dog whined again, then gave a sharp bark and looked over his shoulder in the direction of the garbage cans. Millie saw the paper-wrapped packages again in her mind's eye, but this time she could smell the raw meat.

"I think he just threatened to raid your garbage if he doesn't get something to eat." The dog waged his tail after Millie stopped speaking. She'd heard of Wise who could communicate with animals before. What she'd never heard of were animals with such a complete understanding of human language. Perhaps she'd conveyed her meaning to the dog subconsciously with her mind.

Theo went around the back of the house for a few minutes. He came back with a can of scraps that included fish heads and chicken feet. He put the can on the ground in front of the dog, who toppled it and started nosing everything remotely resembling meat toward him. He left the vegetable scraps alone and went about his meal slowly, surprising behavior for a dog whose hunger was almost palpable. Most would eat so quickly the meal would just come up a few minutes later. This dog seemed to know that would happen, and wanted to prevent it.

"These were going on the compost heap later anyway. You should probably go to the Howe farm tomorrow when they slaughter all of our Thanksgiving turkeys. And there's this." Theo pulled something round with bristles on one side from where it had been tucked into his belt. "He's all tangled. That's probably why he's itching."

"I should bring him to Rachel's now? I should brush him?" She and Bill never had pets. She remembered the Websters had an old mutt who'd died about a year ago. "He probably needs a bath. I don't know how to take care of a dog."

"Well, you're the one who can hear him. He might get depressed, hanging around with a sap like me who can only make things hot or cold. We really should think of something to call him. It seems kind of rude just to keep saying 'the dog.'"

"Oh, he has a name already. Well, at least he gave me a picture of something." She stopped talking to Theo and turned her focus on the dog. "You showed me a grizzly, but why are you showing me the ocean again? Wow. You must have come a very long way if you've seen a grizzly bear. I hope you can tell me why you traveled so far at some point. Do you want us to call you Bear?"

The dog cocked his head as if considering this. She got the impression that the name wasn't exactly correct. Just before he started wagging his tail, she knew he thought it would do for now. "Bear it is, then."

The washtub squatted in the kitchen like a sloshy gnome. Bill wasn't sure which surprised him more, the shaggy red dog or Millie's laughter. He said a silent prayer of thanks for the bath, considering how filthy the red-brown canine was.

"Get in the tub and we'll wash you up." Millie spoke to the dog reasonably, like she would talk to a person.

The dog got in, placing one foot at a time gently on the bottom of the tub. He sat on his haunches, then blinked at Millie and wagged his tail. Okay, maybe the dog had winked. Water splattered on the floor and Bill winced. The dog turned his head, gave Bill a curious glance, then stilled his tail.

"Good job, Bear. That's my brother, Bill. Bill, this is Bear."

"Um." Bill thought a human introduction for a dog made more sense coming from a seven year old girl than one almost seventeen, but he went along with it anyway. "Um, nice to meet you, Bear."

Bear wagged his tail and panted, lifting one muddy paw toward Bill.

"What is that, a command to shake?" Bill raised an eyebrow at Millie, who shook her head. He took Bear's paw in his hand, being a good sport even though he didn't generally like big dogs because they were messy. This one at least seemed well trained. Mother came in with a bucket and some rags and soap. Bill stuck his hand under the tap in the sink, turned it on, and washed the mud off.

"Bear says he'll try not to make a mess, Bill." Millie smiled.

"Wait. What?" He glanced over at Mother, who was smiling so big he thought her face might get stuck that way.

"It seems your sister has developed some sort of partial Mind Wisdom involving dogs." Mother giggled, pouring water into the tub. But she never giggled, barely even laughed most of the time.

"Oh." Bill looked at Millie, Bear, and then the door that led into the hall. "What does Dad think of all this?"

The door swung slowly open while he watched it, revealing Giuseppe on the other side. He shuffled into the kitchen, slippers making a rustling hiss across the wood, and placed one wrinkled hand on the back of a kitchen chair. Bill hurried over to help him settle himself into it.

"Dad thinks it's a welcome development, William." Giuseppe grinned. "After your Wisdom comes in, you can try to learn the minds of dogs, cats, horses, certain birds; any animal with friendly bonds to humankind. But it won't be easy for you. With partial Wisdom, as I've told both of you before, one skill comes naturally because it's the only one."

Millie had taken up some of the soapy rags and

started washing Bear. The smell of wet dog gave way to Palmolive. Bear sighed, resting his chin on the tub's edge. Even when Millie encountered matted fur, he stayed still, flinching only a little. Dirt and coarse red hair coated the first rag, so Millie got a fresh one. She also made use of a bottle of mineral oil and an old bristle brush for the worst snarls. She didn't speak to Bear, but when Millie reached for one of the dog's paws or tried to get at a distant part of his body, he'd move or turn around to accommodate her.

"So are we going to take in every stray that comes to our door?" asked Bill.

Bear rolled his eyes, then gave an incredulous "whuff" that someone else might have dismissed as a sneeze. Bill, however, was suspicious. Partial Wisdom or no, this was the most intelligent animal Bill had ever seen.

And how had Bear known Bill thought dogs were messy, anyway? He had a nagging suspicion that something about this creature or his communication with Millie wasn't normal even if their parents seemed unaware of how hinky it all was. He glanced down at the growing pile of dirty, hairy rags.

"Look at that sour face," said Mom. "I know you're the sort of young man to keep everything tidy, but it's only dirt, William. Why begrudge such a charming animal a bath and a meal? Millie wouldn't bring in anything too dangerous without my Seeing it. We should be happy for her. This kind of Wisdom could prove helpful, not to mention lucrative."

"And that's what I'm doing for Bear here, helping,"

said Millie. "He's been on his own for months now, traveling from somewhere far away all on his own. He's looking for his friends, a man and a cat. Don't worry, I'm sure he'll be on his way once we find out which direction they went." Millie's smile flattened as those last words left her mouth.

Bill tried not to crack under pressure from his mother and his sister. At least Dad wore a neutral expression. He stood there for a couple of minutes, absorbing the ill-will in the room until he finally understood what it was.

By the time the clean water buckets were empty, Bill realized that Millie would be lonely without the dog, that she'd felt alone for weeks and he'd been so caught up in forming that alliance with Tucci and scheming against Finn to notice. He sighed and crossed the room, taking the buckets by their handles to refill them.

Millie and Mom didn't look up as he set the water down near them, but Dad gave him a small smile. Of course Giuseppe sensed Bill's still-waking Wisdom even if he hadn't broached the subject yet.

Bill headed over to the stove and put the tea kettle on, then set the tea leaves in the pot. He got down Father's favorite cup and saucer, turning around afterward to watch Bear's bath while waiting for water to boil. They'd finished removing the dirt, including a heap of small twigs and leaves.

Millie rubbed mineral oil on each snarl in Bear's coat. After that, she took a brush to them in the same order she'd applied the oil. The steamed water whistled, startling the dog enough that he perked his ears and lifted his head. Bill removed the kettle from the stove and steeped the tea, then served it to his father.

Bill didn't know how he'd expected Bear to behave while having his fur pulled and inevitably ripped out at times. He certainly would have placed money on yelping and jumping in the process, if not Millie being bitten. But the dog only whined softly four times during the hour-long process. The snarls Millie had worked when Bear cried all proved so matted they had to be cut out with shears.

With his coat detangled, Bear let Millie rinse him a final time with water. Then he got out of the tub and went directly to the door. Mother opened it and the dog went outside, walking a short distance before shaking what had to be gallons of water from himself.

"Thank you, Bear," said Millie, holding a flannel sheet. "Come back in, and we'll get you a bit drier. Then you can sit by the radiator and you'll be cozy in no time." Bear wagged his tail vigorously as he trotted toward her. He let Millie wrap the sheet around him and rub all over. Once finished, Millie gathered the sheet into a bundle and rose. Bear stood too. He leaned against her, pressing the side of his head into the top of her leg just below her hip bone. Bill hadn't realized how tall the dog was until he saw him do that.

"You're welcome," said Millie, scratching behind Bear's ear. "Go and get warm, now."

Mom held the door to the hall open and Bill could hear the dog's claws clicking all the way into the parlor, but lightly as though he wanted to take care not to scratch the polished wood floors.

He still thought Bear wasn't exactly normal, though

he supposed Millie could have given him a picture of what a radiator looked like with her Wisdom. Father had taught him how Mind Wisdom consisted of reading and sending mental perceptions; pictures, emotions, or all three. He'd said that one of these nearly always came on first and more naturally than the rest. From the way Millie had been talking, she used pictures with this dog.

He looked at his sister now and saw that she grinned even while cleaning the washtub and the floor, a task that usually brought on a scowl. Maybe this partial Wisdom was good for Millie, hinky dog or no.

Bill had seen right through the nearly manic giddiness surrounding his sister since the engagement announcements. It had been like a time at school last year when Millie insisted on wearing a party dress to sit for a history exam. She'd had a brand-new ribbon in her curls and her Sunday shoes on, too.

Bill had thought then that the festive garb had been a sort of armor, insulating her from the boredom and disdain she had for the test's subject. Her gaiety and those private hours spent in Theo's company over the last two weeks had been just like that exam, a front for some kind of ill mood left unexplored.

But tonight Millie displayed genuine contentment. The homey and generous task of bathing a down-at-the-heels dog wasn't usually in Millie's wheelhouse. She'd grown up jumping in puddles, climbing trees, and looking for tadpoles in the pond at the Howe farm. The first thing she'd proclaimed she would be when she grew up was an explorer like Meriwether Lewis, a man she'd always insisted must have actually been a woman in disguise. Even as she matured into a young woman, she remained madcap and impulsive.

Bill and Millie had grown up suspecting that the minds of others were an untamed frontier. They'd figured only one of them would develop full Wisdom and get to explore that uncharted territory. He had a feeling the years of the whole Wise community assuming Bill would be the next Mind Wise had hurt his sister's heart deeply.

She'd be expected to marry and be a mother, not an explorer. Of course Millie would finally be content now that she had the ability to explore something, even if that was the just the mind of an animal. But no. He probably had that last part all wrong.

Millie might consider an animal's mind more of a challenging puzzle than a human's. Bill knew people were complex, but animals, even those that shared their lives with men, were completely alien. She might be exchanging pictures with Bear, but everything the dog transmitted to Millie would need interpretation. It was impossible for dogs to see things the same way as people. For one thing, their visual perspective was closer to the ground. And hadn't Bill read about how dogs couldn't see all the colors and sensed more with their noses than their eyes?

"Sit with me, son." Giuseppe hadn't fallen asleep after all.

"How was the tea?" Bill took the chair opposite him.

"Eh, *mezzo mezzo*. It could have been better if you'd had some with me."

Bill barely remembered what his father's eyes had

looked like when his body matched his actual age, but now they resembled a pair of raisins in a nicely browned roll. That would happen to him someday, when he was younger than his father is now if he wasn't careful. Bill felt like he'd swallowed a brick, but he kept his face as blank as he could. That didn't fool his father.

"You take too much on your shoulders, William." Giuseppe put both hands on the teapot, and poured more of the golden-brown liquid into his cup. By now, it had cooled enough for that. "Too many burdens, and not enough joy in compensation. That makes monsters of men, you know."

"It's just, there's no time to seek joy. I'm not built that way, to go after what I want when so much needs to be done for the greater good." Bill couldn't explain about Gilbert. Even if he'd somehow been careless and Father knew already, Millie and Mom stood at the sink, washing up. He thought briefly about saying a prayer, asking that they'd never find out, but he didn't want to think loudly enough about it for that. God probably wouldn't even hear prayers from a man in love with same, let alone answer them.

"God made you different, William." His father's words made that brick in the stomach heavier. How could Dad not know? "If God made you, He knows your strengths and your shortcomings; your heart, too. He made you as He meant, and then put you on this Earth and into this family. Now it's your turn to make something with that, to make a life."

"But I'm limited in what I can have by what I am." Bill thought his father couldn't possibly know his secret.

Dad had to be referencing Wisdom.

Bill felt Millie's eyes on the back of his head and tried not to shiver. She followed Mom out the door. He wouldn't have to finish this conversation in front of them, at least. But there was no way Giuseppe, so in love with Katherine, could possibly understand one man in love with another.

"I'm incapable of true happiness in this life as it's been laid out for me, I guess, Father."

"Are you? What do you truly want that you cannot have?" Father finished his tea.

Bill fidgeted with the tea things as he thought about that question. All he wanted was to be at peace. He closed his eyes, crushed under the weight of that self-knowledge. He didn't want to be happy, wasn't sure he could handle expressing the kind of bouncy, head-spinning feeling he saw and lately felt in other people his age.

As long as Bill could remember, he'd carefully pulled the string and tape off a present instead of tearing into the paper. As a child, he preferred sitting on a bench with grandparents to playing a game with the other kids. He'd always done his homework and chores before playing bridge with Millie and their friends and kept his room neater than any other teenager he knew. He was conscientious, sedate, dutiful. Peace suited him in a way happiness never did.

But could he be at peace? He would obey his parents and marry Rachel. He didn't want to, but he would because honor bound him. There were no other young men with Wisdom to make a match for her. He also considered her a friend.

They'd known each other since the day he and Millie were born. It would be peaceful, living under the same roof with Rachel. She was respectful and got along with everyone he cared about. She liked the simplicity and quiet out at the Howe farm. He had love for her even if he wasn't *in love* with her. In his heart, Rachel felt like another sister.

But then there was the matter of what he'd be expected to do with her on their wedding night. Bill couldn't be at peace with that sword over his head. How could he do that kind of thing without romantic feelings involved?

The prospect made him want to weep with despair. Bill couldn't marry Rachel and then shirk his duty to become a father. He'd have to get as many children on her in as few years as possible, too, because of the rapid aging that came with Mind Wisdom's talent to erase or overwrite memories.

Could he bear all that if Gilbert shared his feelings? Perhaps he could tolerate his familial duty if only romantic love existed somewhere in his life. Maybe his best friend in the world sat in his room across the street, as equally sickened by his own version of the same situation. Perhaps what Bill really wanted was just to love and be loved in return.

Bill already knew that emotions were like a Nor'Easter. Only the thoughts that inspired them could be controlled and that cost too dear a price. He could hide them away but only for so long. Maybe Father was trying to tell him that his feelings were moot. What mattered was what he did with them.

"William?" Guiseppe cleared his throat. "Are you back? I asked what you cannot have."

"I changed my mind, Father." Bill grinned. "I can have anything I want."

"Oh?" His father's eyebrows climbed the ladder of his forehead. "And why is that?"

"Because I'm the only person who decides what I want in the first place. And it's up to me to go out and get it." Bill took the tea things to the counter and set them by the sink.

"Are you sure, son?" Giuseppe started to rise from his seat. Bill pulled the chair out for him, let him shuffle toward the door, then replaced the chair. He held the door open for his father, waiting until he got to the door of his study. He'd been sleeping in there the past few nights to spare his knees from the stairs. Giuseppe looked back at him down the hall expectantly.

"Yes. There are few things I've been more certain of in my life." Bill spoke once more before letting the kitchen door shut. "Goodnight."

In his mind, he heard Giuseppe's voice. "Rest well, son."

I love you, Dad, he said without speaking. Bill's telepathic answered settled the question of his Wisdom coming in. He sensed unadulterated approval.

And I you, son, came the silent answer. *More than you know.*

Even though it was the night before Thanksgiving, Bill already knew what he was most thankful for.

"Bless me, Father."

"Gladly, son." Father Francis let out a sigh so raspy Jimmy worried that he might just croak there in the Reconciliation closet. "But have you sinned?"

"Oh, yeah, Father." Jimmy folded his hands and bent his head over them. "I sin all the time. Selling hooch is breaking the law and so is working for my Boss." He held his breath, trying to keep the rest of it in.

"Jimmy, you only just confessed to those things this morning. Man's laws are not Gods and that is why this Church is Sanctuary. Do you want me to repeat what I said about alcohol and how drinking or selling it is no sin?" A faint rustle came from the Father's side and Jimmy imagined him smoothing his cassock.

"I know, Father." All of Jimmy's breath had rushed out with that sentence so he took another one. Deep, like he was about to go diving in the waters he regularly navigated. He supposed getting wet was one way to look at the job Bianco had given him. "Well, I guess I haven't exactly done the thing yet that needs confessing, Father. I'll have to, though. But I'm worried I might not get a chance to come to you otherwise."

"And what troubles you about this future sin, son?"

"The idea that I'm the only one who's troubled by it, Father." Jimmy pressed his forehead against the top of his folded hands, something he hadn't done since he was a kid. "It's murder, Father. Cold-blooded and to order like a plate of fancy vittles. I don't know if I can go through with it. Don't think I'll be allowed to live if I walk away, either."

"Jimmy, remember when you were ten and I caught you sneaking into the Rectory?"

"Yeah, Father. I remember that." Jimmy chuckled but it came out sounding more like a sob. Maybe the Father wouldn't notice.

"I let you go, but you didn't leave." Father Francis cleared his throat. "Please refresh an old priest's memory, Jimmy. Why?"

"Because I still had your cufflinks, Father. I stole them."

"Yes. You stayed to give them back. And this is why theft is a different kind of sin from murder. Can you tell me why?"

"Because you can take stealing back, Father. It's venial."

"And murder?"

"Ain't no way you can take that back. I get it."

"Do you, Jimmy?"

"Um, I think so, Father. But I ain't the brightest bulb, you know."

"On the contrary, my son, you've got more brightness about you than most in your Boss's employ. This is why I think you've guessed at what I'm going to say. The best way to repent this sin from the future is not to commit it in the first place."

"But what if the Boss kills me?"

"Then you will have died with a clear conscience and a soul worthy of God's Kingdom."

"That's harsh, Father."

"The Lord tests His children at times, Jimmy. Perhaps this is one of those for you."

"I don't know, Father. My being where I am, it protects people. My hooch ain't poison like that swill down in New York. You said it yourself, the hooch ain't a sin and neither is breaking this law that bans it. If the Boss loses me, who knows where he'll get his stuff from. How many innocent people in this city will die?"

"Tell me then, Jimmy," said Father Francis, "can you be sure your Boss will not murder you anyway?"

Jimmy couldn't answer. Memories of his trips to Plymouth, his mostly harmless flirtation with Esmeralda Cavalcante, and the Boss's reaction after his last run barraged his mind.

"He wouldn't do that, Father. I'm too valuable." But Jimmy knew the words were lies as soon as they left his lips. "Thank you, Father. I think I gotta go now."

"Jimmy?" The Father coughed. Jimmy waited it out. "Was there something else you wanted to tell me?"

"Yeah, Father." Jimmy unfolded his hands and stood. "I lied just then. I ain't worthy to be here, not of nothing."

"Jimmy—"

"Don't, Father. Worms like me don't belong in God's House." He pushed past the curtain, blinking in the kaleidoscope sunlight coming through the stained glass. Over his shoulder on the way out, Jimmy murmured, "I'm just a nightcrawler under Bianco's heel, Father. Don't waste your time on me."

Jimmy still had no idea how wrong he was.

Millie was glad Bill insisted she wear a hat before they'd even made it to the end of the block. She hated the hair squishing contraptions, but the cold was more like January than November and she actually needed one. What's more, once she actually left the house she wouldn't have bothered going back for it. She looked back over her shoulder for Bear.

Millie let the dog out about a half-hour ago, before the sun was up completely. He still hadn't come back. She knew Mother would look out for the dog, let him in if he came to the door, but it was below freezing out. She wouldn't want to be stuck outside on a morning as cold as this and she didn't want to think of Bear stuck out here all day either. Maybe it would warm up once the sun rose.

She reflexively walked faster as they passed by Theo's house, then felt silly. They'd come close to settling things the night before, though she couldn't be sure with Bear interrupting them. She'd gone over there to apologize to Sarah anyway and would have to keep trying even though Theo thought their friendship a lost cause.

Other than the cold, the sun shone bright and beautiful. The sky was that clear and pale shade of blue that never showed itself in summer. Cherry and birch trees reached for the sky with bare branches but the oaks and maples still wore half their foliage. She couldn't see the grass in most of the open spaces under its blanket of red, orange, and gold leaves. More of these sights graced the landscape the further they walked out of the town proper. Maybe Bear had stayed out to enjoy all of this. Millie gave herself permission to stop worrying about him.

Bill walked along without speaking, his head somewhere else. Her brother's expression told her that he looked inward. Millie couldn't help but shake her head. They couldn't be more different if they'd been strangers. Any time they met new people they heard lectures about how twins were so similar.

"Aren't you two lucky," people would say, "to have one other person in the world just like you." They weren't even identical, as if that would make a difference. If she had a nickel for every time someone made that assumption, she could laugh all the way to Uncle Finn's bank.

Maybe someone like Carl Jung would write a book about twins someday and educate people. Millie wondered once again whether Jung was from a Wise family. When she'd shown Dad a copy of "Psychology of the Unconscious," he'd had the same idea.

She caught sight of someone approaching them at the last intersection before reaching the Howe farm. He had a hat and scarf on, so she couldn't see his face or hair, but she knew who it was immediately. She'd recognize that saunter anywhere.

"Gil!" She waved as she shouted, breaking her brother from his reverie. Gilbert sprinted up the cross-street toward them. They all stopped at the corner, where Gil leaned forward with his hands on his thighs. Bill went to his side, to make sure he wouldn't topple over.

"Million and Billion," he puffed, drawing the scarf away from his face. Running and Gilbert had never gotten on well together. Cold, dry weather always seemed to make it worse. "Haven't seen either of you in a brace of weeks. I hope we're not starting a trend."

"We looked for you," said Bill, "any trend is on your head."

"It's all Plymouth Cordage's fault. They offered me extra money to stay late. And then yesterday, Sarah." He caught Millie's eye, then looked at someone behind her. She turned and saw that Rachel had come down from the farm to meet them.

"What about Sarah?" asked Rachel. She lifted the lid on her basket to pull out a battered looking Thermos, then held it out toward Gilbert. "Coffee for your thoughts?"

"I asked her for help with the manifest records and some time slips from Cordage. She came to me with a sordid story about how Little Miss Millie here walloped her, so she fell and cut her hand." He looked Millie in the face with a scrutiny he usually reserved for books of poetry. "So, did you rough up my flat tire... I mean, fiancee?"

Millie would have laughed out loud at the insult just a couple of days ago, but her conversation with Theo and the stink-eye Rachel aimed in Gil's direction made her friend's meaner-than-usual quip seem unnecessarily cruel. Sarah might not be the most interesting person to talk to, but Millie had more of an idea about what she went through on a daily basis than she had before.

She wondered how much of Sarah's interest in math had been a way to distract her from a very reasonable fear of her mother or brother burning her house down. That might also be why she always wanted to tag along with the rest of them everywhere. Millie wondered if she'd end up the same way, constantly unable to sleep without worrying about a house fire. A shiver that had nothing to do with the chilly morning air took her.

"Yes, I did slap Sarah," said Millie, "and I felt bad about it right away. She didn't do anything wrong, just told me a few plain and inconvenient truths that set me off. And don't call her a flat tire, Gil. We all know you wouldn't have picked her as a wife, but she's in the same boat. How would you feel if she started calling you a blowhard or something?"

"Don't cast a kitten, Million," said Gilbert. "I wouldn't refer to her like that around anyone but the three of you, anyway."

"Don't say it around me either," said Rachel. "I won't listen to rude remarks about her personality or any of the rest of us for that matter. We're not children anymore." She took the lid off the Thermos, turned it over, and handed it to Gilbert. Then she opened the insulated canister. The foggy aroma of hot coffee permeated the chill air, completing the idyllic feel of a New England country road in late autumn. Rachel didn't pour yet, just gazed at Gilbert and raised an eyebrow.

"Sorry, ladies," said Gilbert. "It won't happen again."

Rachel nodded, turning her lips up in a grin that didn't touch her eyes. Coffee steamed as she poured it into the lid-turned-cup. Gilbert took a sip, closing his eyes as he swallowed.

"Sorry, I didn't bring any more coffee," Rachel said. "Papa was expecting Gilbert to come because it's time to slow everything down in the root cellar, but we didn't know you'd be visiting. It's been years since you've come on turkey day."

"Our mother sent us down for some offal from the birds because last night, Millie— Oh no," Bill's mouth made an oval shape as he groaned. "Millie, maybe you should stay here."

Rachel and Gilbert blinked, looking from Bill to his sister and then at each other.

"Yeah, maybe I should keep away, all things considered." Millie felt like the village's missing idiot. Bill was right.

"What are you talking about? Are you saying your bearcat sister here can't handle looking at a couple of buckets of turkey gust and a side of blood?" Gilbert kicked back the rest of his coffee and held the cup out for a refill.

"Last night, I met a perfect gentleman who told me he needed help." Millie watched Rachel pour the Thermos's dregs into the cup. "I gave him food, water, a bath and let him sleep in my bed."

Gilbert blinked owlishly, shaking his head in shock. Rachel's mouth dropped open and a strangled little sound came out of it. Bill chuckled.

"His name is Bear." Millie smiled as she dropped the pretense. "I think he's some sort of Irish Wolfhound. Apparently, I have some kind of partial Wisdom that lets me communicate with him."

"You can hear animals now?" Rachel replaced round eyes and mouth with a sunny smile. "Yes, you should stay away from the turkey slaughter. None of us need to be there, actually. We could go to the orchard and cart in some apple wood for the smoker instead."

"Is there time to get more coffee first?" Bill looked at the thermos and licked his lips.

"We can go on up and get it." Rachel's eyes lingered on Bill's mouth. "We have to go up to the house anyway, to get to the root cellar."

They all started walking together at first, but Millie slowed her pace. What if they'd already started killing the birds? Would she be able to hear them in her head even when she couldn't see them? She shuddered a bit thinking about that. She'd never considered inadvertently experiencing pain, suffering, or even death second-hand. She had even more respect for her father now.

Gilbert minced his steps until he walked along next to her. "So Sarah didn't tell me she said anything to you but hello. What set you off? If you want to talk about it at all, I mean."

"I made her angry first." Millie's defense of Sarah would feel trite if she didn't admit this now. She told Gil the whole story. "At the end I said something about how Wise girls back in the Pilgrim days didn't have to watch the mundane ones leaving for work or college."

"Oh God." Gilbert winced. "Tell me you didn't mention Radcliffe."

"Uh, I did." Leaves crunched under their feet. "Why?"

"She got an acceptance letter at the beginning of the month." Gilbert sipped coffee.

"What?" A college acceptance letter was nearly as much of a scandal as having a child out of wedlock for Wise families. Wise didn't up and send out applications to colleges on their own. Their parents did it for them, but only if they had enough other children already married. "She never said she tried to get in."

"She didn't have to." Gilbert rolled his cup between his hands. "Mrs. Pickering wrote them a letter. She got her own education there before she married Mr. Pickering. They only take married ladies if they live off-campus locally."

"So, Sarah still wants to go to Radcliffe?" Millie couldn't imagine anyone wanting to go sit in a classroom for four more years, but Sarah was an odd bird.

"Do you still want to be an explorer?" Gilbert glanced at her. Her answer to that question must have been plain on her face, because he nodded.

"But she never told any of us that she wanted to go to college. Not even once." Millie thought he must be wrong about this somehow. One of them should have noticed. But that line of thought only insulted Sarah's intelligence and downplayed the disdain the group had always had for its youngest member.

"Why would she?" Gilbert glared down into the

dregs of his coffee. "We only would have poked fun. Remember how we used to tease her about randomly doing sums like others might quote poetry? Dull people have dull dreams."

Gilbert was right even if he was being a prick about it. It was only natural for Sarah to keep secrets from people she must have sensed didn't care. For all that they had a desire to escape Plymouth in common, Millie realized that Sarah was as different from her as the moon was from the sun.

"Gil, I asked you not to talk about her like that." Millie thought having more compassion for Sarah was important, though she couldn't put her finger on why. "I mean, you're marrying her for goodness sake. Stop razzing her already."

"This isn't about her anymore, it's about me. I don't want to get married at all. It's nothing personal." Gilbert's glasses had fogged over from his breath and the hot coffee. He handed her the Thermos cup and removed them to wipe them down with his handkerchief. "Sarah wanted to grow up and study mathematics, I think that's dull. You wanted to be an explorer, I think that's dangerous. Rachel wanted to be a nurse like Florence Nightingale, I can't stand the sight of blood. All I want is to be a bachelor and write witty stories, like Oscar Wilde or Mark Twain. Someone's well-read author uncle, who goes on outings to Boston and attends matinees at the Majestic Theatre."

"God, Gilbert." Millie tucked a stray curl behind her ear. "Do your parents know?"

"Doesn't matter if they did. I'm an only child now."

He put his glasses back on, then started folding the handkerchief. He tucked it in his pocket. "If I had seven siblings like Rachel, maybe they'd consider letting me go."

"Well, couldn't you and Sarah get married and then move to Boston?" Why wasn't this solution as clear to Gilbert as it seemed to Millie? "She could go to Radcliffe, and you could get box seats at the Majestic if we manage to get one over on Finn." Millie handed the thermos cup back to Gilbert.

"She'd never put up with that sort of thing." Gilbert tapped the cup with his pinkie. "You saw the reason why, of course. You wouldn't have slapped her otherwise if you hadn't. That girl has a puritanical streak a mile wide. It's why she loves math with all its strictures."

"Um. And this is a bad thing?" She wondered whether she'd ever fall in love with anybody herself. "Doesn't that mean she wouldn't want much from you than to be left alone?"

"Sarah doesn't tolerate anything but strict discipline from those closest to her. Just look at Theo for an example." Gilbert turned the cup over, letting the last drops of tepid coffee scatter on grass and fallen leaves. "She'd run our household like she's running a set of equations."

"What does that mean?" Millie waited to hear where Gilbert would take this analogy.

"It means she and I have had a few long talks since our parents handed down our life sentence. The first thing she told me was how she would not tolerate drinking, smoking, or any rumors about the, er, masculinity of her spouse." Gilbert sighed, strumming his fingers on the empty cup. "Sarah might seem harmless because she's mousy and scrawny and got her head in her slide-rule. Fact of the matter is, she's not harmless at all. She's harsh and absolute, like a theorem. Stronger than she seems, too. Calculating with more than just the numbers."

"She's using some hinky equations then," said Millie. "For some women, being able to chase her dream could be a fair trade for letting her husband live like a confirmed bachelor. As long as he'd do something about the family obligation of having children at some point after she'd gotten that Radcliffe parchment."

"You forget, this particular woman is infested with lines like bars on a prison cell." Gilbert tapped his temple with the cup. He looked like he hadn't slept in weeks. "Suffice to say, Sarah imposes order on anything she touches. I wish I were marrying you or Rachel. You can be reasoned with and Rachel just wants to make people happy."

"There are too few of us," said Millie. "There'd be no one for her to marry if one of us married you. All the families want as many grandchildren as possible after losing so many men in the Great War."

"She's got a sibling. Why should she have to marry at all or even marry one of us for that matter?" Gilbert's shoulders slumped. "Eventually, the Wise are going to have to get a little wiser to modern times. Sarah and I will just have to suffer for the next hundred years." He looked up, then handed the Thermos cup to Millie.

"Give this to Rachel, will you?"

Millie looked up, finding that they'd reached the old yellow farm house. Bill was already on the steps starting to sit down.

Rachel's jaw clenched even as she spoke. "I'll send Papa around back to meet you at the bulkhead, Gilbert. You two stay here and I'll get the coffee. We need to get out of here before they start putting the turkeys down."

Millie mounted the steps, handed Rachel the cup, and plopped herself next to her brother. She knew every knot and imperfection in the board she sat on. The familiar surroundings weren't comforting. She'd never been this restless.

She thought she'd even take an acceptance letter to Radcliffe over staying in this little town.

Bill had been relaxing on the porch for almost five minutes before his sister started in on the drama.

"We're might have trouble with Sarah," said Millie. "It's probably my fault."

"Look, I heard some of what you and Gil were talking about. Sorry, voices carry. So, she wants to go to Radcliffe. She could just wait seven years and go after she's had a couple of kids. I bet they'd still take her then."

"But I had to go and rub her face in it. Now she's a howling mess and it's all my fault."

""Wow. I'd better ask Rachel for an extra wheelbarrow so we can push your enormous head through the orchard." He rolled his eyes and sighed.

"Yeah, that made me sound like the queen of the prima donnas." She stuck out her tongue to show there were no hard feelings. "Still, poor Sarah's so miserable she won't even let me apologize. What are we going to do about it?"

"Nothing." Bill heard the door open behind him and footsteps on the porch.

"What do you mean, nothing?" Rachel spoke, then closed the door.

"I mean, we can't do anything about Sarah's situation or her feelings. Except apologize." He made sure to clarify enough in case Rachel hadn't heard the start of the conversation. "And she's not accepting those. So we do what we can. Nothing." Bill stood up and stretched.

"And we should take your word for it that there's nothing at all we can do?" Millie's skepticism was louder than Independence Day fireworks. She stood, then went down the steps.

"I bet Dad had one of his talks with you about life recently." Bill stretched his arms over his head, yawned. "None of us can make Sarah's decisions for her. Even if she let us try and help, the choices she makes are still hers."

Rachel came down from the porch, passing Millie. Bill followed as she went around the side of the house. He jogged ahead when he saw the wheelbarrow she'd been off to fetch. Millie sprinted all-out, passing him with ease. He let her grab the handles and trundle along with the empty barrow. She'd pass it to him as soon as it got heavy enough to blister her hands.

"So it's like when she stopped helping me with Geometry," said Rachel. "After a point, she saw that I wasn't ready to understand the concepts. Once I'd memorized the equations, there wasn't anything else she could help me with. It was up to me to understand them or not."

"That's a good way of putting it." Bill walked along without stumbling. His feet had learned the path from the Howe house to the orchard years ago, a good thing since he'd resigned himself to living here. "We all knew the engagements were coming. We all knew there'd be mixed feelings. Somehow, none of us were prepared for the reality. And it all happened in the middle of the Finn crisis. We're all chasing our tails over who's marrying who and how everyone feels. We're forgetting about Finn."

"That's right," said Rachel. "Bad enough to be stuck in a loveless marriage, but worse having the town controlled by your paranoid uncle the Seer and his band of Irish Mobsters. I'm getting nowhere with information, even when I'm not too distracted to look for it. There's nothing about what happened to those two Italian men and Cloris Mullins anywhere I'm able to look. The real version of events might just be unrecorded. Maybe even erased."

"Millie's not going to be happy to hear this, but we might want to ask Sal Tucci." His foot inverted slightly and a rich cidery scent met his nose as he stepped on a hidden windfall. They'd reached the edge of the apple orchard.

"You're right, I'm not happy." Millie dropped the handles to pick up a fallen branch and plunk it into the barrow. "I think asking him for anything is asking for trouble as bad or worse than whatever Uncle Finn could cook up." She rubbed her wrist. "I mean, they're both Mobsters so I don't get how one of them is somehow better than the other. Anyway, I have Bear around now in case Finn puts his hands on me again, but guns kill dogs."

"Tucci doesn't have a gun." Bill didn't feel guilty for the lie. His Wisdom could convince Tucci to leave easily if he turned out to be a problem. Mind Wisdom was easy to use on mundanes like him. "Look, tactically speaking, it's sound thinking to pit Sal Tucci against Uncle Finn. In a month or two, Tucci might just decide to leave town anyway if there's no money here for him. Finn can't be convinced to do that at all. But if Tucci makes Finn burn some of his assets, he's weaker when we try and deal with him." He leaned down and placed another branch on the barrow.

"Call me superstitious, then." Millie dropped in two branches this time. "The last time a Tucci lived in town, he died. Hell, maybe that's what started this mess in the first place." She took the handles again and wheeled the barrow further into the orchard. "Sarah would warn us about calculating the probability of a coincidence or something."

"At this point, what other options do we have?" Rachel pulled a Thermos out of her basket and handed it to Bill. "The information from the dockmaster's log leads to the Supper Club, which is run by another Italian with a name from the cemetery. The manifest only tells us the name Howe didn't come from any of the colonists, even though this farm was here since Old Colony days." She paused to set down her basket and grabbed three branches. "Gran and the names in the Bible only lead us to more questions. We need to find," Rachel tossed a branch in the barrow, "the," and another, "answers." And Rachel's last branch clattered against the rest.

"I guess I'm outnumbered, then." Millie took the thermos from Bill, uncapped it, then took a swig right from the bottle. "Gilbert will side with Bill. Theo'll think he can deal with Tucci too. Sarah's totally justified to go against me now." She tilted the thermos again, drinking more deeply this time. Bill wondered whether Rachel had spiked it.

"I just wonder something." Rachel got another thermos from the basket and tossed it to Bill. "If Tucci's so useful, why isn't your uncle trying to manipulate him? None of us or our parents are going to help Finn bring the Irish Mob to town. Tucci's throwing money around, too, eating at the diner every day."

"Uncle Finn hates Italians." Bill opened his thermos and drank. The hot coffee infused his chest and belly with more than the expected warmth. He smacked his lips, inhaling, but didn't taste or smell a hint of alcohol. What had Rachel put in the coffee to make it so invigorating, then? "You should hear some of the things he's called Father under our own roof. He wouldn't work with Tucci in a million years. In fact, he's more likely to try and roll him for the money he's got and dump him on a cargo boat. In the ocean, more likely"

"Well why hasn't he done that, then." Millie tipped her thermos back and drained it. "If I were a big guy, I'd have run Tucci out of town already myself."

"Thought you were scared of his nonexistent gun." Bill dodged as Millie made a grab for his thermos.

"That'd be easy if I were a man." Millie picked up a branch. "I'd sneak up on him in the john. Think fast!" She chucked the apple wood at his head, and he ducked it neatly. "Give me all your coffee, Chiavo, or you sleep with the fishes!"

"No way." Bill smirked, playing along with the jest.

"This coffee's too good for a two bit hoodlum like you. I'm the Boss here. Threaten this tasty beverage again, and I'll have my wiseguy here bump you off."

Rachel chuckled, and dumped the armload of branches she'd been gathering into the wheelbarrow. "That's wisegal to you, Mister Boss. I'll be a gangster, but not a guy. Hey, if Ms. Cavalcante can do it, why can't I?"

"Finally, Jimmy!" Esmeralda Cavalcante's knees wobbled for the first time in eighteen years. It had nothing to do with the sight of Jimmy himself. What his arrival meant for her club was of far greater importance to her. "You've got my order, right?"

"Hi, Ms. Cavalcante." Jimmy's face looked pale, drawn like he hadn't eaten much lately. He blinked long lashes that drew attention to the darkening circles under his eyes.

"I think it's about time you started calling me Esmeralda." She stepped forward, one hand on the brass rail between the upper seating area and the small bar.

"Ms. Cavalcante, I couldn't." He cut his eyes away toward the floor. "I have orders to keep things proper enough to pass a chaperon's muster, you understand."

"Indubitably." Esmeralda's gut twisted as she thought of Jimmy's long absence. What kind of work had cousin Giacomo given the rumrunner besides the usual? "It looks like someone's been running you ragged. Sit down and eat something."

"Yes, ma'am." Jimmy rested his weight on a barstool as though it was the most comfortable seat he'd taken in weeks.

"I'll be right back."

Esmeralda stepped into the steamy kitchen. She nodded as she passed her Head Chef, set a bowl atop a side-dish, and began ladling white chowder into it. One filled, she sprinkled fresh parsley on top and set a hunk of fresh bread and round spoon at the side.

"Miss? I could have gotten that for you."

"Don't worry, Etta. It doesn't have to be fancied up." Esmeralda smiled at the statuesque woman. "This isn't for a customer, just Mr. Delaqua."

"Oh." Etta Franklin smiled back, her white teeth shining out from between dusky lips. "Tell that lucky kid I said hello."

"Sure thing, Etta." Esmeralda balanced the soup on one arm and pushed back through into the restaurant proper.

It was a shame she couldn't have Ms. Franklin out in the front of the house on occasion to greet diners like Head Chefs generally did in fancy restaurants. No law prevented her from working at the Plymouth Supper Club as might have been the case south of the Mason Dixon, but Esmeralda knew that her cousin wouldn't tolerate public knowledge that the woman behind the Club's delicious food was Mulatto.

Esmeralda shook her head, marveling once again at how she and Jacky had grown up so differently under the same roof. She set the soup down in front of half-Puerto Rican Jimmy before her anger at Jacky's hypocrisy made her drop it. She'd never repeat any of the words her cousin had used in reference to Etta if she lived a thousand years.

"Thanks for the grub, Ms. Cavalcante." Jimmy picked up the spoon and made short work of the soup, then used the bread to mop up the dregs.

Esmeralda busied herself tidying the back of the bar while he ate, peering into nearly empty cabinets and scrutinizing the low levels of alcohol in the remaining bottles. Cousin Jacky's beef with his rumrunner had nearly shut her down. She wasn't sure he cared, either. Something was definitely even more rotten than she'd thought in the state of Bianco's organization.

"Jimmy." Esmeralda decided to take the plunge and get some answers. As usual, she phrased it carefully. "Why are you so late with the shipment this time?"

"The Boss had an emergency and needed me on it." Jimmy stared into his empty bowl.

"A liquid emergency?" Esmeralda raised an eyebrow, which didn't do her much good with Jimmy not even looking at her.

"Well, not exactly." Jimmy poked the last stub of bread crust on the side plate with his spoon.

"Is the situation over and done now?"

"Ma'am, I can't say for sure." Jimmy finally looked up at her. "I'm not sure and I can't say are probably two different things, though."

"I'll go and tell Etta that you gave me a huge hint because her soup is that good, Jimmy."

"That ain't the only reason, Ma'am."

"Are any of those other reasons things you can tell

me?"

"One is. You've got a good head on your shoulders. You can see things for what they are. And I know you're watching this whole dog and pony show very carefully. That makes me easier than I have any right to be just recently, Ms. Cavalcante."

"Wow, Jimmy." Esmeralda grinned. "I think that's one of the nicest things any man's said to me in years."

"Really?" He blinked. "How so?"

"You didn't say anything to imply that my competence is extraordinary simply because I'm female."

"That's, um, blunt, Ma'am, if you don't mind my saying so."

"You're a breath of fresh air."

"Thanks, Ms. Cavalcante." He set the spoon in the bowl and then waved at it. "Your chef's the bee's knees. Tell Etta I said that, would you?"

"Sure. Oh and that reminds me. She asked me to tell the lucky boy that she said hello."

"I don't feel lucky most of the time lately."

"Don't worry, Jimmy. Yours always has a way of turning on a dime."

"I hope so, Ms. Cavalcante." He looked around at the empty dining room. "Say, aren't you going to need more help in here, what with the holidays and the new stock in?"

"Yeah. And I'm not sure where I'm going to get it, either. I'm not exactly the most popular employer in town, you know."

"Yeah, but I got a hunch that the right thing will fall into your lap sooner or later, Ma'am."

"I hope your gut's as accurate as usual, Jimmy."

"Maybe it'll be me?"

"Jimmy, I thought you wanted to cool it with the flirting."

"That's not what I mean. I meant maybe I could stay here in Plymouth for a while. Help out a bit, maybe at the door or something."

"What would my cousin think?"

"Nothing good. You're right, Ms. Cavalcante. I guess I gotta go back. I'll head down to Fall River tonight."

"Thanks, Jimmy. Listen, if you need anything I want you to ring Etta in the kitchen. Tell her you need your lucky charm back. I'll call in an order so you have an excuse to come up here and get away for the day."

"Thanks, Ma'am. I appreciate it."

"You're a good egg, Jimmy. I wish my cousin understood that."

"Maybe he will."

But Giacomo Bianco's days of greater understanding and compassion for others had gone out to sea on a riptide, never to return.

The Webster girl usually either tagged along with that lunkhead brother of hers, or else played third wheel to Rachel Howe and his half-guinea niece. The lunkhead brother had taken a job at the docks and Finn smiled. Maybe Theodore would snap and torched the place. Sarah couldn't follow him there and she'd avoided the other girls since that day at Brewster Gardens. Finn would have gone after her then, but the Howe girl walked her home.

He'd thought about approaching her as she came out of the school but a man loses stature in the community when found skulking around school girls. She'd spent every weekend at the Elmwood house. Gilbert had managed to make sure Sarah was never alone for weeks now, a smart move on his part. But not today.

Finn was down at the diner having steak, eggs and coffee and planning on over-tipping Helen in hopes she'd let him give her a tickle one of these days. He'd also gotten a good look at the fat dago who'd been eating all the apple pie. He reminded Finn of someone but figured that was because all guineas looked the same with their schnozes and greasy looking hair. He'd seen the Webster girl across the street, heading into the library. She'd been all by herself.

He left six dollars on the counter which was five more than what his meal had cost. Staring that dago right in his beady eyes, Finn only smiled when fatso looked away first. The bell above the door jangled as he left the diner and headed toward the library. When he walked through the door, he saw the Webster girl turn a corner in the Reference section.

She was some kind of honor student, a whiz with numbers like Cloris had been. She even looked like her aunt, the hair and the eyes anyway. This girl was skin and bones and Cloris hadn't worn glasses, but the resemblance was there in what he could see of her face. He hesitated. Could he actually exploit a girl who practically wore his dead wife's face?

The main thing he'd Seen about Sarah Webster was her bitterness and anger. He Saw her fight with Millicent before he'd witnessed the end of it in person. He also Saw her open a letter with Radcliffe letterhead and then stain the fancy paper with tears. And he'd Seen her showing the letter to the Elmwood kid, who'd reacted like the pompous ass he was. What if she broke down crying in his arms, like Cloris did the night the Italians killed her? But his wife had been a sweet soul, content to stay home and make babies. Sarah Webster wanted no part of that life, resemblance or not.

Finn let his feet carry him to the Reference section and past the spinster at the desk. He turned the same corner the girl had and found her seated behind a thick book filled with charts and tables. Beside her right hand sat a stack of graph paper, a pencil, and a worn-looking slide-rule. He knew that instrument. In profile and holding that rule she looked even more like Cloris than he'd originally thought. Finn swallowed the lump in his throat and took a seat across from her.

Sarah didn't look up, though her left finger had paused over the column of decimals. Finn blinked at the numbers, thinking there was something familiar about them. Had he Seen them before, or only seen them? He watched her write numerals down on the graph paper where she had an equation set up. Only two spaces for variables remained. Again, he had a sense of deja vu. The only time he got those was when he Saw something in a dream.

"What are you trying to solve for?" The question came out with less confidence than he'd intended.

"Did you know that not all equations have finite solutions?" Sarah didn't look up. There wasn't even a hitch in the motion of her finger as she flipped to a different page and scanned it. "Haven't you ever heard of stochastic processes?"

"No." Finn realized he'd hesitated. "What are those?"

"Are you sure you have no grasp of random variables?" She still wouldn't look up, but he noticed the corners of her mouth curving in that direction.

"Absolutely." He smiled as he spoke, letting it come through in his voice. Maybe she was warming up to him.

"Don't you realize that's a double negative?" He heard the scorn in Sarah's voice. She hadn't been laughing with him, but at him.

Finn was stuck. This girl was too smart, genius level even, but he hadn't expected her to be this good at dodging his questions by asking him about complex math. Of course, he probably shouldn't have tried engaging her about the subject that was her forte. One of her hands still had a bandage on it. That must have been one humdinger of a cut if it hadn't healed fully in almost a month. She had to be angry at Millie, still. Finn decided to regroup and flank.

"I notice you're injured. What happened to your hand?"

"Just one chance in a series of random variables that became the most probable outcome." Sarah answered without a question this time.

Finn wondered whether he was getting anywhere. He still had no idea what she was talking about. It was bad enough when blowhards like the Elmwood kid tried fooling with him, now a girl was making him feel like he was all wet. He stopped himself from getting too angry. This was the tag-along, the mousy bookish girl the rest of the kids didn't want around. What would she do if someone started treating her differently? He decided to give her a line, but not the usual sweet talk.

"You're the bee's knees with the numbers. A regular Jane College." Finn gave her his best smile.

Sarah's finger stopped moving again, but she didn't write anything this time. "You know, your aunt had a head for numbers, too. You look so much like her. Now that I hear you talk, you also sound like her." Dammit, she did remind him of Cloris. Also himself. Sarah was almost as much of an outsider as he was.

Finn couldn't sit here and manipulate the girl anymore, Irish ascendancy or no. It stung, that truth, like the chill of the grave. Finn closed his eyes and let the words in his head match the ones he spoke aloud for the first time in close to fifteen years.

"Sorry for bothering you, Miss Webster. I just miss my wife, you know?"

He heard the scratching of her pencil on paper, then a rustle and a shuffle. She must have found her number and gone to the slide-rule to solve the equation. Instead of the scratchy sound he'd expected to hear, she made a little gasp. The leathery nutmeg scent of old books got stronger, the air heavy with it. He felt her hand, the one with the bandage, cover his. Finn Mullins opened his eyes.

"How did she die?" asked Sarah. She had stood up and was leaning across the table. Some of the amber brown hair that matched her eyes had come loose from a barrette on the right side of her head. It was the same shade as his dead wife's. Her hand felt warm like Cloris's, too. Warm hands, cold heart.

Sarah Webster looked at him, head tilted like a raven examining some shiny answer. Her expression was much more familiar than some literal bird's. It was the face he made right after he'd Seen something. That was how a person looked when she'd brushed her mind against Fate. He couldn't speak. He wasn't sure he could move.

"No one ever talks about her." She spoke those words deliberately, gripping his hand tighter. "No one tells me anything, a feeling I'm sure you're familiar with. I'm tired of waiting for the rest of them to pretend to notice that it bothers me. So tell me about my aunt, your Cloris.

How did she die?"

Finn Mullins was Seeing in so many different directions, it was impossible to tell which of them was his ideal outcome with her. Everything depended on what he said next. He chose one.

"Giuseppe Chiavo killed her." His Sight narrowed absolutely. He knew exactly what to say to her now. "Cloris was so much like you. She also chased a dream, something she didn't end up getting. Don't you want to go to Radcliffe?"

"More than almost anything in the world." Sara's pencil scratched again as she laid out another number on the graph paper with a hooked left hand, like a boxer laying out his opponent in the ring. She nudged the slide rule. "Don't pretend you can do anything about that."

"But what if I can?"

"I'm engaged. I must get married and have children. That's not something anyone can change." She nudged the slide rule again. "Hmm."

"You've been hiding that partial Wisdom, haven't you?"

"I don't have to do much to hide it, actually. You're the first one to notice the whole two years I've had it. Congratulations, you get a Kewpie doll."

"Getting magic that early is prodigal, you know that?" Finn definitely felt like he'd found a prize much better than some cheap carnival doll.

"Yes. But I don't care. I don't want Wisdom, I want my degrees." Sarah's words opened another vista to his Sight. Finn Saw a solution.

"I can make that happen for you."

"There's no way. Gilbert already said he won't move us out of Plymouth and his family's the one with the means to do that. And you know I've got to marry him. There's no one else."

"Oh, but there is, Sarah Webster. There's me."

She looked up, fumbled her pencil, dropped it.

"I don't know how marrying you instead of Gilbert Edgewood would make a difference." Sarah bent at the waist to pick up the pencil. Even from that angle, she looked like Cloris. Finn Mullins licked his lips, Seeing that he stood at the verge of getting everything he wanted. He let her catch him staring when she stood up again. The girl would have to get used to his tastes and desires. Best to let her understand that now.

"That's not true and you know it." Finn knew he still had to clinch the deal, get her agreement. What had he been thinking? Scaring her off by leering wouldn't help. But she'd rely on her numbers, sure bet. "I'm going to win this time and winners get to call the shots. Do another one of those calculations and you'll See I'm right."

The girl sat back down and worked with the charts, the paper, and the rule. Finn Mullins leaned his chin on one hand and watched the clock tick out two and a half minutes. He looked down expecting to see the top of her head.

Instead, he drowned in eyes the color of puddles reflecting autumn brown leaves. Who had who, exactly? Finn was almost sure partial Sight was less powerful than his full version. At least, that's how it had been with him and his sister. He pressed his hands together to stop them trembling.

"Maybe I'll marry you, Mr. Mullins." Sarah turned her head, peering at him with just one eye, like a sparrow this time instead of a raven. So, he'd shocked her too, then. "But you can only win this with my help. And you won't get that unless you can show me some proof that you intend to make good on your promise about Radcliffe."

"How do I prove that?"

"I hear you've got loads of money." The girl's lips curled up like hair beside a flame but her eyes held no trace of a smile. "Pay my entire tuition. Rent or buy an apartment with my name on the note. Do those things and we've got a deal."

Before he left, Finn rummaged through Cloris's hope chest. He made sure to leave package containing a token of his affections addressed to Sarah on the Webster doorstep. And that's how Finn Mullins found himself driving to Cambridge instead of present in Plymouth on the day that his nephew chose a side.

Bill had only ever walked past the Plymouth Supper Club. He'd done so at night and seen patrons staggering out the door, so he knew Esmeralda Cavalcante served illegal alcohol. He figured that Captain Delaqua from the dockmaster's log was her supplier. If Bill noticed it, so could the police. But they hadn't.

Tucci wouldn't stand a chance operating here even if Uncle Finn wasn't trying to help the Irish Mob move in from Boston. Sal said he came back to Plymouth because his father had worked here. The headstone in the cemetery verified that. If Tucci wanted to set up a below board business, Bill had to find out how Ms. Cavalcante did it without police interference.

He was surprised that single Mafiosos from Providence hadn't come sniffing around, looking to horn in by proposing to the widow in business. For someone like Bill whose family arranged marriages for generations, that idea was a no-brainer. She had to have an intimidating male relative with high standards keeping both assassins and suitors away.

The name Frederico Bianco graced one of the older headstones in the cemetery. Bill knew now why that name sounded familiar. He'd seen the name Giacomo

Bianco in the headlines of the Fall River Herald. Maybe he sent the Cavalcantes and the Tuccis and Frederico here to establish the Supper Club. Giacomo Bianco, Crime Lord of Fall River, must be the picky relative, then.

Bill walked down the alley next to the Supper Club. It smelled like the gravy Father used to make before he got too weak for cooking but tainted with gone-over greens and stinky cheese. The alley was only just wide enough for a box truck with a wooden fence blocking one end. It would be next to impossible for passers-by to see the goods during a delivery. He heard a woman's voice giving orders.

"Get the labels off those crates." The shrewish voice was commanding and confident instead of cajoling or whining. "This cologne routine might be fine in Boston and Providence, but we serve food here. If anyone sees Colgate Cashmere on the boxes in our trash, we'll attract buzz we don't want."

The sound of paper tearing met Bill's ears as he passed the dumpster. A young man maybe a year older than him ripped paper into tiny pieces. Next to him sat a stack of crates labeled with names and logos of popular colognes and perfumes. He put the tiny bits into a sack that was the source of the rotten vegetable smell. The man pulled the label off another crate and tore that one up too.

"No loitering," said the female voice that had spoken before.

Bill looked up to see the woman it belonged to. She was taller than average for a lady, with her hair cut in a short style fashionable ten years ago. She wore a day dress with a drop-waist like armor, its colors glaring and whirling in a brightly distracting kaleidoscope. Bill skimmed her surface thoughts, snagged the one that he needed, and ran with it.

"I'm not loitering," said Bill, "I'm looking for work." He gave her his best big friendly smile. "I'm William Chiavo. I heard you hire part-timers. The docks and Cordage don't, but I like working with people better, anyway."

"Hmmm." She studied him, then picked up an empty tin can and tossed it up and down in one hand. She smirked and there was nothing friendly about it. "I could use another waiter. It gets busy in here after Thanksgiving. Think fast!"

His hand stung as he caught the can before it hit him in the face. Whatever else Esmeralda Cavalcante was, she had an arm that could have struck out half the New York Yankees. The Sox should let her on the team to break the Bambino's Curse. He smiled again, mostly because normally he wouldn't have. But waiters smiled, no matter what anyone literally or figuratively threw at him.

"Good. You're not a klutz like Eric, here." Esmeralda jerked her chin at the young man tearing labels. Her smirk turned serious again. "Be back here at six. Wear black trousers and a white shirt with long sleeves. If you don't pick up waiting tables tonight, you're out of here before close. Now scram."

"Yes ma'am." Bill didn't have to feign excitement. The rush from intercepting the can had gotten his blood going. He turned and left the alley before Esmeralda either changed her mind or decided to exercise her pitching arm again.

Bill headed home to make sure he had an appropriate set of clean and pressed clothes. On the way, he saw Sarah crossing Main Street carrying her slide rule. Her brow had more furrows than one of the Howe's fields, her glasses sat low on her nose, and her coat draped over her shoulders like an afterthought. Her lips moved and though he couldn't hear her from that distance, Bill knew she recited a sequence of numbers. There was something off about her, something different that he couldn't put his finger on at first.

After overhearing Gilbert's conversation with his sister, Bill felt a new sympathy for Sarah. He crossed the street, pacing his steps to catch up with her. He could hear her footsteps now. They were different too, in a way Bill couldn't figure. He watched her back as she dodged smoothly around a lady looking in a shop window. He had to copy the movement a few moments later and then, Bill understood. Sarah usually dragged her feet, stumbling at times, bumping into people and even buildings because numbers always occupied some part of her mind.

Bill got close enough to make out the book of graph paper under Sarah's arm. She'd been in the library then, working on some incomprehensible calculation or equation. This had happened more frequently since she started High School and Bill wondered whether being that big a genius differed much from having Wisdom.

Both of those things made a person different, isolated

even. Sarah wasn't Wise, but being from one of those families plus her genius-level understanding of mathematics made her different from everyone else in town. None of the Wise had her talent or harmony with numbers. Anyone who understood mathematics had no idea Wisdom even existed. Out of all of them, Sarah was the most alone.

Bill felt a rush of urgency, a need to catch up to his friend, tell her someone understood before it was too late. Too late? For what? He suspected his Wisdom picked up on something, maybe the cause of Sarah's change in comportment.

He tried leaning on her mind as he had with the dock-master and Tucci, and Bill found resistance he hadn't expected. It was like the time he'd leaned on a latched screen door as a little boy. The metal mesh felt rough against his skin, but molded to his shape. He'd felt the warm air on the other side of the screen, heard sounds and voices, but not as clearly as if he'd gone through the door.

In her mind, Sarah sang. It wasn't a tune like any music Bill had ever heard. Her thoughts floated out of his reach and weren't words as he'd expected, but numbers arranged in a patterns Bill couldn't discern. He understood one of the concepts driving her thoughts, though. Probability.

Had Sarah calculated the odds for something? An equation drifted by so complicated Bill didn't recognize its operations. The lens of Sarah's thoughts made it obscenely beautiful. Had she solved this glorious thing? Was that the cause of her elation? The surface of Sarah's mind was as alien as the surface of Mars.

Bill only knew that he'd be too late even if he caught up with her. One other thing he recognized was her utter faith in the idea that she finally belonged somewhere. Sarah had found some purpose, a secret place in her own personal scheme of things that she guarded like a dragon with hoarded gold.

Bill's contact with Sarah's mind shattered. He didn't know when he'd stopped walking, but it was long enough that he lost even that screen-door impression of her. He walked again, continuing on his way home at double Sarah's pace.

When Bill reached the street they all lived on, he headed straight to the Webster's house to find no one at home. The position of the sun told Bill he had less than an hour to get clothes, dinner, and his rear end back to the Supper Club. Sarah was out of his reach for now. He'd just have to try and catch up to her later.

Giuseppe heard his son come home again and tried not to let Bill's noisy mental anguish distract him from the thoughts in Theo Webster's mind. Giuseppe loved Bill more than his would-be son-in-law, so he got the gist. His son's chaotic thoughts were more interesting than the tight focus Theo maintained but that focus was more important because if Theo lost control the entire block could burn to ashes in minutes.

"Put your hand on the surface of the water, like this." Lucinda Webster stretched the scarred fingers of her right hand apart, flattening her palm. Fire Wise were not entirely immune to the changes they made in temperature. Eventually, they all had burn scars on their hands at least. Some that worked with cold like Theo practicing now even lost fingers to frostbite.

"Calm yourself, Theodore." Giuseppe sensed the sinking fear that Lucinda's scars often caused in her son. "Focus only on cooling the water, as your mother explained."

Theo took a slow deep breath, then exhaled. Giuseppe was the only person who could hear the young man count to ten as he breathed. He flattened his palm in imitation of Lucinda, then extended his arm so his hand hovered above the bowl of hot water. Carefully, he lowered it until he made contact with the liquid. Giuseppe sensed the effort Theo made not to flinch. He shut his eyes.

Giuseppe kept counting with Theo in his mind. *One, two, three, four, five. Pull the heat into the hand like you pull the air into your lungs. Six, seven, eight, nine, ten. Bring the heat up through the arm so it spreads without burning.* Giuseppe opened his eyes, and saw the flush on Theo's cheeks first. He looked like he had a fever.

Lucinda was focused entirely on the bowl of water which no longer steamed. A sheen of condensation grew on the sides of the bowl, from the top down. Now, she spared a glance at Theo. It wasn't until the surface of the water frosted over that she smiled.

"Good job," she said. "We'll take a break. Keep Mr. Chiavo company while I go help Katherine with her icebox." Even after nearly eighteen years acquainted and the engagement of their children, Lucinda Webster still didn't feel comfortable calling him Giuseppe. He knew it was more because she thought she'd butcher his name than any of the old animosity that Finn still nurtured. Still, he thought the Wise here were probably more *calabrese* than the ones he'd left back in the old country.

Lucinda left the room and Theo deflated, sinking into the nearest chair. He looked more relieved than exhausted, which was good. It meant he was strong, had endurance his mother lacked.

"You'll have an easier time of it than she did eventually." Giuseppe smiled. "I know, Theodore. You don't believe me. It's true that I wasn't there. But

Katherine knows. She watched your mother develop her Wisdom, and she'd fall asleep after a lesson like this one. You look like you could go out dancing, come home afterward, and still find the strength to chop a cord of firewood."

"Thanks, Giuseppe." Theo wiped his damp hand on his handkerchief.

"In fact, perhaps you should go out this evening." Giuseppe nodded. He'd finally had time to make sense of half of the turmoil inside Bill's head. Most of that had to do with the Plymouth Supper Club. "Yes, that outing would be a good idea."

"Um, I beg your pardon?" The handkerchief dropped from Theo's hand.

"I'd like you to go dancing this evening. I know it sounds strange, but I'm asking you to do me a favor."

"Do you a favor? By going out dancing?" Theo picked up his handkerchief and tucked it back in his pocket without folding it.

"Yes. Bill's got a job there, starting this evening. He's only just getting his Wisdom, however, and," Giuseppe grimaced. "Well, you know what that can be like. For one of the Mind Wise, being in an enclosed space with lots of people is less than ideal. He knows this but doesn't care about the danger he might be in. I'd feel much relieved if friends of his were on the premises."

"How did you know?" Theo meant about Bill's job. "Weren't you kind of distracted when he came in?"

"Yes. But I'm just so used to hearing him, it's second-nature." Giuseppe beamed.

"Okay." Theo looked like he'd say something else but

Lucinda came back from the kitchen, yawning.

"You've got ice in the ice box again," she said. "Maybe in a few weeks it'll be cold enough to save money and my energy by keeping things in the shed. Come on, Ted, help your tired mother back home. Goodnight, Mr. Chiavo."

"Good night, Lucinda, Theodore." Giuseppe didn't have the strength tonight to get up and see them out, but knew they wouldn't be offended. He heard a door close upstairs and then a jumble of footsteps creaking down from the second floor.

"Dad," said Millie just at the same time as Bill said "Father." Each of his children tried to squeeze past the other through the door to the dining room.

"Slow down now," he said. "You both know how we resolve situations like these."

Bill and Millie faced each other with their hands behind their backs while Giuseppe counted aloud. "One. Two. Three!"

Bill's right hand was flat with the palm down, indicating paper. The corners of his mouth turned down when he saw Millie's first two fingers extended to resemble a pair of scissors. Giuseppe remembered how just a few years ago she would have let out a Bronx cheer, but all she did now was nod and turn to face him.

"Dad, have you seen Bear? He wasn't back when we got home from the Howe's. He's still gone, and it's starting to get dark. Can I take a Daylo and look for him?"

"I haven't seen him," said Giuseppe, "but he's bound to be hungry soon and come back. If he's not here in the next fifteen minutes, go ahead and look around for him."

He had known already that Millie's newest friend wouldn't be back all day. Something about the dog's thoughts made Guiseppe think Bear was more than what he seemed. Bear was looking for someone or something, possibly under some kind of compulsion. All he had been able to tell for certain was that Bear meant no harm. He'd let Millie unravel the mystery of the dog on her own.

"Okay," she said. "Thanks Dad. I'll go ask if Mom's seen him." She hustled out the door and he heard her footsteps fade in the direction of the kitchen.

"Bill?" He noticed his son wore a crisp white shirt.

"Father, I've got a job."

"I know. Plymouth Supper Club." Giuseppe smiled and then lied. "I don't need Wisdom to recognize a uniform."

"Okay, that was easy." Bill smiled. "But aren't you worried about me getting in trouble with the police?"

"William, haven't you noticed that the law has not touched the Plymouth Supper Club for years?" Giuseppe smiled broadly enough to make his face ache. The near constant pressure on his mind as he resisted Bill's natural ability to read it would wear him out if he didn't give his son a plausibly benign answer.

"I did." Bill tilted his head. "So why, then?"

"It's been fixed by Ms. Cavalcante and her Boss." Giuseppe shook his head, letting the smile drop down from its alpine heights. He concentrated in an image of money changing hands, bringing it to the front of his false thoughts.

"That makes sense, I guess." Bill shrugged. "But I'm still surprised you're okay with me working in a speakeasy. Aren't you going to tell me to be careful, keep my mind shielded, and not believe everything I hear?"

"Of course not. Why repeat all the things you already have memorized?" Giuseppe said nothing about his request of Theodore. He couldn't without affecting Katherine's outcome. Bill would have to think his father lied deliberately to him, get angry, and react accordingly. A good father shouldn't save his own heart and damn his child in the process. "You go ahead and be yourself. That's more than enough, William."

"Thanks, Father." Bill was always too subtle and serious to fidget, but performed his closest facsimile. Giuseppe knew nervous on his son when he saw it, of course, but the folk at the Supper Club wouldn't recognize it. "If it were Millie coming in to tell you she'd gotten this job, would you be this calm about it?"

"Of course not."

"But didn't you support suffrage?"

"I still do."

"Then why? Why treat your daughter differently than your son?"

"Because she is Millicent and you are William and none of that has anything to do with which one of you is a girl. Equality is different from equity; your needs are different. If she'd grown into the same temperament she has now but as a boy that would still be true."

"I don't understand." Bill shook his head. "I think I should, though."

"Individual people are different from each other. It's

not a question of suffrage. You and Millie both need food but if your mother were cooking to comfort both of you she wouldn't cook just one dish. Your favorite meal is chicken soup. Millie's is sausage and pancakes. When both of you need a father's advice, should I give her chicken soup advice just like yours, or sausage and pancake advice? When it comes time for you to advise others, will you serve them all the same meal for equality's sake, or treat them with equity?"

"Okay. That makes more sense." Bill glanced at the clock on the mantel. "Thanks again, Father. I'll be home after the Supper Club closes."

"Cold tea," drawled Bill in his best Gilbert Edgewood impression, "marvelous! And for you sir?" The man ordered "sonic tonic" which meant he wanted gin in it. Bill nodded and double-timed it to place the order with Esmeralda, who was mixing the illegal drinks that night. The hardest thing so far this evening had been not laughing at the code-names for all the beverages.

The Plymouth Supper Club did serve actual supper, which people ate because the food was as good as fancy restaurants in Providence or Boston at a quarter of the price. Everyone seemed to be on as much of a liquid diet as a solid one, staying for hours after they'd finished their food to imbibe glass after glass of illicit spirits.

Esmeralda put his drinks on one of the small trays and he went back to deliver them. Then, he headed to the next table with a huge smile on his face. Bill's own serious demeanor didn't fit this vocation so he'd fallen back on imitating the character of the most gregarious person he knew. He wondered what Gilbert would think if he could see Bill now. Small talk wasn't something he normally engaged in, but it helped the customers feel easy enough to order something that could get them all arrested.

Some of the tables had groups of couples, but there were also a large number of single men. Most of these were looking for single ladies but those were rare as unicorns. Esmeralda visited each of those single patrons and perhaps that had helped seven years ago when the proprietress looked less careworn. About a quarter of these flirted back, but Bill wasn't fooled. Their surface thoughts told him the flirters hoped for a drink on the house.

Ironically, the Plymouth Supper Club could use a female touch, something for all those lonely fellows to look at. Bill had never been particularly inclined toward ladies, but he recognized the potential to increase business with the right sort of attractions. A few dolled-up girls who could sing or dance would draw more patrons. That could open a door for Sal Tucci to do business in Plymouth. He'd pass that information along to him for sure.

The place wasn't set up for a big band. The only stage barely left room next to the small piano. Esmeralda had booked a group of four musicians; a drummer, a man with an upright bass, a sax player, and the pianist. They weren't amazing, but good enough that couples danced to their music. Bill liked his job at the Supper Club, at least so far. His face ached from all the smiling, but at least it wasn't a boring place to work.

A group of three came in and sat at one of the tables. Bill took two steps forward, intending to greet them as he'd done for all the other guests in his section, but he stopped as soon as he recognized them. Theo and Gilbert grinned and waved while Sarah sat with her eyes on the table linens. The guys wore suit jackets and Sarah was in the yellow party dress she'd worn to the winter dance at school last year.

"What are you waiting for Chiavo?" Esmeralda tapped his shoulder as she walked by. "Get up there and do   your   job." He continued on his way toward the table of people he'd grown up with. What if they wanted alcohol? Bill rankled at the potential for awkwardness. Sarah did, too. She glanced up, noticed all the single men, and clutched one of Gilbert's hands in both of hers. Gil rolled his eyes like the Supper Club was dull as a History lecture, but Bill noticed his lip curl and knew better. Gilbert was nervous, not bored.

"Hello, Bill," said Theo.

Bill hid in his new waiterly skills like a front line soldier in a foxhole.

"What brings you in tonight?" Bill shifted his weight from one foot to the other. "I didn't expect to see you here. Our, er, specials and Flame Wise don't exactly mix."

"Relax. I won't order anything I shouldn't," said Theo. "You went with me when I got hired at the docks, and gave Gil a pep talk when he went to work at Cordage. We're just here to support you on your first night on the job."

Gilbert nodded his agreement. He couldn't sense Theo lying, but Wise and their relatives were harder to read than regular folk. Bill wasn't about to lean on Sarah's weird mind while he was at work. He had to keep his head in the waiter game, not other people's thoughts.

"Well, thanks, then." Bill wanted to ask where Millie was, but Esmeralda was giving him her hurry-up look from behind the bar. "Anyway, can I bring you something? We serve coffee, tea, and plain tonic without any sauce, and the food's the cat's meow." He gestured toward those with his hand.

"Bring us the succotash and a pot of regular tea with four cups, please." Theo looked around the room. "Wow. There are loads of guys from the boats here."

"Four cups?" Bill was confused. "But there's only three of you."

"No, there's four of us," said a familiar throaty voice from behind him. He moved out of Rachel's way, and turned around to hold the empty chair out for her.

He hadn't seen Rachel wearing anything in years besides practical homespun hand-me-downs. Because Rachel was two years older than Bill and Millie, she'd graduated High School before either of them went to school dances. Rachel wasn't wearing the kind of dress girls wore to school functions, anyway, even though it was definitely made for dancing.

The dress she had on was lavender satin and sleeveless, with bead and fringe embellishments that caught the light and the eye when she moved. Her hair was pinned under itself into a mock bob. A feather fascinator on a ribbon graced the left side of her head.

Rachel looked like the girl in the Arrow shirt ads. He felt thoughts about her that he didn't share coming from most of the men in the room. Gilbert's ideas were similar to his own though even more detached, but Theo's were like the rest. He was the only one fighting them down, however.

Sharp prongs of envy brushed by his mind, so strong he almost gasped. Even Rachel seemed to waver under them as she took a seat. They came from the women in the room, of course, with two exceptions. Sarah exuded relief while Esmeralda's pragmatic mind calculated how much that dress might have cost.

Bill wondered the same thing himself. The Howes couldn't buy something like that so where had she gotten it? But he was a waiter, not a woolgatherer. Bill imagined a big brick wall, filling his mind with that bulwark against the swell of reaction in Rachel's wake. Bill couldn't afford to lose his job because of everyone else's feelings.

"I'll go get your tea," said Bill. He had no idea what else to say to his friends who, for the first time in his life, had no idea what he'd just been through. As he left to place the order he could hear Sarah let out a nervous giggle which Theo shushed. Esmeralda still gazed in Rachel's general direction.

"Chiavo." Esmeralda leaned in to whisper. "I've got a funny feeling about those four. Water down whatever they're having."

"They only ordered some food and regular tea," said Bill. "And I know them."

"Oh," said Esmeralda, "well that's fine, then." She looked a bit more at ease. "Do you know why they're here?"

"Probably to celebrate. The two fellows just got their first paychecks." Bill tried sending soothing thoughts around Esmeralda's head to help cultivate her ease. It wasn't direct meddling; that would cost him months or years of his youth. Instead, Bill just shifted the mental environment around her.

While Bill waited for his friends' order, he remembered his Wisdom lessons. General energy influenced people, their emotions waxing or waning with a crowd consensus. It's why mobs went mad with anger and theatrical performers evoked tears or laughter.

The order came up and Bill filled his tray and carried it along. He looked up, but before his eyes went to Gilbert as he'd intended he got hooked by Rachel's gaze. He managed to keep walking and set everything down in silence just in time.

Bill could still see the placid face she showed to the world, but in her mind, Rachel wept. She wasn't mourning dead brothers or the sisters sent halfway across the country to marry. Her heart was breaking, because the magic she'd tried to make tonight had turned into something horrible. All the men wanted her except the one whose head she'd set out to turn.

She'd loved him since the day she ran home in tears from the train station after her favorite sister went to Chicago. He'd come up the street to meet her with a bundle of uprooted daisies clutched in his grubby hand saying "I'd be sad too if they sent my sister away." But that was Bill's own memory. He'd been the one who gave Rachel daisies that day, because he could imagine all too easily how she felt. He knew her current pain himself now and her anguish was so palpable it nearly blinded him. There was only one thing to do. He leaned through the miasma of dismay, and whispered to the woman he was not in love with but had to marry anyway.

"You look beautiful, like a girl in a painting." He wasn't lying, either. Bill could appreciate her beauty aesthetically, just like Millie's.

As he left their table, Bill glanced over his shoulder and saw Rachel smiling. He grinned back, but shot a glance at Gilbert before turning back to look where he was going.

"Watch it, kid." A fine-featured man a few inches taller than him sidestepped to avoid an imminent crash with Bill's empty tray. He smelled strongly of Aqua Velva.

"Sorry, sir." Bill couldn't help it, he blushed. For a guy with Mind Wisdom, he sure had trouble sensing people before crashing into them. He headed back toward the bar to look over the rest of the tables. The man followed him.

"Heh." The cologne-scented man smirked. "I can't blame you, kid. That's one hotsy-totsy Sheba over there."

"What, my fiancée?"

"Wow, kid." The man leaned against the bar and barked out a laugh. "I heard the cats and kittens in this town got hitched young, but holy smokes! You won some kind of crap shoot right there." He stuck his hand toward Bill. "Name's Jimmy Delaqua." So this was the punctual captain. Perfect.

"Bill Chiavo." He shook Jimmy's hand. Esmeralda stepped up beside them.

"That girl is engaged to you?" She nodded in Rachel's

direction. Rachel looked up, blinking. Esmeralda smiled and waved at her.

"Yes, ma'am, she is." Bill smiled at Rachel, too. Theo noticed them looking, then leaned over to say something to Gilbert.

"A girl that pretty ought to be on the stage. Can she sing? Dance maybe?" Gilbert whispered something to Sarah, who then took out a pencil stub and scrap of paper and started scribbling.

"If you want to ask her yourself, I can introduce you."

"That'd be the bee's knees." Esmeralda gave him a tap on the back, propelling him in the direction of his friends' table.

As Bill approached, Rachel's eyes widened. Theo and Gilbert stopped whispering. He saw Gil blink at Esmeralda's garish dress, and Theo give Jimmy a once-over, his eyes lingering in the area under his left arm. Bill had figured Jimmy was armed and Theo just confirmed it for him. Sarah didn't look up from her scribbling or make any other indication she noticed what transpired.

"Theo Webster, Gilbert Edgewood, Sarah Webster, and Rachel Howe," said Bill, "I'd like you to meet Jimmy Delaqua, recent acquaintance, and Esmeralda Cavalcante, my boss." They all looked up now, though Sarah did so only briefly before jotting down a few more numbers under a radical sign. Theo, Gilbert, and Rachel stood up, all smiles. Bill felt the tension radiating from them like heat from a fireplace.

"So good to meet you all," Esmeralda's eyes sparkled and her cheeks were flushed. Bill knew she was preening like a swan after he'd called her his boss. By leaning on her mind just a little, he could feel Esmeralda's ambition surging around her like a rip-tide. "Miss Howe, William here tells me the two of you are engaged to be married."

"Yes, ma'am, we are." Rachel's smile was bright but it was her rush of joy that nearly blinded Bill. Keeping his Wise senses open right now was like staring at the sun. He tried to hold out, keep on reading the others, but wasn't sure how much more exposure he could take.

"Well, it seems to me he's a lucky fellow. Bill here seems like a good egg so you're lucky, too. Do you mind if we sit down?" Esmeralda glanced around the table. Everyone nodded except Sarah, who still scribbled away. The boss-lady took the seat beside Rachel, but Jimmy just leaned against the nearest wall. "Bill is doing an excellent job tonight at the Supper Club. His skills could take him far in the hospitality industry. We're looking for more help here, though. Entertainers, actually."

"More specifically," said Jimmy, "a song-and-dance act, or even better, a torch singer to go with those cats down there honkin' on bobos." He waved a hand vaguely in the direction of the small band camped around the piano.

"Rachel does." Sarah sounded like she was blurting out an arithmetic answer in the classroom, though she hadn't looked up. "She sings Helen Morgan's tunes when she thinks no one's listening." Bill tried to read anything he could from Sarah, but nothing came through.

"Sarah's caught me out." Rachel took Sarah's revelation in stride, even though Bill could tell she was surprised and slightly embarrassed. "I haven't ever performed in front of people, though."

"Her voice is even prettier than she is." This time, Sarah's tone was thick and sweet as divinity. Her hand scribbled numbers faster. Bill noticed she had lead smudges on her hand. Something still blocked him from reading her thoughts or feelings. He set his shoulder against the wall next to Jimmy, and then leaned once again on the strange terrain he already knew made up Sarah's mind.

It was dark in there this time, uncomfortably warm like hothouses at midsummer. The ground thrummed under his feet in perfect time with a rhythmic recitation of numbers coming from off to his right. The numbers were important, they made sense themselves and also made everything Sarah saw and heard sensible.

A pattern lived there, one just at the edge of Bill's understanding. If he could only get more of a sense of it from Sarah's perspective, he might figure it out. He leaned more heavily with his mind, got closer, realized the importance wasn't within the number sequence but in Sarah's ability to predict its pattern.

Bill gasped for breath gone absent.

"Get his tie off!" Gilbert's voice. The music stopped abruptly.

"He needs air." That was Theo.

"Lay him on the floor." Rachel. She'd know what to do for whoever they were talking about.

"Kid was fine a second ago." Delaqua.

Hands held Bill under his arms, and then he was on a flat cool surface. So it was him they fussed over. Sarah's mind had done a number on him, then. His entire field of vision was still blank and dark green, but whatever he lay on countered the heat. A thin hand pressed against his forehead, more soothing than any compress his mother had used for his childhood fevers.

"I'll get him some water too." Esmeralda's footsteps clicked away and then back again. The band resumed playing.

"Oh, Bill." Hands loosened his tie and he smelled cider and cinnamon. Rachel again. One of her hands circled his wrist, first two fingers over the inside, checking for a pulse. He felt the weight of his head settle on something soft but yielding and covered with a pebbly sort of surface. Her lap beneath the spangled dress? She hummed a little along with the music, then started adding the words. As she sang, all the dark emptiness lightened and filled with sound.

> "My heart is sad and lonely
> For you I sigh, for you dear only
> Why haven't you seen it
> I'm all for you body and soul."

Bill hadn't realized his heart had had flopped and flailed like a fish out of water until he felt it begin to slow and steady. His mind wrapped around the song's lyrics, Rachel's sentiment behind them. The emotion ran through like a current, clear and singular but diffuse, having been used by numerous men and women to express their unrequited love over the years. The memory of numbers warred like an army with the lyrics Rachel sang.

"He's coming out of it." A cool hand not unlike his mother's brushed his forehead. "Bill? Are you all right?"

"I'll be fine." He sounded more like his father than himself. Bill tried to open his eyes, but realized they hadn't ever closed. He lifted his arm to get a look at his hand, and felt like it carried the weight of a steamer trunk. He half expected to see papery skin with liver spots, but the appendage looked the same as it had last time he'd checked. Someone hoisted him to a chair.

"Here." Gilbert held a glass of clear liquid out in front of him. "It's water. Small sips." Bill held the cup to his lips and took a little swallow. It was so cold it felt like he'd cut his mouth. One of the other waiters set a plate down in front of him. The golden aroma of chicken chased away the last remnants of what he'd sensed in Sarah's mind.

"Eat." Esmeralda brandished a fork in the direction of his right hand. "That's Etta's recipe, it'll put some ballast in your gut."

"Thanks." Bill took the fork and then a bite of Chicken a la King. "This is outstanding, Ms. Cavalcante, thanks. I'll be able to get back to work in a few minutes." He took another bite, bigger this time. How Etta wasn't famous for cooking this, he didn't know.

"Get a load of this kid." Jimmy chuckled. "Faints dead away, but keeps his manners." Bill tried to chew a decent number of times before swallowing. He didn't want to ruin his new good image, but the food was delicious and he hadn't realized just how hungry he was.

"What did I tell you, Jim?" Esmeralda nodded in Bill's direction. "Kid's got class, and he's one of us." Bill didn't bother mentioning his half-Irish heritage because he wouldn't be involved with this illegal business for much longer, anyway. He slowed down the breakneck pace of his meal, taking another small sip of water.

"Excuse me, Ma'am?" A little man with his shirtsleeves rolled up stood at Esmeralda's elbow, trying to get her attention.

"What's eating you, Goldfarb?" Esmeralda turned to glance at the little man, then followed his gaze. He was looking directly at Rachel.

"Is that young lady the one who was singing up here a minute ago?" Goldfarb stretched his hands, then clenched them shut.

"One and the same." Esmeralda's lips curved into a smug little smile.

"Is she up from New York, or maybe Boston?" Goldfarb rubbed his hands together.

"No, she's a local." Esmeralda turned to Rachel. "Ben Goldfarb, this is Rachel Howe. Miss Howe, Mr. Goldfarb is in charge of entertainment here at the Supper Club, and he tickles tunes out of those old ivories." She nodded down at the piano, which now had an empty bench.

"I could have sworn it was ten years ago in Chicago, and I was hearing Helen Morgan for the first time." Goldfarb extended his hand toward Rachel. "You could do anything with that voice, Miss Howe."

"Thank you." Rachel took his hand but he raised it to his lips and bent over it instead of shaking.

Bill's fork clicked against an empty plate and he looked up to find his water glass empty too. He'd barely been aware he was still eating. Setting the fork down, Bill stood up. As he headed toward one of his tables where the glasses looked only a quarter full, he heard Esmeralda and Rachel make an agreement for her to sing on Friday and Saturday nights starting this weekend.

The cloud of concentration around Sarah thickened so much, Bill sighed relief when his friends left. He wasn't sure what had disturbed him more, Sarah's mental effect on him, or the bright hard smile she'd worn since spilling the beans about Rachel's singing. He'd need to discuss Sarah, and soon. She was definitely up to something involving all those numbers. But Bill wasn't sure who to start with.

After bringing refills to one of his tables, Bill helped another close out its tab for the evening. He thought about asking for Theo's help with his sister, but tossed that idea with the dregs from some dirty glasses. He knew if someone came to him with a line that Millie was batty, he'd bust them in the mush. No one could afford Theo losing his temper and Millie had already pushed that envelope with him.

Millie herself, then? She might give a repeat performance of slapping Sarah around. For all Bill knew, that was what had bent her out of shape in the first place. Millie would take him seriously and even sympathize, but she was rash and jealous of his Wisdom, too. If he told her it was already coming in, she might react badly, get enraged, or go into a funk. They couldn't afford that either.

Rachel was too tender- hearted. She'd believe Bill, but then she'd also want to have a cozy chat with Sarah about her feelings. Bill wanted more information first, because Rachel would treat Sarah as an ally. Bill wasn't sure she was one anymore. Sarah's mind was such a bizarre place, like something out of Lewis Carrol's stories. He couldn't risk giving her new information if his suspicions were true.

Gilbert, then. What else were best friends for?

Millie had just put her coat, hat and scarf on to go and look for Bear when he came scratching at the kitchen door. She let him in and watched him trot directly to the metal dish she'd used to feed him last night. He sat on his haunches, grinning at her.

"Wow, Bear. You don't beat around the bush, huh?" She went to the cold pantry and got some of the offal they'd brought from the farm. After that, she unwrapped it and put it in the dish.

The shaggy red dog yawned before he started eating and Millie got a picture in her head of a short young man with dark hair and blue eyes. It was the same as the one last night but there was a scent along with the picture, a sort of metallic smell like recently cleaned armor. Millie had never seen a suit of leather and mail before, let alone smelled it, but Bear must have at some point.

"You went searching for your fellow again today, is that it? I'm sorry you still didn't find him." She filled another dish with water and placed it on the floor near Bear.

Millie watched him eat as pictures flowed from his mind to hers. He remembered eating deer and birds with a fluffy black and white cat. The small man bathed in a lake, and Millie blushed. She never imagined the second man she saw naked would be through a dog's eyes. He had a cross-shaped scar on his right shoulder that looked like it came from a branding iron.

Bear's head bumped against her hip, jarring the image lose from her head.

"Oh, so you're finished." He waved his tail and perked his ears, then whined at the door. "You want to go out and keep looking? I'm coming with you this time, okay?"

Bear's tail flapped like a bird's wing, beating against the back of her leg at a pace she could do the Charleston to. Giggling, she put her hat and scarf back on. Millie added gloves to her wintry ensemble, then went out into the frigid night with the dog.

He sniffed the air, catching a scent which he conveyed to her. It smelled musty and leathery, with traces of incense like the inside of the Catholic Church after a big Mass. Millie followed him down their street and out toward downtown Plymouth.

They passed the docks, the library, and the diner. Bear surprised Millie by turning his nose up at the church to double back toward the water again. The dog had to be getting closer to whatever the source of the smell was. As it got stronger she noticed more things about it.

Millie got the impression that whatever he tracked was an item with paper older than the U.S. Constitution or even the Mayflower Manifest. She pressed his memory of the smell for more information but there was none. Bear had the trail of an item he'd never seen before. It was as though he'd been given the scent, like she'd read they did with bloodhounds at Scotland Yard.

"Is it something that belonged to him, Bear?"

He cocked his head again, and she felt that same contemplation from him that he'd had when she'd guessed his name.

"I'm only partly right again, then. I'll try and do better. I know you haven't seen the dang thing but somehow you know it's important by its smell. Where do you remember it from?"

A man passing by from the direction of Plymouth Cordage stared at Millie like she belonged in a sanitarium. Then, his gaze traveled to her legs and she narrowed her eyes before giving him Hell.

"Haven't you ever seen a girl talk to her dog before?" The man glanced at Bear, who growled. His eyes widened and he blanched before scuttling across the street and hurrying away.

"You didn't need to scare him that much, Bear." The dog gave her a skeptical look, and she got an image of a burly man in leather armor ripping at the bodice of a young redheaded woman in a homespun dress. "Oh. Okay, maybe you did. But how did you know?"

He sniffed, then whuffed.

"Wow. I wish I had a nose like yours, Bear."

He tilted his ears in what she'd come to recognize as his expression of confusion. Then, he stared at Millie's forehead, between her eyes.

"I can't read people, big guy, only animals. Maybe even just dogs. People are going to be Bill's department."

She got a picture of herself and her brother from

Bear's perspective. The dog showed her and Bill doing a long list of activities, running, jumping, climbing, even eating a sandwich. In all those tasks, Millie went faster, farther, higher and ate more than Bill. Classic dog loyalty. She laughed.

"Okay, Bear, whatever you say. Thanks, buddy." She pulled off a glove to give his ears a scratch and noticed they had stopped next to the alley behind the Supper Club.

Bear stood and pointed down the alley, directly at the service door.

"It's in there? Did you know Bill's working at this restaurant right now?"

Bear whined and rolled his eyes.

"Of course you did. You smell him. So, you think this whosiewhatsis you're tracking is in there?"

Bear wagged his tail and grinned.

"How about your fella?"

Bear's tail went still.

"Well, one is better than none I guess." Millie examined the door and found that it didn't even have a knob or latch on the outside, just something that looked like a doorbell. "I'm going to try and get someone to open this. They might not be okay with letting a dog in there, though. Is there anything you can show me so I have a better idea of what to look for?"

Bear sent Millie an image of thick yellowish parchment, then an old leather hide folded over it. Slowly, that leather molded against something flat and rectangular.

"A book? That's the only thing I can think of with old

parchment that might be inside a restaurant. I'll look for one of those, then." She walked up the three steps to stand in front of the door, then pressed a button that rang a buzzer inside.

The door opened, revealing a man in an apron. His annoyed expression faded from his face as he looked at Millie.

"Well hello there," he said.

"Hi, big-timer." Millie pitched her voice low and throaty, doing her best imitation of Rachel. It worked; the man gave her a huge smile. She dimpled, cocking her head so her curls would bounce. "Would you be so kind as to let me and my dog in for just a few minutes? I need to powder my nose and it's too cold to leave my poor poochie woochie out here."

"Uh." The man looked around her with a puzzled expression. "Miss, I can let you use the restroom, but, um, your dog must have run off."

"Oh." Millie let her mouth drop open in a coy expression of disappointment, and leaned toward the man. "If only someone were kind enough to fetch him for me, I would be ever so grateful."

The fellow ran out into the alley, only stopping himself long enough to grab a coat off the rack beside the door. Millie slipped in, leaving a wedged wooden stopper in the door. She didn't feel bad about lying to the Supper Club employee, but locking him out in the cold wasn't something she felt comfortable doing.

She'd stepped into a store room. One set of swinging double doors had little round windows, clearly marked with a sign reading "Kitchen, R. Franklin, Head Chef."

Another door stood slightly ajar and she spied a sink and toilet inside. A third door was closed. That one had a placard engraved with "E. Cavalcante, Manager." She went to it and tried the knob. It turned, and the door opened without even the slightest creak.

Before going into the Manager's office, Millie turned the light on in the powder room and shut the door. That would hopefully keep her cover story intact if the man came back before she finished. She felt a sense of approval like an "I told you so" in her mind, and realized Bear was still with her somehow. She went into the office and pressed the light switch, then closed the door.

Esmeralda Cavalcante's office was covered in paisley. The walls were papered in it with shades of pink, purple, and gray. Red and purple paisley fabric draped the chairs in front of her desk. Esmeralda's own seat behind the desk was upholstered in paisley, either a custom job or an import from somewhere Millie vowed never to order from. A large plush red and blue paisley rug covered the floor nearly corner to corner. Even the lamps had paisley shades, causing the light in the room to diffuse in shades of soft violet.

In addition to the usual furnishings of the desk and chairs, the office had a filing cabinet and book case. A sumptuous chaise draped in the same garish pattern as the chairs sat beside the shelving unit. The filing cabinet was locked. The book case was filled with works of fantastical fiction she wouldn't expect a hoodlum lady to keep.

Millie read off titles. Macbeth and The Temepst by

William Shakespeare. The Scarlet Letter by Nathanial Hawthorne. Frankenstein by Mary Shelley. Dunsany's The King of Elfland's Daughter. War of the Worlds, The Time Machine, and The Island of Doctor Moreau by H.G. Wells. J.M. Barrie's Peter Pan and Wendy. Dracula by Bram Stoker. The collected works of Hawthorne and Poe. Every volume was a recent edition, even the oldest stories. They all bore the wear of several readings.

Millie went to the business side of the desk. A blotter, a pen, and an inkwell squatted at the right and on the left sat a box of envelopes with a roll of stamps. Nothing here looked like an old leather-bound parchment book.

She sat in Esmeralda's chair, bumping her knee on the side of the desk with a hollow sound. Drawers, of course. What a stooge, not even thinking to look for drawers in a desk this big. Millie smacked her forehead lightly with her palm, then rolled the chair back to have a look inside the desk's compartments. In her head, she heard a barking laugh and wondered how a dog could find humor in a situation involving furniture he didn't the have hands to manipulate. She almost laughed aloud herself before remembering the covert nature of her mission.

Down on the floor, Millie opened the lowest and most out of the way drawers first. Nothing but invoices for food and soft drinks in one of those. The other drawer had a glass beside a bottle of rum draped with more paisley fabric. Of course. Millie tried to imagine what Esmeralda Cavalcante looked like and could only envision a stringy paisley matron.

Bear added the scent of rum and Colgate's Cashmere

to that. Millie wondered again how the dog could listen in and thought about walling him off from her thoughts. He gave her an image of his own sad puppy face as though begging her not to. He seemed awfully accustomed to this kind of communication for an animal she'd only encountered yesterday. She wondered for the first time whether the man Bear searched for was Wise just like her father.

She rummaged around in another drawer and her hand brushed something cold and hard wrapped in fabric. Bear made a warning growl in her mind, so Millie peered into the space where her hand had been. Peeking out from under a red paisley scarf was the pearl-handled butt of a revolver. It was compact and fancy, so small it couldn't be more than a 22. It was probably a Palm Pistol or a Pepper Pot, both guns she would have chosen for herself if she'd been allowed to carry one. Her father referred to them as ladylike guns.

Millie picked the gun up, using the paisley fashion accessory to cradle it and keeping her finger well away from the trigger. Something else made a thunk against the bottom of the drawer as the fabric slithered out in her hand, but she stayed focused on the little firearm. The last thing she wanted was for it to go off and attract attention. Even worse if she hit herself, too. The safety was off, so she flicked it back on.

Sure enough, the gun was loaded. She peered into the drawer and found another firearm. This one was a .38 special, absolutely not ladylike, also with the safety off. She flicked it on and stifled a sigh, then wiped both guns with the scarf to get rid of any fingerprints she might have left before returning them to the drawer. Whatever else Esmeralda was, she had to either live dangerously or be as paranoid as Uncle Finn to keep her guns like this. Even a gangster should realize how impractical it would be to shoot herself accidentally while writing a letter or paying a bill.

Millie had searched all but two drawers. She decided to skip the mirror-image of the one on the side of the knee well and open the long thin drawer just under the surface of the desk. Bingo. There was a little volume the size of a prayer book, and even with her human nose Millie could smell incense and old parchment.

The book's leather cover was brown and mottled with age. She opened it, and the pages crackled. It must be ancient. She got an image of a short man in monkish brown robes and a skullcap, perched on a stool in front of what could only be a slanted wooden writing desk. Pots of ink in every color she could think of lined a sort of level shelf at the top. The little man reached up to dip a quill into a red pot, then bent to the first page of a brand new book exactly this size. Millie knew this vision came from her canine friend, but the perspective looked over the man's shoulder. That was impossible for any dog, even one of Bear's size.

She was too intrigued by the book she held to follow the trail of her thoughts about Bear. Millie gazed down at the page, and saw an elaborately decorated first letter done in red and black ink with yellow crosses and green leaves adorning it. She started to read, and realized it was in Latin, her absolute worst subject. She started to close the book, but got that begging puppy face from

Bear again. Millie stayed her hand and looked at the jumble of words again.

She could read them with no trouble. The book seemed to be a series of tales about Hrafin of Mercia, a powerful noble warrior from the days before Arthur united Briton. The first one told how Hrafin encountered a monster, and in the course of defeating it, Changed with a capital c. Millie had just started reading the next section, which appeared to tell more about the nature of creature Hrafin became. She heard someone outside the office. Millie tucked herself into the knee well and pulled the chair in after her as far as she could.

"I'll just get the smelling salts in case it happens again." That was a woman's voice just outside the door.

Millie tried desperately to recall whether she'd seen any smelling salts in or on the desk but couldn't. She heard a click as the door knob turned. Too late, she remembered that the lights had been off when she entered. She'd have to hope the woman either didn't remember or was too distracted to notice.

Footsteps came toward the desk, but stopped. Millie peeked out under the wood panel over the knee well, seeing a pair of feet in large metallic paisley-printed shoes pointing at the book case. There was a rustle of fabric and the clinking of metal on glass. Millie got an image of a hand with rings on every finger clutching a small blue bottle. Now where did that come from? The feet clicked away toward the door, which clacked shut behind the garishly shod lady who could only be Esmeralda Cavalcante.

Millie almost stood up, but stopped before she

brained herself on the underside of the desk. She crawled out from the knee well and was immediately beset with the pins and needles of outrageous bad circulation. She flipped the book open again to read another page and a much more modern piece of wood pulp paper fell out from the back.

"Esme," it said in a scrawling hand, "You'll remember this book from our parochial days. I need you to hold on to it for me. I can't let the group this book is about discover that I know this much about them. I'll come visit after Christmas and get it back. The situation here in Fall River should be resolved by then. Fondly, Cousin Giacomo."

Millie opened the drawer she'd found the book in, rifling through it until she found a large envelope with traces of excelsior inside and mumbled a word she hoped her mother would never hear her say. She found no addresses on the envelope that had most likely contained the volume. Still, there was only one Giacomo she could think of who was connected to Esmeralda. Giacomo Bianco, the crime lord of Fall River. Someone like that wouldn't send a book this important by parcel post.

She didn't have time to sit and think about this. Esmeralda could come back any minute. Millie put the empty envelope back and closed the drawer. As she was about to come out from behind the desk, she saw a small silver key next to the inkwell. The drawer she'd taken the book from had a lock. She locked the drawer, then stuck the key in her coat pocket with the book and the note. Now it would take Esmeralda a while to be sure the book was missing. She'd probably spend hours trying to find the key and open the drawer, though there hadn't been anything else there with it. She might not even try looking in that drawer until Christmas.

Millie shut the light off once she was next to the door, then listened for any indication that there were people out in the store room. A scratching sound came from the door leading into the alley, followed by a canine whine.

"That must be the dame's dog." Millie recognized the voice of the man who'd let her in, and the creak of the alley door. "C'mere, boy," said the man. "Be a good pooch and come to Eric. Jeepers, don't you want to get warm?" Dog claws rattled on linoleum and then the pavement outside. "Dammit!" A blast of frigid air rushed under the door. "Gimme that back, you crazy mutt!"

Millie heard the man's footsteps clatter down the steps outside and the door slammed after them. She crept out of the office and closed the door quietly, stepping as softly as she could toward the bathroom.

"Millie?"

She wanted to jump out of her skin, but turned her head instead to find her brother.

"Bill."

"What are you doing here, trying to get me fired?" He looked weary and a little pale.

"No, just trying to powder my nose." That was her story and she was sticking to it. All the suspense made her have to go for real, anyway. Maybe she'd tell Bill about her adventure, but definitely not here.

"Well, jeez, Mill. If you wanted to come in and do

that, you could have gone through the front and asked for me." He sounded more tired than annoyed. "I work here now, in case you don't remember."

"It was so cold and I had to go so bad, I forgot." She shifted her weight from one foot to the other, which was not even remotely an act at that point. "And Bear's outside. You couldn't get him into a place like this."

"Still. I could have let him sit in the foyer behind a philodendron or something, he's so well-behaved. Hell, Ms. Cavalcante would probably like him." Bill snagged a stack of napkins from a shelf.

"Um." Millie pointed to the powder room. "I still have to. You know."

"Oh!" He shook his head. "Okay. We'll talk later."

He walked through the swinging double doors to the kitchen just as she put her hand on the door knob to the powder room. She went inside, glad of her ruse now that she really did have to go. As she washed her hands, Millie heard the door from the outside open and close again. She came out of the powder room, turning off the light as she went.

"Sit. That's a good boy. Wow, you're a big fella." The man leaned against one of the shelves, panting.

"Bear!" Millie rushed to the dog's side and leaned over to put her arms around his neck. "Oh, thank goodness you found him." She straightened and turned to face the man. "He could have caught his death out in that cold. Thank you ever so much, Eric." Oops. She'd only overheard his name. Couldn't have him think she was there spying on the juice joint.

Millie flung her arms around Eric's neck, then

attacked his cheeks with a flurry of little pecking kisses. She meant to throw him off-guard, not initiate a petting session, after all. He smelled like coffee and the cold from outside. Millie pulled away before he even had a chance to get an arm around her waist. Eric's cheeks flushed and he leaned more heavily against the shelves than before.

"Ya ya ya you're welcome, Miss…Um." He acted just like the boys at school did whenever they saw Rachel.

"Mullins." She didn't want to get Bill in trouble.

"Eric Kovach," he managed. "You ever need help here again, just ask." He gave her a dazed grin. He was nice looking in his way, with curling brown hair and amber eyes. Nowhere near as handsome as Theo, though.

"Thanks. Now I hope I'll get in trouble again." Millie dropped a wink, smiling as she swallowed a guffaw. Bear found all of this far more amusing than any dog should. She stuck her hat back on her head and pulled her gloves on. Her new friend Eric watched as she walked out the door with her dog. Millie could swear she almost saw herself through his eyes. But that was nonsense for anyone like her who wasn't Wise. She waved but didn't look back.

When things went sideways, Gilbert Edgewood went back to his plants. Predictable for the most part, flora presented a more comforting presence than fauna. They never judged, didn't keep secrets, and had no agenda. Their needs were simple, too. Everyone else knew plants needed water, light, and good soil. Every Edgewood, Wise or not, knew they also craved companionship, but weren't too picky about the company. Plants were better people than he was himself.

Gilbert paced rows in the burlap-covered conservatory, running his fingertips over and along leaves, stems, and twigs. These garden denizens would wither and die if they weren't brought in. As his hand caressed a pygmy lemon tree, Gilbert got a sense of its life before the glass-walled room was built. That had been before he was born, so this tree must have belonged to his grandfather. Most of the plants in the conservatory hadn't been around that long.

He paused, letting the tiny tree convey how dark it had been in the basement with only the light from dingy panes. Sending back sympathy and gratitude that the little tree was still here, Gil felt a flow of unseasonable growth energy. He hadn't meant to do it, but he thought they'd get more lemons than usual this summer now.

Turning down the next row, he breathed in the scent of cooking herbs. Even though Gilbert and his father always asked before taking their leaves, those plants projected a nervous energy whenever someone approached. He couldn't blame them. A person might bring water or be coming to take leaf or stem away with them, sometimes both.

He tried to focus on soothing thoughts, but that got harder every day. Sour regrets had plagued Gil since he said Sarah's name to Finn Mullins at the Old Colony Club. The basil plant trembled before him.

"Don't worry, I'm just here for a visit," he said.

Despite what most people thought, talking to plants was no waste of time. Even a mundane's voice had power to move them. The words weren't important, but the tone and intent were. Gilbert had been twelve when his father had shown him old Nana Roma's rose garden downtown. She didn't have a drop of Wise blood, yet the plants were gorgeous, healthy in a year with terrible pests and drought problems. And what was the difference between her garden and the one next door? Nana Roma sang hymns to her roses.

Pacing down the last row, Gilbert finally came to his favorite, a hibiscus that produced purple-blue blooms every summer. He reached out to run his hand along its braided trunk, which had been one of his father's first projects as a Wood Wise. Father had been a prodigy, getting his full Wisdom two years earlier than the rest of his generation. Gilbert knew all his life that he'd fall short of filling dad's shoes. He probably deserved to go barefoot, figuratively speaking.

"I really screwed the pooch, ladies and germinators." Gilbert put one hand in his pocket, touching the letter with horrible news. He was about to read it again, when someone tapped out "shave-and-a-haircut" on one of the windows. He sighed, letting go of the paper. That could only mean one of two things; Millie or Bill. He rapped a quick "two bits" in answer, then went around the corner to open the door.

"What can I do for you at this late hour, fearless leader?" He stood in the doorway, hoping that Bill wouldn't want to come in. At least it wasn't Sarah again, but Gilbert would rather be alone.

"Can I come in?"

Horsefeathers.

"Sure. But don't feed the plants." Gilbert moved aside and let the man go through, holding his arm out to grant Bill passage into the conservatory. Holding back all his negativity around his best friend made him glad he'd already curbed them for the plants.

Bill's fainting episode this evening confirmed his suspicions that Bill's Wisdom was in like an overworked doctor. Gil didn't want his thoughts read if he could help it. There were just some things even a best friend shouldn't have to deal with.

"You have time to listen to something?" Bill shifted his weight from one foot to the other. Whatever trouble he'd scaled on the way here must be bigger than a molehill.

"Me and the corn are all ears."

"I'm getting my Wisdom," he said. "So far, I can only

read mundanes. But that includes Rachel. And Sarah." Bill's forehead furrowed, and he sighed. "Rachel's fine, a little worried that I don't want to marry her which isn't far off— I'm rambling, sorry. It's Sarah. Something's wrong with her. Her thoughts and feelings are like nothing Dad described. Her mind." Bill pinched the bridge of his nose, closed his eyes, shook his head. "God, I don't know how to say it. She might not be normal."

"Is it full of numbers, her head?" Gilbert closed his eyes to keep them from rolling. Of course Bill would panic the second he saw a mind that thought mainly in the abstract. "I mean, she's a super genius, you know. Always talking about probability and the odds of something-or-other. Her heroes are Pythagoras and Gauss instead of Clara Bow and Betsey Ross. What did you expect, dreams of movie stars? She'd probably rather meet Albert Einstein than Buster Keaton. Ugh, now I'm rambling."

"I thought the same thing. But yesterday, both times, it was like something out of H.P. Lovecraft in her head. The math was there, aligning with something huge that I couldn't wrap my brain around. I would have loved getting nothing but logarithms, believe me."

"Wait, both times? You mean, you saw the odd in the bird once and decided to take a stroll down disturbing lane again?"

"Well, yeah." Bill's eyes popped wide open. "Oh no. You don't think it's contagious?"

"Um—" Gilbert hoped not, especially considering the letter in his pocket. "no?" He didn't want Bill running off to wake up his father or Mrs. Webster.

"Are you sure? My head is like a different place all the time now." Bill had stopped staring at the door like he might bolt for it but there was still a little twitch under his eye.

"Full Wisdom does that." Gilbert adjusted his glasses. "It's halfway like March; blows in like a lion but doesn't walk out like a lamb. You never feel the same as you did before it came in. There's an extra sense we get that's on all the time, like a light without a switch so you can't shut it off. That's why you have to work like a horse to block it. Even when you put a wall up, some still gets through. Plants are simpler than people, I have it easy."

"Okay." Bill's head drooped. "I wish Father explained it like you just did."

"Now what do you mean about her head being full of spooky? Was it really like Lovecraft or more like Poe? Sarah turns up her nose at most fiction, especially anything fantastical."

"Not full of horror stories." Bill took a couple of deep breaths before continuing. "Her head was full of horrible things."

"She's all gloom and doom? Are you saying she's depressed?"

"No. Look Gil, just let me finish. This isn't easy to describe."

"Fine. Speak on, Macduff."

"I'm going to start from the beginning. I was on my way home after getting hired at the Supper Club. Sarah came out of the library and something about her was different." Bill paced over to one of the philodendrons. He reached out as if to stroke one of the leaves with his index finger, but stopped short.

"Sarah's usually odd." Gil shrugged. "Nothing touches her, and she doesn't touch anything else. Nobody cares about numbers the way she does."

"We all act annoyed every time she gets out paper and that slide-rule." Bill sighed. "Maybe we shouldn't."

"Well, sure, but all the teachers love her. She doesn't need us."

"Yeah, I thought so too." Bill tapped his finger lightly against the philodendron's pot. "The teachers give Sarah some support, but not enough because none of them are Wise. The Websters taught Theo and Sarah, because Fire Wisdom is dangerous. Part of that was to make sure whoever didn't get Wisdom knew what to do if their sibling went bonkers. Sarah needs structure like this plant needs water and sunlight."

"Fire Wisdom is the bummest of the bum deals."

"My father would disagree with you. But don't change the subject. Sarah's an outsider, even with us. She can't blend with the mundanes and we've spent our entire childhoods making her feel like the oddball."

"Hey, at least you don't have to marry her."

"Gilbert, jeez." Bill's fists clenched. "You're thicker than the oak in front of the Howe place. Sarah's a wreck over something. This is serious."

"Horsefeathers." Gilbert snorted. "She did it to herself. There's another side to this story besides poor Sarah's algebraic brain. How many times did Millie try and bring her along to climb trees, or Rachel to choir practice? There was a time Theo wouldn't go anywhere unless she tagged along. She'd act like we took her away from her charts and calculations. Yeah, she's a weirdo. Remember when we all talked about our heroes? All of ours were people who went out and did actual things. You remember who Sarah's hero was?"

"Yeah, Ada Lovelace. Fine." Bill crossed his arms over his chest. "She's always been different. Seems like the one thing she's got in common with the rest of us is the mile-wide stubborn streak you're demonstrating right now. I'm not her defense attorney, just explaining how it's affected her right lately. You're the one who has to marry her. You don't want to know what's wrong with her? She might be dangerous. I'm trying to protect you, Gil."

"So speak plainly, Bill. You think I need to be spoon-fed? Cut to the chase. What's her damage?"

"She was less timid tonight than usual. I think Sarah found something at the library today. I have no idea what it was, because all her thoughts are numbers. But there was this giant equation in her noggin and she'd almost solved it." Bill's face started turning red, and he twiddled his fingers. "Also, she had this expression, like finally someone understood. I thought maybe she was with a person who gave her a new perspective."

"Do you know what kind of equation it was?"

"It looked like the probability stuff she's been going on about for the last few years. Much bigger than that, though."

"Did the equation make you pass out in the Supper Club?"

"No, the numbers were all from outside the library. She had some kind of epiphany there. And like I said, she wasn't alone."

"Well, I guess the library's the proper place for eureka moments." Gilbert shifted his weight from one foot to the other, wanting to reveal that letter but not the shame of dropping Sarah's name.

"I bet whatever happened helped her get close to solving that equation. Someone else in town is as odd as her, lonely too. I can only think of one person who fits that description. Uncle Finn." Bill's nose crinkled as though he'd just smelled something rotten.

"Eww, right?"

"I peeked in her mind again at the Supper Club, hoping to learn more. I wanted to know why she started talking about Rachel with Ms. Cavalcante."

"Yes, that was strange. Sarah's usually mum for months around anyone new, especially someone as intimidating as Esmeralda."

"Exactly. Sarah just started volunteering information while doodling numbers on that paper. I saw them later when I cleared your table. They were from that equation in her head."

"But Sarah just complimented Rachel."

"I know. She acted helpful, which makes sense because Rachel sticks up for her the most. But there was something off about it." Bill wiped his brow, sweating boulders, like he had in the Supper Club. He opened his coat and fanned himself with the lapels.

"Sit down, Bill." Gilbert pulled a stool from under one of the rows of plants. "None of this passing out, either. I'm tone deaf."

"Think of the hottest day you can imagine." Bill put

the stool against a wall, sat down, then let his coat slide off his arms and slump to the floor. "Then think about being in here with none of the shades drawn. After that, imagine you're wearing a blindfold with your eyes open."

"My God. No wonder you ended up on the floor."

"I'm not done. You're hearing a constant stream of numbers spoken in a pattern but you can't understand them. The person speaking them does, though. What's more, she knows the pattern even before she recites it."

"So it's a prediction? Like the guys in the papers who chart the stock market? Like Sight?"

"Sight?" Bill pulled out a handkerchief and wiped his brow again. When the cloth came away, it revealed furrows in his forehead. "I didn't think of that before. But yes, that makes sense. Maybe she's a Seer."

"So you think she's got Wisdom? How'd she end up like that, then?" Gilbert used to love Bill's wild theories and flights of imagination but this one freaked him out.

"Sight Wisdom is supposed to be all pictures." Bill sighed and leaned back against the wall. "But pictures are abstract, just like numbers. It's not too crazy to imagine that Sarah's been hiding her ability."

But Gilbert thought it was crazy. "Would she get something like that this early, though?" He'd never consider these ideas if not for the letter in his pocket. "Most partials don't get anything until they're adults."

"Millie's got it and she's sixteen. There have been cases as young as twelve. Partial Wisdom is more powerful the younger it comes in." Bill slumped on his stool, eyes glittering. "But from how hard it was to look in her head, she's got a powerful version."

"Are you saying what I think you're saying?"

"I'm saying she's some kind of prodigy with the maths and her Wisdom." Sweat trickled down his face like he was standing in rain. He looked feverish. "Sarah acts like someone with Sight. She doesn't take risks without serious calculation and her thoughts aren't linear. She's not normal in the head."

"Well, but how do you know what a normal head looks like, Bill?" Gilbert put one hand in his pocket, clutched the letter.

"Rachel's head is normal. So's Esmeralda Cavalcante's."

"And mine isn't?"

"Wait." Bill stared at him and Gilbert felt a strange itching at his left temple.

Gil tried not to scratch his head, practically clamped one hand to the inside of his pocket and the other to his hip. He focused on one thought; the curtain in the front window that they always used as a signal. Gilbert remembered his mistake, how he'd screwed up and answered Finn Mullins with Sarah's name. He didn't want Bill to see that in his head, or anything about the letter Finn left for Sarah.

"So, is my brainpan normal or what?"

"It's different from Rachel's and Esmeralda's." Bill frowned. "Probably just because you're Wise and they're not. Yours was more like Sal Tucci's, actually."

"You read his mind?" Gilbert managed a laugh that didn't sing with nerves. "What's in there, Boston Cream Pie?"

"Well, yeah. Lots of food. The man's always hungry." Bill shrugged. "It's actually kind of boring in there. There's this sense like he's hiding something. You had that, too, Gil. I could tell that you've got serious problems on your mind. So spill the beans already."

"I guess it's about time." Gilbert leaned against one of the tables, taking comfort in the nearness of a geranium. "I have something you need to see but first there's something you have to hear. Bill, it's my fault. I ruined everything."

"What are you saying here, Gilbert?"

"I'm saying she's all messed up because of me." Gil gripped the side of the table so hard his nails gouged dead wood. "Finn kept on asking me questions. I panicked and dropped Sarah's name."

"No. Way." Bill's eyes went glassy.

Gilbert checked in with the plant nearest Bill, a Thanksgiving Cactus. Its energy trembled and shrank away from Bill. The little buds and blooms on it drew in, trying to protect themselves. His head itched again, that communication with the plant apparently opening a door in his mind for Bill to walk right through. Straightening, Gil slapped the side of his head. He put himself between Bill Chiavo and the plant.

"How dare you." Gil put his hands on his hips, glaring down at Bill. "Get out of my head!"

"Okay, fine." How much more sweating could Bill do before he just dried up? His skin had turned a delicate shade of green, maybe he needed water. Gilbert refrained from getting a hose and dousing Bill's head with it.

"Never invade my mind again, William Chiavo." Gil grabbed a watering can anyway, for the plants. Watering them would help them resist the negative energy this conversation generated. "I'll tell you everything, just give me time to talk, okay?"

"All right." Bill listened as Gilbert related his entire encounter with Finn at the Old Colony Club.

"I still don't see how that did anything for my uncle besides give him a reason to try talking to Sarah."

"You're just saying that because you feel bad about trying to invade my mind."

"No, it's true." Bill shook his head. "All you said was her name. Anything else Uncle Finn Saw must have come from things she said."

"That brings me to the second act in our little family drama." Gilbert set the watering can down. "Sarah gave me this letter tonight, on the way home."

Fishing the letter from his pocket and handing it over to Bill sent a flood of relief through Gilbert's heart. For weeks, he'd lay awake reliving that moment on the steps at the Old Colony Club. Maybe he'd sleep easy tonight.

Bill unfolded the letter and read it, his eyes moving from side to side like twin pendulums. At the end, he hung his head.

"I can't believe this," he said. "Finn wooing Sarah, sending her that dress. At least she didn't wear it."

"I'm sorry, Bill." Gil thought Bill should be the one apologizing but his old friend looked so downtrodden by recent events he couldn't help it.

"It's not your fault, Gilbert." Bill didn't even look at him. Gilbert waited for an apology that never came.

"So whose fault is it?"

"It's Millie's." Bill's eyes glittered with rage and unshed tears.

"Really?" Gilbert held no sympathy for Bill, only brittle disappointment. His friend's greatest flaw was evading blame. Taking a deep breath, he picked up a hose, and turned the sprayer to the mist setting to water the hibiscus. "Not yours?"

"What do you mean?"

"When you take charge, you take blame. Responsibility comes with perks and downsides, just like Wisdom."

"I don't get how Millie's mistake is my fault." Bill glanced from the hose and back to Gilbert again. "And I don't understand why you're watering plants when you said you'd tell me everything."

"Listen hard, then. I lead all the plants in this room, first of all." He walked down the row, spraying as he went. When he turned the corner, he spoke again. "Second, I'm responsible for them. Me. if I don't give them water, they curl up and die." He sprayed and let the words flow with the water. "In exchange, these plants give me comfort, some small measure of sanctuary in a world that would hate me if it knew all my truths. So yes, Mr. Chiavo, I'm watering my plants." He turned another corner and kept talking with his back to Bill. "I'm also telling you that you need to water us, too. Or else."

"Or else what, Gilbert?"

"Or else I'm out. Our friendship is over." He paused to lean his face closer to the spray so it would hide his tears before he turned around again.

"But Gil, I'm in love with you." Bill looked up at him from the stool, his face waxy and pale.

"The feeling is not mutual." The top of Gilbert's head felt light, as though a helium balloon had lifted the top of it right off. His toes and fingertips chilled like they'd touched a glacier. "I told you to stop! Get out of my head!"

Bill's eyes bulged and his mouth gaped like a fish out of water. He looked half dead, broken, like he'd been shot in the heart. Gilbert felt a stab of pity and shame. He hadn't thought his anger would hurt Bill so badly, though he'd told nothing but the truth.

"I'm sorry, Gil." Bill leaped up without even taking his coat and hurried out the door into the frigid night. The hose coiled on the floor at Gilbert's feet, a puddle of water stretching under half the tables in the conservatory. He didn't remember setting it down or leaving it running.

Apology died on Gilbert's lips. He wasn't sure why he felt so bad for his oldest friend, or why he hadn't shown Finn's letter to Bill. After bending down to shit off the sprayer, he felt around in his pocket for the envelope. It wasn't there. The only possible explanation was that Bill had wiped the last few minutes from Gilbert's mind.

He sank to his knees and wept into his hands, mourning the death of his closest friendship. The shrubs and herbs communed all around him, pulling away the anguish, grief, and regret to replace it with a salve of quiet growth.

"Bless me, Father, for I have sinned. It's been six weeks since my last confession."

"Child, what is your sin?" The Priest's voice sounded light, unburdened. Bill recognized Father John.

"Father, I messed up. I made my friends take on a huge risk and now we all might suffer immensely because of it."

"What mistake was this, Child?" Father John didn't sound too concerned. Bill had a hard time taking the Priest seriously. He was just a year older than Gilbert.

"I thought my uncle was up to no good. Instead of confronting him, I sent my friends to spy on him. And that only made things worse."

"Is your uncle sinning?"

"He's greedy, looking to take everything we have, control our lives."

"My son, I'm not sure what you're confessing to, exactly." Father John's fingers tapped against the wall between him and Bill. "You're trying to stop another man from sin, not committing it yourself."

"Asking my friends to spy on someone isn't sinful?" Bill blinked.

"Your friends decided whether to spy and how to do

it if they so chose. Your part in it is minor at best." Father john sighed. "Look, my son. You're here for a reason, clearly in crisis. But I'm having trouble figuring out how it pertains to a sin against God or His Church. Unless there's some point you haven't made yet."

There were a half-million things Bill wasn't telling Father John. The trouble Bill always had with Reconciliation never changed. He couldn't confess about Wisdom or the way his family lived because of it. He couldn't talk about Uncle Finn directly. And he definitely shouldn't talk about Tucci, Ms. Cavalcante or the Supper Club. He reached for the curtain, about to give up and go home to cry in his pillow. But then he remembered something he could confess, maybe even the real reason he'd come here in the first place.

"I'm in love with my best friend. I told him tonight and he said he doesn't love me back."

The other side of the booth silenced so completely that Bill wasn't sure Father John still breathed until he checked the Priest for surface thoughts. He stopped short of reading them, then sat and prayed; not for his soul, not even for Gilbert's. Bill pleaded with God, asking Him to guide Father John. He thought the young Priest needed it. If only the old Father, Paul, hadn't retired two years ago. Paul had been unflappable and pragmatic, approaching moral issues with a grounded logic impossible in a man his replacement's age.

And Bill finally understood that he wasn't so different from Father John. He had no right to lead his friends, no experience, no weight of years to temper his judgment. He always scoffed and scorned, called Millie impetuous.

But it was he who'd acted rashly tonight. Bill had sinned in pride and his friends' mishaps were now his burden to carry.

"Perhaps your friend understands more than you do that romantic love between two men is a sin in the eyes of the Holy Church." Father John's voice had lost all of its buoyancy. He sounded weary now. "Perhaps he even seeks to spare you both from damnation with his rejection."

"You don't know him, Father."

"Maybe I know someone like him. You presume too much, Son." Father John tapped on the wall again, a sign Bill believed signaled contemplation. After a pause, the Father continued. "But your other problem, the doubts about crossing your uncle. Do you understand now why the situation disturbs you?"

"Pride, Father."

"Yes." Father John chuckled. "It goeth before a fall. Have you fallen recently, Son?"

"I have, Father. After my friend rejected me, I stole from him."

"And so we come to the real reason you're here. Pride has made you assume your feelings were returned. And when you found they were not, you lashed out at someone who trusted you. Can you return what you've taken?"

"No, Father." Bill hung his head. "I destroyed the thing utterly."

"Then you must make amends by doing the right thing by him and the other people in your life." Father John cleared his throat. "What is your ultimate goal now that you've explored how and why you fell?"

"To get up and walk again, Father. Keep on going because these people are counting on me."

"I will give you a warning, then. This time, you have got to walk humbly. Slow down. Look down too, for that matter. Remember that you fell. Remember your mistakes and make them into armor. We're young. What's more, we're human. We're bound to err. But mistakes can teach us if only we let them."

"Okay, Father."

"I want you to stop and pray for guidance like I believe you were doing a few minutes ago. If you stop to pray, answers will come to you."

"But Father, what's my Contrition?"

"Slow down and walk humbly, as I said. Encourage your friends to that end as well. Try to help them as best you can, not by removing their burdens, but by offering to share the weight."

"Yes, Father. Thank you."

"Thank you, Son."

Walking back out of the Church, Bill wondered why Father John had thanked him. After the mess he'd made this evening, he wasn't about to read the Priest's mind. But Bill didn't have to. He understood just by the emotion in Father John's voice that he was lonely. Maybe all leaders suffered so.

Both Mom and Dad already lay asleep in their

bedroom by the time Millie got home. That was unusual, but Millie's little old book had her too excited to wonder why she wasn't in trouble for breaking curfew. She went into Father's study. The light was brighter in there and she strongly desired the company of the large radiator. Bear went directly over to the big metal box and laid down directly in front of it. She had to settle for a seat off to its side.

She sat down in the wingback chair, kicking her shoes off so she could put her numb feet up on the ottoman. Warmth from the heater caressed her toes. She sighed contentedly and opened the book for the second time. Giacomo Bianco's note marked the place where she'd stopped reading in Esmeralda's office.

Hrafin had become some kind of creature the book called Changed. He didn't age, bronze and stone weapons couldn't hurt him, and he was stronger than any mortal man. Basically he was Achilles without the heel. Bear made a chuffing sound.

"Okay, Bear. He's not like Achilles, then. I don't get why it's such a big deal to you." She kept reading. Hrafin struck terror into the hearts of anyone he spoke to. This was because he'd grown a mouth full of dragon's teeth. Millie laughed out loud. "What a crock. Dragon teeth? Applesauce!"

Bear whined, rolling his eyes. He chided her. Millie paused until she could figure out why.

"Yes, you have a point. Here I am, brain linked with a dog, and I laugh at the idea of a metaphor related to dragons." Millie tried to put her skepticism aside about the nearly immortal protagonist and read the tragic tale of Hrafin and his Lady, Ælfwynn of Mercia. It reminded her of the old *Ballad of Matty Groves* or *Little Musgrave.*

Bear's own master was the subject of the book she'd stolen. Is that why the dog thought it so important? She stopped to scratch Bear behind the ear and get one of the sweets Dad always kept hidden in the end table. After that, Millie turned back to the book to find that Hrafin believed Changed were at risk of being cursed by their perfect memories with scant hope for redemption.

Millie had never been too enthusiastic about church, but believed in the idea of souls and the stain of sin. Too much cruelty changed a person. That was one reason she objected so strongly to Bill's involvement with Tucci. She wondered if that was part of Uncle Finn's problem as well.

Bear sidled up to the chair and put his head in her lap. He looked up at her as though trying to say that he knew what she meant about cruelty. If he really was the companion of this Hrafin from the book, no wonder. He touched the volume lightly with his nose as though urging her to keep on reading. But Millie had questions.

"Is Hrafin like me? Can he understand you with his mind like I can?"

Bear only blinked.

"Then it must be you who's special. You understand people?"

The dog blinked again. She was wrong on both counts, then. He nosed the book a second time, so Millie kept reading.

They made a pilgrimage to Rome and met an older Changed there named Lacertus, who'd sworn service to the Holy Church. He said he'd been a soldier under Augustus Caesar but converted to the Christian faith before being thrown to lions that were actually feral Changed in animal shape. Lacertus had aided human soldiers in Augustinian Just Wars for hundreds of years. Hrafin wanted to help as he could. Ælfwynn had no heart for combat. She'd learned strategy at her mother's knee, but the battlefield wasn't the place for her. Together, the three of them concocted a plan.

They started a Holy Order for Changed and other creatures faithful to the Church. Their plan included scholars, scouts, and combatants. Ælfwynn created the Anchorites of the Cloister, devoted to meditation and recording the history and origin of Changed. Lacertus recruited any he could find for the Undying Knights.

Hrafin founded Rome's Rangers, who brought stories, texts, and tactical information back to the other two branches. There were references to three other books at the bottom of the page, each an in-depth record of the three organizations. She had to know more, find out why Hrafin had abandoned all of that and traveled to another continent. When she turned the page, Millie found the rest of the pages blank.

"That's all? But what happened to them after that? How come there's nothing in the history books about these Orders?"

Bear pushed his head under Millie's hand.

"Yeah. I bet you don't care about that. You just want to find Hrafin. Now I do, too."

The dog wagged his tail. Millie heard the front door open.

"Bill's home." She tucked the book under her arm, then draped her coat over herself from the neck down. Millie listened to her brother's footsteps as he came down the hall.

While Bill paused just outside the door, he ultimately kept going toward the stairs and up them. Millie held her breath until she heard the door to Bill's room shut. Bear's nose was going a mile a minute.

"What do you smell, boy?" It wasn't until she opened the door that the pungent odor of sweat and fertilizer hit Millie. She held the coat up to her face to muffle the sneeze, then shut the study door again as softly as she could. "Phew. The Edgewood conservatory. Ugh. But if he was with Gilbert, why is he so upset?"

Bear leaned his head against her hip bone. She wasn't sure what she'd do without the big fella around. He made her feel special, cared for. And his quest for his missing master inspired her sense of adventure and curiosity.

"I know you want to go back to your Hrafin," she told him. "I aim to help you do exactly that. But I hope afterward that you'll visit sometimes, if you can." Millie yawned.

Bear nudged her toward the door again.

"Yeah, you're right. We should get some sleep." The dog seemed to know she wanted to get into her room as quietly as possible.

The wheels in Millie's head turned with questions about Hrafin, Lacertus, and Ælfwynn. She tried to imagine what life was like for Wise in ancient Mercia and Rome, or even whether there were any back then.

She completely forgot to wonder how she'd known Bill
was upset.

"Eric." Esmeralda Cavalcante tapped one golden paisley shoe against the worn linoleum covering the Supper Club's back hallway. Rosetta Franklin stood in the kitchen doorway, watching.

"Yes, Ma'am?" Eric Kovach gulped, hoping he wasn't in hot water on account of the hot ticket with the dog.

"I need you to get me some information."

"Um, information, Ma'am?" Eric scratched his head, hoping he looked more innocent than clueless. "About what?"

"I need to know more about this Salvatore Tucci character." Ms. Cavalcante whipped a sheet of cream-colored stationery from the crook of her arm.

"But why, Ma'am?" Eric vaguely remembered her saying she'd turned down a business offer from a man named Tucci the month before.

"That's none of your business." Ms. Cavalcante cleared her throat. "I need you to tail the man, tell me where he disappears to every few days."

"Yes, Ma'am." Eric turned toward the door but then stopped and turned right back around. Eric Kovach had a question but wasn't sure how to phrase it so he raised his hand.

"What, Eric?"

"I haven't seen him around, Ma'am."

"So?"

"Ms. Esme," Etta Franklin came to Eric's rescue. "How's the boy supposed to find Tucci when he doesn't know what to look for?"

"You're right, Miss Etta." Esmeralda sighed, the fire in her eyes banking down to a more reasonable level. "Eric, look for the fat, pasty, Italian man in purple. Start down at the diner around sunup."

"Yes, Ms. Cavalcante." Eric hung up his apron and shrugged his coat on for the second time that night. "Thanks, Miss Etta."

"Don't mention it, child."

Eric followed instructions so well, he didn't mention anything all the way out the door and down the street. He passed his apartment when he saw a rose tint at the horizon. Sleep would have to wait until he'd carried out the Boss Lady's orders. When he got to the diner, he stopped and jogged in place for a few minutes to keep warm. Thanksgiving week meant the streets were mostly empty, quiet too, though activity happened if you knew where to look. Eric did.

A night-owl by nature, Eric Kovach knew plenty of things he shouldn't. He understood that his employer and her enterprise were illegal, of course. Eric also knew that Esmeralda was rare, possibly unique, not because of her vocation but due to her sex while engaging in it alone. He knew that the families on the other side of Main Street were peculiar, including that Bill Chiavo kid who now worked with him.

Another thing Eric had discovered was that the dead in the graveyard behind Saint Peter's were restless. Their eternal slumber wasn't disturbed often but Eric knew it had been just a night ago. He'd heard a strange dragging and squeaking sound on his way home. Later, when he'd gone over to see what it was, Eric saw tumbled earth and disturbed floral arrangements near the central mausoleum complex and some monoliths on the south side of the cemetery.

Standing outside the diner, he could see the graveyard now, a shadowy patch behind the Church. He thought about the date he'd committed to memory, December 31st 1922, the night almost everyone in town forgot. But Eric remembered.

Three people had died, got buried right in that cemetery, too. He'd known who they were and how they ended up laying lifeless on top of the ground instead of under it. A few years later Eric visited those graves, when he finally got up the nerve to go over there and look at the headstones. He couldn't do anything else with his knowledge, after all.

One was a woman named Cloris Mullins, another was Ms. Cavalcante's late husband Raul. The other shared a name with the man he waited for now. Tucci, who his boss needed more information about. She'd asked the right guy.

Eric imagined he was still thirteen and peeking out his window again instead of standing in the cold. He had a knack for seeing things he shouldn't. Whether that was a blessing or a curse remained to be seen. So far, his extra knowledge was like that night as far as the rest of

Plymouth's residents were concerned; hidden. But he was nineteen now. The innocent immunity of childhood wouldn't protect him anymore.

Lights went on inside the diner, the cook and the waitress visible through plate-glass windows like actors on a stage. Eric had stopped bouncing and jiving, his attempt to keep warm would have tired him out even if he hadn't just worked a full shift running meals and bussing tables. Maybe he noticed the movement around the corner because he'd gone still.

The squat, stocky figure rounded the bend, a purple fedora perched atop his dark curls. An indigo trenchcoat flapped in gusts off the ocean like a loose sail. Eric watched and waited until Sal Tucci pushed through the door and into the diner. Then, he went around that corner the man had come from and peered down the street.

Eric didn't have to retrace Tucci's steps to know where he'd come from. All the Plymouth natives knew where the warehouses were. But Eric checked for something else that most other people didn't bother with. Clues.

He wasn't peculiar like the people on Chiavo's street. All Eric had were powers of observation and deduction, ones he'd fostered and honed with his love of works by Arthur Conan Doyle and Agatha Christie.

If Salvatore Tucci came fresh as a daisy to the diner at this hour of the morning from the warehouses, that meant he lived in one of them. An eccentric practice, to be sure, but by no means illegal. Eric went all along the side of the street Tucci had come from, checking doors and steps. At number 129, he found an empty Sixlets sleeve. It may as well have been a sign that said "Tucci was here."

Eric tried the latch and it opened. A janitor's cart stood beside a door marked "office." Being a night-owl, Eric was used to the company of people who kept odd schedules. He headed on down and peeked into the gap at the door, which was ajar.

"Hello." Eric smiled at the man with the dust mop.

"Hey." The spindly man gave him a gap-toothed grin.

"I'm sorry to bother you at this hour but my boss asked me to check and see if you had any vacant space for storage."

"'S possible." The man's voice whistled through the spaces left by missing teeth. "Check the list." He jerked his chin at a clipboard hanging on the wall and went back to battling dust bunnies.

"Thanks." Eric picked up the board, flipped through the entries. Tucci had number 131. He left the office and headed up the hall to check out Tucci's space. He found it on the left, understood it'd have a window facing the middle of the building that he couldn't investigate until days or even weeks later.

Leaving the warehouse, Eric decided he was finished actively sleuthing for now. Outside, the diner looked like a beacon, calling to him with the siren song of fried eggs and bacon. But he couldn't afford to be drawn in, not in a literal or figurative sense. Instead, Eric returned to his one-room apartment directly across from Saint Peter's.

As he pulled the door open, he glanced back at the church's cemetery, relieved to find it empty and quiet, as graves and their yards should be. At least once, they weren't that way in Plymouth. Once inside his room with the door locked behind him, Eric Kovach gulped down a stale crust of bread before hitting the hay.

"More coffee?"

"Yes please, Helen." Salvatore Tucci smiled up at the waitress who'd served him for months. He'd have wasted away to nothing without the diner's low prices and substantial grub.

She poured and he smiled, adding cream and sugar until the coffee resembled a cream caramel. Sal and his guest in the warehouse needed the extra calories. Gazing out the east window at the horizon to watch the sun come up over Plymouth was one of best parts of returning to the town. The worst had been his visit to the graveyard where his life both ended and began in 1922.

Losing his father, Louie, had been both the best and worst thing that could have happened for Sal. His Wisdom all came from his mother's side with his dad mundane and unaware of anything out of the ordinary. She had no trouble keeping her secret, of course. Mom had always been content in her own body, only ever switching temporarily to avoid the runaround from auto mechanics or trouble when walking home from her factory job after dark.

Sal's powers had just started coming in when he turned thirteen. His discontent had less to do with the changes every kid that age went through and more with how he couldn't stand the tits and ass making themselves plain on his previously slender and flat body.

The lumps on his chest reminded him of tumors. Sal hated them, felt like his body fomented a slow-motion rebellion, made an impostor of his physique. He'd done everything he could to hide the new reviled attributes, from binding his chest with old bedsheets or curtains to filching Dad's more worn out trousers from the mending pile.

Mom hadn't cared. To her, it was just part and parcel with the power to borrow bodies. She was the one to permanently adopt Sal's nickname and even suggest he could claim it was short for Salvatore.

"It's what I would have named you if everything matched when you were born," she'd said. His mother prayed for his eventual happiness.

Dad continued calling his son Sally, insisting that a man was a man and a woman was a woman in the physical sense, period end of story. But Sal had always been a boy in his own heart and mind. With the power to swap bodies, he had the chance to make his physique match the other two parts. But Mom had sworn him to secrecy about their shared ability. He couldn't tell and so he had to live with the curse puberty had bestowed on him.

His father's death in 1922 had lifted a weight off Sal's shoulders. He could be who he truly was without hiding it, talk to his mother any time of day about his new abilities. And Sal learned everything he could. Mom told him most of the rules in theory but Sal figured out almost all of the practice on his own. Best of all, she never gave him grief when he came home, no matter whose body he borrowed. She always recognized him, too.

Sal waxed nostalgic about his time with Mom after they'd moved to Providence. Then, he saw the kid from the Supper Club come down the street from the direction of his warehouse. He dropped his teaspoon, starting at the clink of metal on tile.

"Are you okay, Mr. Tucci?" Helen stood at his elbow, bending at the waist to fish the spoon out from under the table.

"Yeah, maybe, Helen." Sal waited until she stood up, then jerked his chin at the kid. "Do you happen to know who that young fellow is?"

"Oh, that's Eric Kovach. He works at the Supper Club." She sighed. "Poor kid."

"Poor? How so?"

"Oh, you know." Helen reached back to grab the full coffee pot from the counter behind her. "The usual story. Kid and his mom, left to their own devices while dear old dad traveled for work. They used to live uptown but moved to the wrong side of the tracks. His mother passed over the summer, so he's all alone now."

"That stinks."

"Yeah, ain't it the truth." Helen refreshed his coffee. "Ollie has your usual breakfast on the grill. Is that all you'll want?"

"For now, Helen, thanks." Sal missed the cup and spilled sugar. "Heh. I guess I need coffee to function enough to fix it in the first place."

"Oh, Mr. Tucci!" Helen giggled so profusely the

contents of her pot sloshed and nearly spilled. "You're a card."

"I'm a whole deck, Helen."

Billy the Kid looked more beat than the scrambled eggs back in the diner kitchen. He also looked like he'd grown up a touch after working a brace of nights. Sal wondered whether it was the notoriously late Supper Club hours that had gotten to him, or something else. If it wasn't anything to do with business, he shouldn't care, but he did anyway. Somehow or other, the kid was growing on him.

"Have a seat, my friend." Sal gestured at the chair opposite him with his cinnamon- coated fork.

"Thanks, Sal." Apparently, he was growing on Bill, too.

"So, you got news from the land of bug-eyed Betties and jazz babies?" Sal took a slug of burnt-tasting coffee and grimaced. He poured more sugar in the cup, stirred, then sipped and smiled.

"Yeah, I do. I'm off probation after just two days because Ms. Cavalcante loves me that much. There's supposed to be a humdinger of a party on Christmas Eve." Bill leaned his face on his left hand. "You should go. They've got a torch singer lined up."

"Oh? What are they, running some doll in from Boston?" Bill shook his head. Sal guessed again. "Providence? Worcester?"

"Nah, she's local. Rachel Howe." Bill stifled a yawn. "That's my fiancee."

Sal had seen Rachel around town, delivering vegetables and baked goods. He wondered why Bill seemed so humdrum about her. Could he get leverage here? Something to counter his own secret would come in handy. He had a feeling Bill might discover it even before that nosy Eric kid from the Supper Club.

"You're moving your people in and taking over, I see." Sal winked.

"My people are your people." Bill stopped with the leaning and the yawning. Sal liked that he could tell when the kid started to get serious. "You're the best chance the group of us has got."

Now that was interesting. Even if none of the rest were Italian, a gaggle of Joes and Janes would be extremely helpful. But there was Bill's bearcat sister to worry about.

"Somehow I'm not sure they'd appreciate hearing you say that. Your sister might get angry." Sal raised an eyebrow.

"Millie's got nothing to do with what's going on at the Supper Club. She's busy now with her dog anyway."

"She's got a pooch?" Sal felt a knot in the pit of his stomach. He hoped it was just the coffee. "Cute little terrier or something?"

"Kind of the opposite. He's some kind of wolf hound. Big. Shaggy. She calls him Bear. But someone trained him like you wouldn't believe. Best manners I've ever seen in a dog." Bill thrummed his fingers on the table. "Hope he keeps her out of trouble. Millie's always had a knack for stepping in it."

"I hope so, too." Sal was more of a cat person but believed animal companionship helped people more often than not. Maybe the pooch would mellow Millie out. He shrugged. "Now, what can you tell me about the operation over there?"

"Here's my notes." Bill held out a folded sheet of paper.

Sal took the paper from the kid and opened it. A chart showed numbers of patrons by profession. In one column, there was a tally of alcoholic drinks ordered, along with another tally of soft drinks. It showed who ordered food and who didn't.

"This thing is great, Bill." It was more than that. The chart had the most important information about lucre in an operation he'd seen so far. The last piece he'd gotten were food and drink prices off the menu.

He saw now that Esmeralda could probably raise the rate on soft drinks and food, since it was the higher earning customers who bought those items. That would let her lower the booze prices by a few cents, bringing in even more customers looking to tie one on. He wondered why she hadn't thought of that herself.

Maybe she was deliberately trying to keep the Club's earnings down so as not to attract attention. If she earned too much, cousin Giacomo might take it out of her hands. But the rest of the paper showed there were other problems, mostly with deliveries.

Jimmy "the Hooch" Delaqua used to stay over in Plymouth every time he made a delivery, but he'd gone straight home every time since Thanksgiving. All the paper said was he'd had extra work to do for his boss back home.

"Bill, what's this extra work of Jimmy's?" Sal took another bite of French toast, waiting for an answer.

"He didn't say." Bill rubbed his eyes. "Only mentioned it was straight from his Boss back in Fall River, though."

"Interesting." Sal folded the chart and waved the waitress over. "Coffee for my friend here, put it on my bill, Helen."

She nodded and gave them a movie-star smile. Well, she gave Bill a movie-star smile. Bill was Captain of the U.S.S. Oblivious when it came to dames. If he cared to bother, he could give Jimmy a run for his money in that department.

When his coffee came, Bill dumped some sugar in, stirred it, and took a slug. "Thanks, Sal. I needed that more than I thought."

"Never underestimate the power of magic bean juice." Sal held up his own cup in a toasting gesture.

"To magic beans." Bill took another sip.

"I'll drink to that, kid." The world could use a little more belief in magic even if he didn't want anyone knowing about Wisdom. Sal could figure leverage on Bill later. Hopefully, he'd never have to use any such thing.

"I can't believe the nerve of my uncle." Millie stuck the last hairpin in Rachel's up-do, hoping all fifty of the damn things would be enough to keep all that hair up. She'd gotten used to helping with her friend's coiffure over the last few weeks, mostly because she had nothing better to do after Bear left.

"He's absolutely awful." Rachel pinched her cheeks even though she didn't need to. The lavender dress brought the roses out on her face and her lips. Even under stage lights, she'd look spectacular.

"The worst." Millie picked up the glittering rhinestone comb and tucked it into the hair on the right side of Rachel's head.

"Thank God we didn't have to tolerate him on Thanksgiving. We'll have to deal with having him around soon, though. It's almost Christmas." Rachel tilted her head, appraising the comb from the corner of her eye. "Thanks, Millie. It looks good."

But Millie didn't want to be thanked for helping Rachel get ready to showboat. She changed the subject. "Where was he on Thanksgiving weekend, anyway?"

"I don't know." Rachel shrugged.

"Boston." Sarah's voice startled the other two girls.

Her pencil continued scratching out numbers and symbols as obscure to Millie as notes in foreign texts.

"And you know this, how?" Rachel put her hands on her hips.

Millie closed her eyes, a flood of relief soothing her at Rachel's question. The shaky unspoken truce between her and Sarah could be irreparably damaged if she got too confrontational.

"Hmm." Sarah's pencil scratched again. "Gilbert hasn't talked to either of you, then."

"No." Millie could answer this one no problem. "He hasn't spoken to me since the end of Thanksgiving weekend, right after Bear vanished. He helped search, remember?"

The dog's disappearance still bothered Millie. He'd gone out in the pre-dawn hours after Bill's second night at the Supper Club. That was usual, but he didn't come back the next evening. It'd been almost three weeks since, so Millie thought he must have moved on. But that didn't feel like the whole story, somehow. There had to be something else to it, a detail she'd missed or misread in Bear's thoughts.

"At least Gilbert tried to help." Rachel shook her head. "Unlike others I could mention who were too busy to chase after a dog." She shot a glance at the door to the tiny closet they used as a dressing room before Rachel's performances.

"Hey, don't go insulting Bill, now." Millie snorted. "He's my brother. I'm the only one allowed to rag on him like that."

"Okay, I'll stop." Rachel elbowed Millie. "But Sarah

avoided my question."

"Yes, Sarah did." She kept at the equations while speaking about herself in the third person. "Maybe Sarah doesn't want to talk about it because she thinks it's none of your business."

"Finn Mullins is everyone's business, Sarah. You know that." Rachel leaned in the doorway, peering down at the jumble of equations. Millie knew better and didn't bother. "Everybody knows that he didn't send you all these fancy dresses I'm borrowing on a whim."

"Yes, I suppose you're right." Sarah tilted her eyes up, meeting Rachel's gaze. "He's asked the elders for permission to marry me."

Millie's head spun so hard it made Rachel's outburst sound like a muted saxophone instead of words. It made perfect sense and none all at the same time. Uncle Finn wanted an in on organized crime and getting control of the Supper Club was the way to do it. Buying out Esmeralda Cavalcante was impossible because of her cousin Giacomo down in Fall River, so the other option was marrying the widow. So why pursue a union with Sarah?

Sarah Webster had no blood connection to anyone Italian, that's why. He hated Italians too much to marry one even for personal gain. Finn Mullins was tying himself to the Irish Mob and an Italian wife would be a black mark against him with them. So it had to be one of the unmarried ladies in this very room. Millie was a direct blood relation and half Italian besides.

"Why not Rachel?" Millie put her hands over her mouth too late.

"Millie!" Rachel blinked.

"No, her question makes a lot of sense for her level of understanding." Sarah was back at her numbers again. "I'm sorry if that sounds horribly big-headed of me. Well, no. I'm not sorry at all. My head is expanding all the time, you see."

"You've got partial Wisdom." Millie reached behind her for the chair only to remember that Sarah still sat in it.

"How long?"

"Since right before I turned thirteen." She shook her head, then scribbled another number. "Your heads are so far up in the clouds you didn't notice, I guess. Even Theo didn't catch on. But I See."

"You're not really going to marry Finn Mullins?"

"Well, he's offered me the chance to go to Radcliffe."

"Oh Sarah." Rachel hung her head. "You couldn't."

"I could." Sarah's pencil scratching paused. "I shouldn't. I wouldn't. But I definitely could." She chewed the eraser, then thought better of that and went back to calculating God only knows what. "The truth is, I'm still not sure how everything will turn out for me. But this conversation is supposed to happen right here and now. That's what matters."

"You're not making any sense at all, Sarah, you know that." Rachel backed away from her as though she were venomous. Millie used to wonder why the Oracle at Delphi always stayed alone up there on her mountain. If she acted anything like Sarah, it was no wonder.

"I know. But that's okay. You've got to head out there on that stage and rehearse."

Rachel nodded and made her escape through the curtain, leaving Millie and Sarah alone together. That wasn't such a great idea but then Rachel never had been a rocket scientist. Millie took a step toward the doorway but Sarah stuck one hand out, blocking her passage.

"No. You've got to stay here."

Before Millie could ask why, she heard Rachel out in the narrow hallway apologizing to Esmeralda Cavalcante. From the sound of things, they'd almost knocked each other over. The second to last place Millie wanted to be was stuck in an ex-closet with Sarah Webster. But the last place she wanted to be was in the path of Hurricane Esmeralda. She stayed put.

"Good." Sarah still didn't look up. "Now, here's some information for your ears only."

"Fine," Millie growled. She burned with anger at the fact that Sarah wouldn't even look at her but she turned ice-cold once the other girl started speaking.

"Your dog friend's not what he seems. He's going to put himself in harm's way and there's nothing you can do to stop it." Sarah stopped writing and tapped her lower lip with the eraser. "You'll feel it when it happens, too; see everything, including where he is and where they bring him after. You have to go after him, even though it's too late to help him. It'll be right on time for all of us. Also, when Theo needs me, you tell him that if the problem won't work, try the inverse. Do you understand?"

"I'm hasty, not slow, Sarah." Millie gripped her upper arms, digging her fingers into the wiry muscle there. "I get it. But why should I trust you?"

"Because I want the best possible outcome, just like you do."

"That's hardly a reason." Millie glanced at the paper under Sarah's pencil. "If only there was some kind of proof."

Sarah looked up. Not directly at Millie's eyes or even her face. Her eyes focused somewhere else, maybe on a future no one else could see. But was that projection good for everyone or only Sarah? Where did her loyalties lie? Millie scrutinized the other girl's face, finding no tell.

"You ought to play high-stakes poker, Sarah, you know that?"

"Except they don't let women play, at least not around here." One corner of her mouth turned up, haunted by the ghost of the tag-along kid she used to be. "It's a good thing they don't. I've got an unfair advantage. But there's no proof except for these." She gestured at the paper covered edge-to-edge with smudgy equations. "No offense, but I don't think you'd be able to decipher them."

"None taken." Millie wasn't sure Ada Lovelace herself could have made sense of those scrawls. All the same, Millie was inclined to take Sarah at her word on this, though she couldn't put her finger on why.

"Everything depends on whether you follow my advice or not, Millie." Sarah bent her head over the tiny round table again, flipped the paper, started in on the other side. "We're all in your hands, at least until that thread of fate's been woven into the tapestry."

"So, whose hands is it in after that, then?"

"I've got a ton of work to do before I even begin to figure that one out."

"Oh." Millie understood somehow without asking that Sarah referred to literal figuring. Her partial Wisdom must be limited by having to generate and solve these monstrous mathematical complexities.

Rachel's voice wafted in through the curtains. Even muffled and at a practice with just the piano, it sounded lovelier than she looked. Millie knew Bill wouldn't care much about either. She sighed.

"Look at the three of us."

"A series of beautiful disasters."

"That's probably the most poetic thing I've ever heard you say, Sarah."

"I said nothing." Sarah's brow furrowed. "Look, I need to concentrate. Head on out and see how Rachel's doing, okay?"

Millie Chiavo left the room but didn't make it to the front of the house.

Just like one of her equations, Sarah had set her up.

"Miss Chiavo, is it?" Esmeralda Cavalcante stood between Millie and the door to the dining room, arms crossed and foot tapping.

"Um, yes?" Millie did her best to look as demure and meek as possible. Millie's best was most other girls' worst in that department. She was about as meek and demure as a bull in a china shop.

"Next time you need to use the restroom, come in through the front door."

"I'm sorry, Ms. Cavalcante—"

"Don't you dare Ms. Cavalcante me, you little—missy. I know what you've been up to in here."

"You do?" Millie felt like she'd been dipped in arctic water for the second time that evening. Had Esmeralda find out about her pinching the book?

"If I ever catch you leading poor Eric on again, you're in hot water." Esmeralda waved one finger at Millie, like she'd been a bad dog or something. "That poor kid has enough to worry about without some snooty girl making fake eyes at him."

"Fake eyes?"

"I know you're engaged to Mr. Webster. Your brother told me all about how much time you've spent with him. Leave Eric alone!"

"I'll take your advice seriously, Ma'am." Millie fully intended to avoid meeting Eric Kovach again, something she didn't bother mentioning to Bill because it hadn't seemed important. But it sure was to Esmeralda. "He's lucky to have you looking out for him."

"I suppose he is at that." Esmeralda still seemed wary, regarding Millie with one eye and her head turned like a crow. "Where's your dog?"

"Run off, I guess." Millie sent a silent prayer, hoping Ms. Cavalcante hadn't overheard Sarah's predictions.

"You miss him?"

"Yeah." And she did, more than she missed Theo, if she wanted to be honest with herself. Millie expected Esmeralda to say something about how he'd turn up again. She did no such thing.

"It's below freezing out, has been all week and will be straight through to the New Year. He doesn't stand much of a chance."

"Thanks for being honest, I guess."

"Listen, girl." Esmeralda put her ands on her hips, leaning forward slightly as she spoke. "This world doesn't like speaking plain to a woman when she's still young and pretty. Take honesty where you can find it, especially when it comes from your gut."

"So why's your gut telling you to shower me with all this, um, practical advice?"

"Because you're not listening to yours." Esmeralda jerked her chin at the door leading into the alley. "You aren't welcome here, in case you hadn't noticed. I want nothing to do with you, my fondness for your brother and Miss Howe notwithstanding. Now get out of my Club and don't come back."

Millie blinked, her mouth dropping open. She shut it, then turned on her heel and pushed through the door without bothering to shout a farewell to Sarah. Her wariness of the local organized crime element hadn't prepared her for abject rejection from one of its major players. Sarah's equations had probably counted this possibility anyway but if so, she'd said nothing.

Out in the cold, Millie Chiavo finally understood what Sarah Webster had known for years. Being an outsider was like looking through glass at food when you hungered. Rachel's muffled voice rising in song as she practiced her torch songs only drove this fresh bitterness deeper into her heart.

More than at any other time in the last three weeks, she longed for Bear's companionship. A single tear trickled halfway down her cheek before it slowed, grew icy, then vanished into the dry air as completely as the dog had.

Eric hadn't seen Sal anywhere besides the diner in three weeks. The stakeout was boring and cold but Ms. Cavalcante paid him well for the information so he kept at it. When he caught a glimpse of the large man on his way from the diner to the warehouse, Eric followed. Maybe he'd finally be able to afford an apartment that didn't overlook the creepy cemetery with the next cash bonus.

About a year after they'd moved there, Eric and his mother had gotten the fright of their lives. One night, the dead of St. Peter's had risen. But that wasn't even the most dangerous part of what they'd seen, huddled together beside the drafty pane of glass.

Raul Cavalcante had shot a woman. After that, another man shot him, and his buddy, Louie Tucci.

"Never tell anyone what we saw outside St. Peter's, boychick." Mama had smoothed his hair, then rested her hands on his shoulders, that's how he knew she was serious.

"But it was an accident, I could tell." Eric had seen the short man in the fedora point, send her out from behind the mausoleums at the middle after he'd done something to the policeman with them.

"Oh, bubbala, that means bupkis to these goyim. All they'd care about is that you're a witness and that'd put you on their bad side."

"But you wait tables for Mr. Cavalcante."

"I know, and that's because with wise guys like that, you want to be on their good side without them noticing you too much." She'd sighed, looking into his eyes. "Promise you'll never tell."

Eric was a good boy, so he followed his Mama's direction even after she died. But it wouldn't stop him from trying to do the right thing now. He had to stay on Ms Cavalcante's good side, even if investigating Tucci was dangerous.

When Eric had tried getting to room 131's window from outside the building, he hadn't had much luck. The week before, the toothless janitor let him into an empty space on the pretense of interest in renting it. That room was across the middle of the building from 131 but Eric still hadn't been able to see in Tucci's window. He'd put curtains up, of course. Salvatore Tucci was no slouch in the brains department.

Walking without a sound was impossible but Eric only had to hide his own footfalls in the echo of Tucci's. Left, right. When the big guy got to the double doors, he glanced over his shoulder. Eric expected this and ducked out of the way in time. At least, he thought he'd been fast enough. Tucci didn't shout or flee, anyway.

The door on the right had locked automatically, because it was after even the janitor's hours. But Eric had tampered with the door on the left the same night he'd pretended at renting, making the lock stick. Eric eased it closed quietly behind him.

In the hall, Sal Tucci was nowhere to be seen. That didn't bother Eric one bit and he proceeded down the hall quietly until he got to room 131.

At the door, Eric heard the clink of breaking glass and an underbreath curse. He leaned over, peering through the keyhole only to find an expanse of purple pinstripe fabric blocking everything. Did Tucci hang curtains over keyholes? No, just a large tuchus temporarily blocking the view. After the rattle of a dustpan, Eric could see.

Tucci had a cot in there and someone lay sleeping on it. Before he got more than the impression of a narrow chest rising and falling under an old army-issue blanket, the door swung open, hitting him in the face.

"Huh. I expected the bearcat, not you."

The light behind the bulky figure erased its face but it still had Sal Tucci's voice. Sort of. Eric thought of standing, running, pushing through the warehouse's front door and out into the frozen night free as a bird.

He couldn't even stand.

Eric Kovach had no choice but to lay there as Tucci dragged him into the room with the cot. When he found himself strapped down on another like the one he'd seen through the keyhole, Eric's senses returned.

Turning his back to Eric, Tucci fiddled with something. Eric turned his head, checking on the sleeper beside him. The angular face rested, its soft jaw at ease. Full lips and drawn cheeks gave the face a muted sort of beauty. Dark, loose curls tumbled like a dropped bouquet on the pillow.

"Why?" Eric's voice croaked out like a toad's.

"Because a man's gotta do what a man's gotta do." Tucci's voice creaked and cracked, too.

Eric cast his gaze in the man's direction, then promptly blinked. Tucci's flesh pitched and heaved like a storm-tossed boat. It looked to Eric like his shape wasn't holding somehow, as though something about him strained against containment.

Tucci turned, bent over the woman on the other cot with a filled syringe in one hand. He held the lady's hand in the other, curling his fingers around it as he murmured softly in Italian. Eric didn't understand any of it. The woman's arm and face did the same strange dance as the man's Once his speech ended, Tucci jabbed the woman's arm with the syringe, injecting his blood into her.

"You're gonna have to take a nap too, kid." Sal Tucci set the syringe down on a table, then reached into a case and produced another. "Sorry."

He drew up a dose of something from a vial and bent over Eric, who was too shocked to fight back or even scream. The needle burned when it went in, like that time Eric hit a wasp's nest with his baseball bat on a dare and got himself stung.

He'd hit something even worse this time and once that realization set in, Eric was on the nod. He dreamed in that medicinal twilight until his untimely end.

This year, Christmas Eve was a record-breaking night at the Supper Club. That's why Bill had only just finished cleaning up at half-past four in the morning. He glanced over at the table where Esmeralda Cavalcante counted stacks of bills, debating whether to approach and ask whether he could leave yet. The phone rang.

"Supper Club." Bill Chiavo had finally gotten the hang of answering the main phone. That was usually Eric's job but he'd been gone for the last couple of days with no explanation.

"Ms. Cavalcante?"

"Mr. Delaqua?"

"Yeah, kid." Jimmy coughed. "Put her on. It's an emergency."

Bill set the phone down and got his boss. She picked it up with her usual greeting of "yeah, what do you want?" After that, her face paled. She clutched her rhinestone necklace, tangling the neckline of her dress along with it in a white-knuckle grip.

"I'm taking that in my office, Chiavo. Hang it up when I get there."

Ms. Cavalcante hurried back through the doors, leaving the piles of money unattended on the table. Bill knew something had to be very wrong. After only a month, she couldn't trust him that much. Then again, he had full confidence in Sal Tucci against his own sister's advice. Should he obey Esmeralda and hang up the phone, or help Sal, who'd pay him for whatever he heard?

When Esmeralda said that she got it, Bill stayed on the line, tapping the handset to make it sound like he'd closed the line. He had experience with that kind of thing. How many times had he and Millie listened in on their parents' conversations? Bill lost count years ago.

"What is it, Jimmy?"

"It's the Boss. Your cousin." Ice clinked in a glass on the other end of the line. "I'm sorry."

"Sorry?"

"He's gone, Ma'am."

Bill sat through a silence so long he wondered if Ms. Cavalcante had fainted. She and her cousin had been close, more like a brother and sister. The bottom of her world must have fallen out just now. But either Esmeralda wasn't as close to Mr. Bianco as Bill imagined or she was made of sterner stuff. Wisdom told him that the latter proved true.

"Okay." Ms. Cavalcante's stern contralto cracked. Then, she let out a long sigh and her usual tone and timbre returned. "How?"

"That whole hinky business I was worried about, it went sideways." Jimmy took a deep, muffled breath. Bill imagined him taking a drag on a cigarette. "Worst-case scenario kind of sideways."

"You never said exactly what kind of business that

was, Jimmy."

"Yeah, I know." Jimmy sucked in a quick breath, like he'd stifled a wince. "We're on a phone, you understand."

"Yes." Esmeralda's voice dripped with rapidly melting patience. "I'll need to hear this in person, of course."

"Um, yeah. About that—"

"So Niccolo's the Boss now and he won't let you come? Is that it?"

"No. There is no Boss, Ma'am." Jimmy took another drag on his smoke. "Them days is over."

Bill listened to dead air. Then, Esmeralda said, "Nico's gone, too?"

"In a manner of speaking."

"So Jacky's house of cards has collapsed entirely." Esmeralda's teeth squeaked as she ground them together. "And that wolf, Mullins, is scratching at my door. Tonight was the fifth phone call from him this week."

"Providence won't accept either of us in charge, neither."

"That's right, on account of your blood and my sex." Esmeralda tapped something against her desk instead of letting plain silence stretch on. A pencil? "There's somebody they'd love to have in charge of this operation, maybe even Fall River's business. The son of a man who used to operate between all three places."

"Tucci?"

"One and the same." Ms. Cavalcante let out a bark of a laugh. "It ain't over until the fat man sings."

"Thought you didn't like that guy."

"He wants to buy in, I want to keep my business from Providence and my life from the Irish. I need you to come and help, back me in front of him when I deliver my terms, Jimmy. How soon can you get here?"

"I can't, Esmeralda. I'm laid up with a busted leg. Gotta get to the hospital."

"Then I'll go down to Fall River, call Tucci in."

"No can do, Ma'am."

"Why?"

"More than a house of cards fell tonight. The Boss's place is up in flames, five-alarm fire and the cops are at the scene. There's not even nobody left alive to run the speakeasies."

Silence fell again. Finally, Esmeralda asked the question in Bill's head. "What the Hell happened there, Jimmy? Phone or not, you must be able to say something about how it got so bad."

"Things ain't what they seem, Ms. Cavalcante. There's more than just men and women on God's green earth and meddling with them ain't smart. That's all I can say."

"You shouldn't be in a hospital, Jimmy. Not if it's as bad as you tell me. The heat will be on in Fall River. Come up here."

"I ain't worried about the fuzz."

"I'm not talking about them."

"Providence? You think they'd move in this fast?"

"Yes."

"Fine, then. I got an associate here who's in the need to know club. Can I bring him?"

"As long as he's copacetic."

"He's not interested in this business. It's the other stuff he's got a stake in, if you know what I mean."

"I understand, Jimmy. What's his name?"

"Fallon."

"I look forward to hearing what he has to say. You can run that boat with a bum leg with Fallon's help and it only takes an hour and change. See you soon."

"Yeah, see you, Ms. Cavalcante."

The two of them hung up but Bill still heard breathing on the other end of an open line. He held his breath, hardly dared to move. Someone else had listened in but he didn't want to give himself away. He thought through all of the phone locations in the Club and came up with one more. The kitchen.

"William?" The chef's soft, low voice confirmed his suspicions.

"Miss Etta." Bill breathed the name out as softly as he could.

"Can we keep this secret?"

"Yes."

"Good." She hung her extension up. Bill did the same.

Turning back to the already clean counter, he made a show of going over it again with a fresh cloth. When Esmeralda emerged from the back of the house, she raised her head slowly.

"Bill, thanks for all the hard work." She stepped over to the table full of money and peeled a few notes off the middle stack. "I might need your help again soon, maybe even as early as tomorrow."

"Ma'am?" Bill's brow wrinkled. The Supper Club was

always closed on Christmas so he had to act confused in order to convince her that he hadn't been privy to the phone conversation.

"There's a set of special circumstances that have come up and I might need you to stand by me while I handle them." She set three five-dollar bills on the bar. "I understand if you don't want to get involved but with Eric missing, I'm short-staffed."

Esmeralda reached over the table again, her hand hovering over the stack of tens.

"I'll do it, Ms. Cavalcante."

"Great. I'll see you at church after the morning Mass." She transferred two of the ten dollar bills from the table to the bar in front of Bill. "You can go home now, Mr. Chiavo."

He collected his pay, hung the cloth on a hook, grabbed his coat, and headed out the door. Even with the extra information, Bill had no idea what the boss lady had planned that could involve Saint Peter's.

Every Christmas, Giuseppe waited downstairs for the children. Ten years ago, they'd rise before the sun to look for their gifts. Over the last four years, their waking delayed, growing later with each passing year. But in 1929, the clock turned back. Giuseppe heard their thoughts as he sat in his study, giving him enough warning to shuffle out into the parlor where the tree sat.

This morning, the clock chimed five-thirty as Millie headed blearily down the stairs and Bill arrived, still in his waiter's uniform, through the front door. Giuseppe smiled at his disheveled children, eyes stinging with love as bittersweet as licorice root. Katherine had Seen this as the last Christmas they'd have together, one that would get cut short.

Giuseppe refused to miss a minute of it. If he didn't show his children love now, he might not get another chance. And so, even with Bill weary and Millie glancing at the door every few minutes for her not-quite canine friend, he celebrated with heart open and mind walled off against the other talents in his house.

His Katie understood. She got down the good china, poured the wine they'd saved for Millie and Bill's weddings, lit the nicest candles, served extra helpings of *pizzelle* with powdered sugar and preserves. And when the children finally ripped the paper from their gifts, he couldn't tear his eyes away.

Bill reached into the box, held the gray fedora with the purple band at eye level before placing it on his head. Picking up the box to put it aside, he tilted his head and peered in again at the item left at the bottom. The maple butt on the revolver was worn but polished to a high sheen. Giuseppe had cared for the gun properly all these years though he'd known he would never use it again.

"It's not loaded, is it?"

"Of course not." Giuseppe gave his son a gentle smile. "I left ammunition in your room, under a shoulder holster in your top dresser drawer. You'll know when to use it."

"Thank you, Father." Bill flipped open the chamber and peered inside. He pointed the barrel at the floor and squinted down it, then nodded and tucked it into the waist on his waiter's apron.

"Papa!" Millie hadn't called Giuseppe that in over a decade. "Oh, but you didn't have to give me this." Her cheeks blazed with color and her curls trembled in counterpoint with her hands. They clutched a compass, also worn but well-kept. "What if you need it again?"

"You'll be glad of it in the future, Millie." Giuseppe closed his eyes, remembering the faded but long savored memory of holding the twins in his arms when they were nothing but little blanket-wrapped packages themselves.

"Thanks, Daddy." Millie wrapped her arms around his neck and gave him a peck on the cheek. He held the tears in, not wanting them to tip his hand. They couldn't know until it was time and that'd be soon enough.

The doorbell rang.

"Do we really have to?" Bill hung his head as he walked to the door.

"You don't." Katie stood in his way. "First of all, you will take care of that gun. It's obvious that's what you're carrying and I won't have it visible in front of our guests on Christmas Day. And second, you are not waiting tables in your own house. Go upstairs and make yourself presentable as a celebrant instead of a servant."

"Aww, but—"

"No buts, William. I mean it." She wagged a finger at him and he headed upstairs. Millie made to follow him. "Not you, Millicent. Get the door. I've got a tea tray to wrangle."

The doorbell rang again.

The door swung open an instant after Millie saw who was on the other side of it. She blinked, not in surprise at the couple standing arm in arm, but at the unexplainable knowledge of who they were before she should have known.

"It's about time." Uncle Finn pushed past her and into the hall. He reached out to pull Sarah's coat from her shoulders, then hang it on the coat tree in the corner.

"Hi, Millie." Sarah's voice came out tiny, almost inaudibly. Or maybe she'd said nothing.

Millie hadn't been looking at her friend's face because

the yellow-gold dress was too distracting. Its spangles caught morning light like a trawler netted codfish and the cut made Sarah look like a film star instead of a girl genius. The design reminded her of something but Millie couldn't place it until she went to close the door. She froze, remembering Rachel's lavender dress. It had looked like this new number of Sarah's, just a different color. She'd hinted it at the Supper Club along with that eerie message about Bear and Theodore.

Uncle Finn's inappropriate courtship of Sarah had begun back then, on the night she'd stolen Esmeralda's book. How had the Websters agreed to such a thing after announcing her engagement to Gilbert? Finn's money, of course. The Edgewoods had none. Money had done a number on their families again.

Millie was sick to death of dollars ruling and ruining lives. She barely spoke to Bill now because of his obsession with burning his reputation at both ends just to get pay from Cavalcante and Tucci. He'd sold out. The Websters had, too, though they'd resisted for a few weeks. Sarah must have known, Seen it in all those calculations. So no wonder she'd given Rachel the first ostentatious gift from her creepy suitor.

"Nice dress, Sarah." Millie put one hand on her hip, then turned her face away from her. She'd sided with Finn after all and Millie wanted no part of that. Through the open door, she watched the rest of the Websters pacing up the steps. She held the door open wide, letting Mrs. Webster and her mister pass through. Theo didn't even look at her and she knew without asking that he felt shame over his sister.

How did she know that? Millie shook her head, squeezing her eyes shut around the implications. She couldn't know. Bill was the one who got the Wisdom. Hers was strictly partial, only for dogs, no humans allowed.

"She's going to lose it again." Theo sighed.

Millie opened her eyes, looked up. Her fiance stood facing away from her, chuckling at something her father had said. There was no way Theo said that out loud in front of Dad, no way she'd hear it over the laughter or with his back turned like that, either.

"Millie, I could use some help."

She closed the door and hurried down the hall to take the tea tray from her mother. Setting it down in the parlor, Millie didn't dare search anyone's faces. The room felt strange, more cluttered somehow. It'd been so free, easy, and open earlier, the way Christmas had always been before.

Biting her lower lip, Millie contemplated this. Every year, the Websters and her Uncle had come over. The Edgewoods, too, though they were conspicuously absent this time. So why did she feel so oppressed? It was like being weighed down with other people's problems.

Millie headed for the sanctuary of the empty kitchen. But shortly after she arrived there, company joined her.

"How do you like your first Christmas?" Uncle Finn blocked the doorway.

"All is calm, all is bright." Millie could have kicked herself. Her mind drew a blank except for the lyric from The First Noel. At least it fit the season. She took a deep breath, trying to prepare some other response in case her

Uncle asked her another question before she could slip away.

"You're not going to ask me what I mean by first?"

"No, nay, never." Seriously? Old ballads? What was next, answering him with sea chanteys?

"Ah, but you were born to play the wild rover, dear niece." He smiled, stared into her eyes.

Millie got a picture in her head like she used to with Bear. But the dog had never shown her anything like this. Hands stretched up through the earth, ground that should have stayed frozen tumbled outward as graves erupted, spewing forth the dead.

"No."

"Yes. I didn't have to show you that one but I thought your reaction might prove amusing." He chuckled. "I wasn't wrong."

"But how?" Millie shivered. "How are you doing this to me?"

"I'm not."

He didn't have to tell her. This wasn't some hidden talent of her Uncle's. It was her own full Wisdom. Millie put both hands over her mouth, staving off the scream in her throat. It cut loose in her mind, though.

And something answered. No, someone. A brawny man with red hair and a beard to match. She got a picture of a house on fire, a haggard man armed with teeth like daggers and a haunted woman whose storied past had finally caught up with her.

Millie blinked, not seeing the kitchen or even her Uncle Finn anymore. All she saw was a snow-dusted countryside, then a cave deep in the woods. The stars showed her where. She got a name. Bear, then Sea. Then Bersi Olafsson. A shaggy red dog morphed slowly into that red haired man who then fell to the ground, choking on some kind of poison. Warm and cold hands moved him from a lawn to a car, then to a boat. And when the sun came up in the picture it blinded her but she couldn't close her eyes.

"Millie!" Something cold doused her face. "Wake up!"

She shivered even more than before and her eyes flickered open. Bill leaned over her, his face a mask of concern. Before she could speak, he pressed a finger to his lips. After that, he stretched a hand down to help her up.

Millie stood up on her own, looking at Bill's hand as though it might bite. Had he known? Had Father? Who else? Mom? Uncle Finn sure had. Was she the last to know she wasn't just partly Wise?

"Here, let me help." Theo pushed past her brother, heat coming off of him in waves. She blushed, unable to meet his gaze or even his touch.

Millie couldn't marry Theo, not now. Two Wise never did, at least not in their circles. She wasn't sure exactly why that was but she was certain of one thing. As handsome as Theodore Webster was, she did not love him. She felt relief but it washed away in the room's mood.

Tendrils of concern, worry, curiosity and even fear brushed against Millie's mind. Listening in on Bill's lessons had done nothing to prepare her for this. Not even her experience with Bersi gave her any idea what

Mind Wisdom was like in a room full of people. Millie had no idea how to build walls. Her mind lay exposed.

"Stop staring at me!" Millie's lips didn't move but when she looked up, everyone had frozen. Well, not exactly. Sarah stood bent over the phone table, pencil scrabbling against the notepad the Chiavos kept for phone messages. Millie turned and fled up the stairs, snatching the compass Dad had given her on the way.

Knowing she might not get another chance, Millie dragged the old rucksack out from under her bed. In the bottom sat a collection of items she'd set aside since her tomboy days. A bowie knife, an old canteen, the army-issue mess kit that used to belong to Gilbert's big brother. She piled a sturdy pair of shoes, clean underwear, one of her school blouses with a sensible skirt, and socks on top of the other items, then reached for the door to her closet.

Her eyes traced the clothes hanging there, dresses and other more impractical items that she couldn't use. Millie pushed past those, whisking hangers aside. At the back, she opened a box. Bill's long johns from two years back, woolen trousers, a fisherman's sweater, a knobby old knitted pompom hat, a scuffed pair of boots. That's what she really needed.

Whipping off her Sunday best took next to no time. The long johns went over Millie's smallclothes, the trousers came after. But she needed another layer between Bill's old undershirt and the sweater. A rummage through her dresser turned up nothing suitable so she turned to face her hope chest, one hand on her hip.

What a funny thing to call it, thought Millie. Hope chest. More like abandon all hope chest as far as her generation was concerned. None of them were even contented. Her own initial infatuation with Theodore's muscular physique was the closest facsimile of happiness. She wondered if any doctor studying the phantom limb sensation had ever considered phantom feelings of the psychological type. But of course, one had. Carl Jung.

Turning her back on the chest, Millie snatched the Psychologist's book off the shelf, cradling it like an arcane tome. That went into the rucksack along with the volume on Hrafin the Changed Knight that she'd stolen from the Supper Club.

Millie had just put the fisherman's sweater on when a knock came at the door. She froze, then shook all over with the knowledge of who was there.

"Go away, Bill."

"But we've got to head over to church for Mass now."

"I'm not going. I feel too sick."

"You can't skip Mass on Christmas, Millie."

"I can go to one that's later in the day."

"You stay put, then. I'll check in on you when we're back."

"Sure, Bill. Whatever you say."

But Millie had no intention whatsoever to stay in that house a moment longer than she had to even after it emptied. She headed out to find the only friend she thought might accept her.

She didn't have to travel nearly as far as she'd imagined, either.

Bill wore pleasantries like a mask. He'd gotten used to that quickly, working at the Supper Club, and it served him well in the company of his parents, the Websters, and Uncle Finn. He also had his walls up, guarding his mind. But he heard Millie loud and clear even through both of the mental and social bulwarks.

She'd leave the house while they went out, a sentiment he'd heard loud and clear outside her bedroom door. Bill knew that his sister was in the worst part of Wisdom; that first full taste, too intense to handle. How had he not noticed what was going on with her?

Swallowing down regret, Bill Chiavo kept his act up for his friends, family, and everyone else at Saint Peter's that day. During Mass, he focused on Father John's sermon about the origin of Christian salvation. For the first time, he gave serious thought to the idea that the three men visiting baby Jesus had actually been Wise like him. How else would they have known to arrive when and where they did?

During Communion, Bill noticed others in the line. Gilbert and his parents. Rachel escorting a hobbling Gram Howe behind the rest of her family. Salvatore Tucci, alone. Esmeralda Cavalcante with Jimmy Delaqua, the latter on haphazard looking crutches with his foot wrapped in a makeshift splint. Another man hovered in their periphery, one Bill hadn't seen before. Tall, stocky, paler skin than any Italian; this had to be the Fallon fellow Jimmy had mentioned on the phone.

He'd get a chance to talk to Tucci after Mass. As Bill tried to catch Sal's eye, Esmeralda intercepted. He'd go and see what she wanted first, then. Bill took the wafer and wine, then headed back to his pew. On the way, he noticed Ms. Cavalcante eyeballing Mr. Tucci. She appraised him like she did a new customer, sizing up the risk that the prospective patron might squeal.

Mass ended and Bill navigated the sea of knees and elbows in the aisle. He drifted like a becalmed sailboat until he reached Esmeralda's side.

"Kid, I need you to make sure Tucci gets this." She handed him a folded sheet of paper.

"When, Ms. Cavalcante?" Bill let down his defenses enough to try getting a read on Fallon's mind and saw a boat in the harbor. Jimmy's. They'd left something important there. Someone, maybe.

"Now." The finality in her tone dropped like a hammer.

Bill ducked and weaved through the crowd, managing to tap the man's shoulder just before he left the building.

"Mr. Tucci, I was asked to give you this."

"Thanks, Bill." Salvatore Tucci flipped open the note, his eyes flicking from side to side as he read it. He smiled, lighting his entire face up. "I need you to stick around for a while, maybe an hour if that's all right. Ask your lady-friend with the gorgeous voice I keep hearing about, too. Tell Ms. Cavalcante that I said yes. If she wants me to catch the Father in time, I can't tell her myself, okay?"

"All right, Mr. Tucci."

"Please, kid. Call me Sal. It's the least you can do considering these new circumstances." He handed the note back to Bill, then turned and let his bulk make way back into the church against the tide of people leaving.

Unable to let his guard down enough to hear Tucci's thoughts, Bill satiated his curiosity by flipping open the note. He nearly dropped it.

Esmeralda Cavalcante had done the last thing Bill ever would have expected of her.

She'd just proposed marriage to Salvatore Tucci.

Salvatore Tucci waited as Father John gave his farewells to the Howe grandmother. His nerves sailed higher and more exposed than Benjamin Franklin's electricity-discovering kite. Did Esmeralda expect a hollow marriage of convenience or one with more substance? Sal had no idea but he would soon find out.

"Hello, Mr.—" Father John squinted as he stuck out his hand for a shake. "I'm sorry. You look familiar but I can't place the name."

"Tucci, Father. Salvatore Tucci."

"Oh, hello. You must be related to Louie. Merry Christmas."

"Yes, Louie was my father." He couldn't lie because he'd need his baptismal record to make the marriage legal. "Merry Christmas to you, too. I wanted to tell you how much I appreciated your sermon on salvation today, Father."

"Well thank you." The Father smiled back. "I hope you found it inspiring."

"I did." Sal nodded. "In fact, it was so inspiring that I was moved to propose to my paramour this very day."

"Oh?" Father John's eyes cut left, then right. "Should I be offering congratulations or condolences?"

"Congratulations, Father. Ms. Esmeralda Cavalcante said yes." Sal gripped the Father's still extended hand in both of his. "But I'd rather accept your good wishes after we're wed."

"And when would that be?"

"Today, if you're willing, Father."

"I can do that. But are you sure you don't want to wait, call the family— Oh. Of course." Father John cleared his throat. "Do you have witnesses?"

"Hello, Father." Billy the Kid nodded from Sal's elbow. "I've agreed to bear witness along with Miss Howe, here." Bill's fiancee smiled and waved.

Sal couldn't get over how smart the Chiavo kid was, like he could read minds or something. He'd lucked out, picking that boy up as an ally. And now, he'd get even more of those and a stake in business besides. This Christmas was nothing short of miraculous for Sal Tucci. His heart swelled enough to make him worry about busting a seam on his jacket.

Nothing could tarnish his bright mood, not even the question ringing through his mind. It wasn't exactly his and he knew it. The thought came from the original owner of the body he currently inhabited.

Why now?

In response, Sal hummed the Wedding March.

Nothing could get him down.

Bill wasn't even sure Father John had done more than

a handful of weddings, let alone one on such notice as this. The Priest was so young, so new to the job. He signed the Church document, placing his signature opposite Rachel's, a new reminder that they'd be here in either late winter or early spring for their own wedding. Standing aside, Bill tried to exorcise those thoughts from his head and get a read on everyone else's instead.

Tuning out the Priest was easy since Bill had been to weddings before and had no interest in the Sacrament anyway. Since they'd just taken Communion, the service got truncated. Just six people stood in the church. The seventh remained seated on account of his injury. Bill started by focusing his mind reading there.

Jimmy Delaqua sat in the first pew with his leg propped up, smelling like a distillery. The first thing Bill felt outside his mental armor was the rumrunner's physical pain. Valiant efforts to put it aside, take his mind off of what came through the alcoholic haze, coated Jimmy's thoughts. Most of those were about a haggard man laying dead on a dark lawn with his throat torn out but most especially the woman standing above.

Viewing that woman through the filter of Jimmy's mind nearly took Bill's breath away. Tendrils of her dark hair flowed against copper skin in a frigid breeze that did nothing to chill her. She turned, moonlight giving her face an ethereal glow. That moment froze in Jimmy's mind, all his care and concern going out to her. Bill found her name. Oguina. And then, the woman in Jimmy's mind's eye smiled and shattered Bill's simple perception.

Long, sharp teeth flashed in the light of the moon but

it didn't mar Jimmy's estimation of her. Bill got the impression that Jimmy knew Oguina would kill him and didn't much care. Jimmy's admiration for her strength, power, and ferocity burned in Bill's brain like a beacon. When another figure held her back and subdued her, Jimmy's relief mingled with faint regret.

Bill left the rumrunner's mind, certain beyond the shadow of a doubt that the "hinky business" he'd mentioned on the phone had to do with Oguina and others like her. He checked the head of Jimmy's large companion and got instant confirmation that this was the Fallon fellow the rumrunner had mentioned on the phone.

The big man had an entirely different set of feelings about the type of creature Oguina was, largely due the the vast volume of knowledge Bill sensed behind his surface thoughts. Howard Fallon had hunted hundreds of others like her, killing many over the course of several years.

Bill wasn't sure what to make of Fallon and his strange occupation so he turned his Wisdom toward Esmeralda. The wedding service was the same as any other contract for her, the vows her lips shaped like signatures on bank documents. She considered Father John's words like a purchase agreement and her new husband a piece of property that also owned her.

Three facts moved Esmeralda's head over her heart. Her cousin, Giacomo Bianco, had died. Salvatore Tucci was Italian and interested in doing her kind of business. She'd received threats from Finn Mullins along with hints that Boston's Irish Mob had taken an interest in points south, including Plymouth.

The realization that someone else approached marriage the same way as he had made Bill feel less alone. New respect for the businesswoman bloomed in his chest alongside a lightness of mood he'd given up on since his own engagement announcement. Bill moved on to scrutinize Tucci's thoughts, expecting much the same thing in the husband as in the wife.

But he was wrong. If Esmeralda's thoughts had given Bill comfort, Salvatore Tucci's conveyed hope. The surface of his thoughts sparkled like water in sunlight, though Bill got the impression of hidden and unexpectedly dark depths.

Pushing further, Bill found himself unable to sink deeper into Tucci's mind. It was like Sarah's or Millie's, as though Salvatore Tucci came from a Wise family. But that was impossible. Wasn't it?

"Bill?" Rachel's cold hand on his arm startled him out of his reverie.

"Hmm?"

"It's over. They're married. Can we head home now?"

"You go on ahead, Rachel." Bill waved vaguely at the door. "I've got to go congratulate the happy new couple."

"Um, okay." Rachel shrugged, skepticism weighing down the corners of her mouth.

Bill headed toward Ms. Cavalcante, who stood in a little knot made up of Tucci, Jimmy, and Fallon. He waited until both of his bosses turned and noticed him before speaking.

"Congratulations."

"Thank you, Bill." Esmeralda nodded.

"Um, maybe we should go somewhere else to talk about this." Jimmy peered up at Bill, then turned his head to raise an eyebrow at Ms. Cavalcante. "Somewhere more private."

"No. I want Mr. Chiavo on board." Tucci nodded at each of the others in turn. "Part of the terms you listed included putting all of our cards on the table. Bill is one of mine."

"What?" Esmeralda narrowed her eyes. "No. He's one of mine."

"Well, I'm working for the same people now, so let's just go someplace and hash things out, okay?" Bill shrugged to hide the effort he put toward calming their turbulent emotions. "I bet Father John has to set things up for the afternoon services."

Eventually, they settled on Jimmy's boat. When he checked the name to see what it was this time, Bill tried not to shudder. The rumrunner had renamed his boat to honor the monstrous woman in his memory.

They all boarded The Oguina, completely unaware that a stowaway slept on board.

The big guy in the hammock gave Esmeralda the heebie jeebies. She couldn't put her finger on why at first. His red hair and large frame had nothing to do with it. It wasn't until they all sat around the folding card table in the ship's cabin and shut their traps that she figured the thing out. Two things, actually.

The big guy didn't breathe. He didn't blink, either; glassy blue eyes remained open, their glitter barely visible from the angle of her view. Esmeralda had a seat facing him but wondered whether one facing away would have been better or worse. She cast her eyes at the table where her hands sat folded with the left thumb crossed over the right. It felt like she was being watched so she looked up again. The seat facing the hammock had been the right choice after all.

Tucci sat across from her. If the unbreathing man with the staring eyes bothered him, his face didn't show it. Instead, her new husband beamed like the thrice accursed day star before her coffee every morning. Would he lose that smile once he realized that their wedding night would be spent going over old ledgers? Even with his apparent better nature, Esmeralda came to this husband warier than she had her last.

"So, we're here because everyone in this room is on the need-to-know roster." Esmeralda set her eyes on Jimmy and his buddy, Fallon. "Mr. Delaqua told me he couldn't discuss my cousin's downfall over the phone. So I will give him this time to explain himself."

"Sure, Ma'am." Jimmy cleared his throat. "The Boss, your cousin, he got himself involved with these monsters on account of his illness."

Jimmy's tale was more of a whopper than the one Ishmael spun about Ahab and the Great White Whale. Howard Fallon interjected at times but that only served to make the concept more unbelievable. Esmeralda would have sooner bought the Brooklyn Bridge.

But then Bill stood up. The kid put his hands on the table and looked her right in the eyes.

"Ms. Cavalcante, every word is true. He's not trying to sell you the Brooklyn Bridge."

She blinked, wondering how he'd known what was in her thoughts. But her pragmatism got the upper hand and she thinned her lips into one straight line. When Raul died, minds had been changed. Literally. She didn't know who or how but always suspected that some of Plymouth's Citizens were not what they seemed. Someone had managed to get the police to turn a blind eye on the speakeasy without money changing hands.

"Mr. Chiavo, what number am I thinking of right now?"

"It's not a number, Ma'am. You're thinking about how the cops never bother you or your Club."

"Bingo, Bill." Esmeralda let the corners of her mouth curl up. "So, we've heard Jimmy's fantastic tale. I bet you've got one of your own."

"Yes." Bill nodded, then folded himself into his seat. "I'm a mind reader. Come from a long line of them, in fact. I think it was my father who set things up for you back in 1922. We call ourselves Wise."

"Ha!" Esmeralda's laugh barked out just before she noticed Tucci go pastier than pasta dough. "You already call yourself wise and you're on the road to being a wiseguy. That's richer than Etta's cheesecake."

"It gets even better." Bill leaned back in his seat. "Your new husband's Wise, too. Or related to someone who is. I haven't exactly figured that one out yet, though."

"So which is it, dear?" Esmeralda's face went flat again. "Are you one of these mind readers or some other flavor of weird?"

"No." Tucci ran one hand over his head and through his hair, a gesture that looked all wrong on him for some reason. Sweat glazed his brow and his stomach growled. "Bill's right, I'm Wise. But I can't read minds, it's something else."

"So tell me, darling," she drawled, "what's your secret super power?"

Before Tucci could answer, the door flew open. Bill's lady stood in the late afternoon sun, which turned her hair from black to deep mahogany. Esmeralda stood up and opened her mouth to object but the songstress beat her to the punch.

"Bill, it's your Uncle Finn. He's got guys down from Boston here in town already, talking about some kind of secret weapon. We have to do something!"

"Okay, Rachel." Bill's soothing tone blanketed the entire room. "If it's okay with Mr. And Mrs. Tucci, I'll go out there and talk to you, figure it out."

"No. Miss Rachel runs along home after she tells us how many men Finn Mullins has." Esmeralda wasn't about to let Tucci take the lead on this. "Bill will follow you when we're done here."

"Six." Rachel shuddered. "One of them has a case the size of a tuba." The girl turned her back and closed the door.

"Tommy guns? Really?" Jimmy shook his head. "I couldn't do much about six guys armed with just revolvers on a good day. Laid up like this, I can't do nothing but die with the rest of you."

"I won't ask you to, Jimmy." Esmeralda counted the rest of her allies. "Is the big Changed fella in the hammock dead?"

"He's not but he's just as useless as I am." Jimmy hung his head.

"If he didn't have that paralysis, Bersi would handle six regular guys without a problem, tommy gun or no." Howard Fallon crossed his arms over his chest. "He'd save all our bacon."

"The Changed are that powerful?"

"Yeah. Even the small ones pack a load of power." Jimmy gazed at the table.

"Maybe he still can help us in a manner of speaking." Tucci stood up. "It'd be risky, though."

"Does this have something to do with your still undisclosed power?" Esmeralda turned her head, looking at Tucci out of one eye.

"Yes. I'm not sure whether it'll work on something like a Changed, though."

"If it's Wisdom, it will."

Everyone except Jimmy was on their feet with guns in hand in seconds. Bill lowered his weapon first.

"Relax. It's my sister." Bill rolled his eyes. "We must have woken her up."

Esmeralda tucked her little pistol away. Howard and Jimmy re-holstered. Tucci kept his out.

"No offense, but your sister's opposed to our kind of business. How do I know she's on our side?"

"I'm not on your side, I'm against Finn Mullins. Is that good enough for you?"

"Yeah, okay." Tucci lowered his firearm. "So, how do you know Wisdom is gonna work on that guy there?" Esmeralda had to respect her new husband's ability to roll with the punches.

"Well, I spent a lot of time in his mind, so I know for sure that it affects people like him."

"Wait, Millie." Bill blinked. "Are you saying that this big guy was your dog?"

"Yeah. I got his name wrong because all I could see were the pictures." Millie reached out and brushed a stray lock of hair away from the man's face. "Bear, then the ocean or the sea. Bersi. I should have known."

"Should haves can wait." Tucci stepped around a couple of Jimmy's crates. Again, Esmeralda wondered how such a round fellow managed to be that nimble. "I'd better try and do what I can."

"Wait." Howard Fallon held up his hand like a cop at a busy intersection. "Changed sleep all day. We won't know if whatever you're going to try works until after sundown."

"Then we let Bill and company get as much information as they can before then." Tucci turned and smiled at Esmeralda. "The rest of you get armed and as dangerous as we can be. After that, I try my thing."

"Sounds like a plan." She smiled back. At least Tucci seemed to have some sense when it came to planning in an emergency.

Bill, Howard, and Jimmy all headed off the boat ahead of her and she'd soon follow, leaving Tucci with the big Changed fellow and Millie Chiavo. The girl sat by Bersi's side, holding his hand and gazing into his open eyes. Esmeralda realized that they weren't empty like she'd thought, that Bersi was aware of everything happening around him. And of course Millie the mind reader knew exactly how he felt, stuck like that.

"I won't need this when I'm him, Esmeralda. Stay safe." Salvatore Tucci strode up to her and handed her his side-arm, holster and all. After that, he waved and turned back to the mind reader and the monster.

As she left, Esmeralda Tucci heard him telling Millie that everything would turn out okay for her paralyzed friend, he'd do what he could for anyone who helped keep Plymouth safe, whether they were Wise, Changed, or just plain human.

As she stepped out of the boat and into the frigid sunlight, Esmeralda considered that perhaps being stuck with Salvatore Tucci wasn't so bad.

"And what I'm telling you is, I had them outgunned already, even the guys you lot don't know about." Finn Mullins narrowed his eyes, one hand wadded up into a fist. The other reached under his coat, caressing the instrument Sarah knew was intended for Giuseppe Chiavo, though her calculations told her it had a 0.78 probability of hitting another mark.

"You bringing that thing here might have tipped them off, Donahue." Liam O'Connell leaned back in the chair he occupied. "In the end, it's only going to make you into a target."

"You can never have too much firepower." Donahue chewed on the toothpick in his mouth. The other five guys from Boston chuckled, elbowing each other and horsing around.

Sarah bent her head over the notepad she'd brought in her purse. Watching the argument wouldn't help her. Only her numbers and the equations they cavorted in gave her any chance of finding the best of all possible outcomes. But she couldn't tune out the conversation and wasn't sure she should. Some of what they spoke about might relate to everything she counted.

Her relationship with Finn Mullins had been a given

in Sarah's grand equation for much longer than any of her friends or family suspected. Everything was as relative as it was eventual. That proof served Sarah well over the years she'd come to grips with her partial Wisdom and the business of hiding it.

What she calculated with it would have stunned them all. But Sarah suffered a Sybil's curse. She couldn't speak of what she Saw until the right time and had to cause all sorts of fusses when she otherwise wouldn't have. The solution to these problems ruled her life.

"What's done is done." Finn shrugged with one shoulder, a gesture that meant he'd seen Donahue's fate and remained unimpressed.

"Tell me about it." Donahue smiled, the toothpick wedged between his bicuspids. "They're gonna need more body bags than at the Valentine's Day Massacre."

"We don't want a bloodbath here." O'Connell spoke up again. "It's supposed to be a minimal casualties kind of operation."

"Maybe you don't, O'Connell." Donahue scoffed. "But you ain't me."

"Gentlemen, please." Finn put his hands on his hips, which Sarah never had found particularly interesting. "We'll have exactly the outcome we're meant to. I've invited an old associate of mine to join us. Meet Jack Houlihan."

Reaching toward the door to his kitchen, Finn turned the knob. It swung open on creaky hinges Sarah would be sure to fix in a few months when the house was hers. Sarah knew a great deal about the man who walked with hitching steps across that threshold but nothing at all of what he looked like.

Mr. Houlihan had broad shoulders, a rumpled suit, and a rash of stubble across his cheeks and jowls. Gray close-set eyes tilted from side to side, appraising everyone in the room. They didn't pause on Sarah but her numbers told her that she hadn't escaped his notice.

"So what's your boy Houlihan packing?" Donahue snorted, rolling his eyes at his boys. "I don't see any heat on him."

"He's got something more effective in hostile takeover situations than your shiny toy guns. He used it seven years ago, in fact."

"Let's see it, then." Donahue jeered, lifting his chin.

"All in good time." Finn leaned one hand against the table Sarah sat at. She knew he'd be looking down her shirt and managed to remember Radcliffe and stop her imminent shudder.

"Jack Houlihan, huh?" O'Connell turned his head to peer at the man he'd named. "Sounds familiar."

"It should if you were here back in '22." Jack stood lopsidedly, like one of his legs was shorter than the other by at least an inch. He probably told anyone who asked that it was from a bout of Polio but Sarah knew better. She didn't want to think about that man and his horrible borrowed legs, though.

"I was the lookout back then." O'Connell folded his arms over his chest. "Too green to play with the big boys, don't you know."

"And now?" Finn raised an eyebrow.

"Now, they think I'm too small a fish to swim in the big stuff up Boston way so they stuck me with your sorry excuse for a coup." O'Connell's act of sardonic verbal rebellion reminded Sarah of Millie.

"I guess that means you get a surprise like your friend Donahue here."

"Don't worry, I love surprises."

Sarah didn't. She kept scratching numbers on the notepad, desperate to find O'Connell a better outcome than the one she'd seen for him already. The grand equation swallowed her so completely that she lost all sense of what went on around her.

When she looked up, Donahue and O'Connell had gone. Houlihan and Finn sat in the far corner, murmuring out something like a conversation. The lopsided man gave her the creeps even more than Finn Mullins did. She glanced at her numbers. The probability that Houlihan had Wisdom in some dire and unknown way was 0.97. Each of them could have been the apex villain of any piece. Together, they raised the danger stakes for her friends and family exponentially.

"Anyway, Jack, that's the size and shape of it now." Finn glanced at Houlihan's legs. I'm glad you got my gifts and used them to get here."

"I'll need more if this doesn't go down tonight." Houlihan shook his head. "They don't last forever. None of them do. But if I can get my old lady back, I'll be set for a long time. She's got gams like you wouldn't believe."

"Don't worry, I think you'll have plenty of fresh options to choose from in the near future. And partnering with me is the right choice. I See you reuniting with said lady friend within the next year."

"And you know what you're talking about when it comes to future events." Houlihan winked, then threw his head back and guffawed. "I'll take your word for it."

"Finn, I'm tired." Sarah stretched, pencil in one hand and notepad in the other. She made sure to stick her chest out as far as she could while she did it, too. Getting out of here and back to her friends was paramount now.

"Oh." Finn stood up. "Jack, I hope you don't mind staying here while I take care of Miss Webster."

"Not at all." Houlihan gave her a once-over that rivaled the ones Rachel usually got. "Congratulations, you two crazy lovebirds."

"Thank you, Mr. Houlihan." Sarah eased her features into a simpering smile. She tucked the notepad and pencil into her handbag.

"Me and Sarah are going to be extremely happy very soon."

"Sounds great." Mr. Houlihan shook his head, his tone flat. "I'll see you soon, Finn."

Sarah let her fiance usher her down the hall but he stopped her before they reached the front door. Crushing her against his chest, he planted his lips over hers. She let him do what he wanted, understanding as she had the week before that submitting to him in a physical sense meant he wouldn't bother trying to See her motives. She couldn't afford that and neither could the rest of her generation.

Her body responded as it had every time he'd touched her since their official engagement, as biology intended. Finn moved her into the study and pressed the issue between them as far as it would go. She let him have his way, mostly because the part of her that was Sarah wasn't really there.

Her mind went back to her grand equations, the numbers whisking away until she understood her urges as just another function of her mortal coil, like hunger or thirst. Anyone would have evoked the same feelings of fire and ice in her body but she let Finn Mullins think he was special.

Everyone wanted to feel special, after all. Everyone except Sarah who, more than ever, just wanted out.

When she came back to herself, Finn had left her at the gate outside her parents' house. She shuddered, more unsettled now with the full physical reality of what she'd done than she'd predicted earlier.

Instead of heading in, she crossed the street.

"This is what's happening, so listen up." Bill Chiavo let his front door slam behind him to make sure everyone paid attention. "Finn's Boston guys are here. With guns. I don't know what they're doing but I bet it's nothing nice."

"And you expect us to stop them how?" Gilbert raised an eyebrow, tucking scraps of Christmas wrappings and ribbons into a paper sack.

"We'll have help, mostly you'd be back up, Gil."

"What do you mean, help?" Theo put his hands on his hips.

"He means that the Tuccis are going to fight Finn

Mullins, they just want insurance." Rachel brushed past Bill and snatched the paper bag from Gilbert's hands.

"Tuccis?" Gilbert wrung his now empty hands, watching Rachel on her cleaning warpath. "What did he do, split into two fat Mafiosos?"

"He married Esmeralda right after Mass." Bill shook his head. "He's Wise, too. Got a power that's going to put him on the front lines."

"Farther front than a guy who throws fire?" Gilbert looked from Bill to Theo and back again.

"Yeah, try bullet-proof." Bill tilted his head. "That's what Sal Tucci has to offer."

"Wow." Theo folded his arms over his chest. "He's got me beat by a country mile."

"So, will you help?"

"I don't know, Bill. Things could get out of hand." Theo closed his eyes. "I could get out of hand."

"I won't let that happen. Just like how Dad doesn't let it." Bill focused on keeping his hands open and at his sides. The last thing he wanted was to let them see how worried he was that they'd refuse to help. Behind him, the door opened and closed softly.

"You say this like you didn't fall over in the Supper Club, Bill." Gilbert shook his head. "You can't be our Fearless Leader if you can't even stay on your feet."

"I'll be there with him, just like last time." Rachel's hand on his shoulder felt almost as comforting as Millie's presence would have been.

"What are you going to do then, Rachel? Serenade us?" Gilbert rolled his eyes. "See, this is why I'd rather be in Boston's Theater District instead of tangled up with this nonsense. With Sarah's new engagement plans, I'm almost free of it. Now Bill and company want to tie me back in? You need to do some better convincing or you can count me out."

Gilbert's animosity hit Bill like an arrow to the chest, with precision and fury. Bill felt the deliberation in his friend's attack, the way he'd felt Sarah's obsession with her equations. But this time, he did not fall.

Rachel's hand on his shoulder replaced all of Gil's bile and bitterness with an almost cotton-wrapped calm. Though she didn't make a sound, Bill's Wisdom let her voice into his head where her love and care for him magnified his Wisdom. And though it contained a distinct carnal element he did not share, Bill found a warm and friendly love for her in his heart. He mingled them and then projected it at Gilbert and Theo.

The other young men froze. Theo lowered his crossed arms. The peaceful stillness in that room unfolded like empty streets on New Year's Day, numb but brilliant with promise. Gilbert's eyes softened behind his spectacles. Bill wasn't sure how long they all stood that way but those moments felt more magical than his other uses of Wisdom ever did.

A rattle and bang at the door shattered the effect. Sarah staggered past Bill, Rachel, and Gilbert, running aground on her brother's chest. She hid her face there, as though hiding from something. Her usually flat hair stood in tangled and windswept peaks, her coat only just barely covering the shoulders of a shimmering dress more appropriate for a juke joint than a Christmas afternoon. One fist beat against Theo's left bicep while the other clutched an ink-stained piece of graph paper.

"I don't have much time." Sarah's muffled voice rode a breathless sense of anguished urgency. "Theo, you and Gilbert have to help Bill. If you don't, everything goes wrong."

"I don't understand." Theo wrinkled his nose as though Sarah stank of something, but put a comforting arm around his sister anyway.

"I do." Rachel's hand dropped from Bill's shoulder and she stepped toward the trembling girl. "You've been hiding something from your brother, Sarah. It's time to tell him now."

"Y-yeah." Sarah's answer choked out on a sob. She turned her head, leveling a bleary eyed gaze at Gilbert. "Partial Wisdom. Sight, and I used it to get you out of Finn's mess. You owe me, Gil." She closed her eyes, avoiding meeting the gazes of the people she spoke to, as always. "I did my part. You're not free of this town until you do your share tonight."

"Your predicament hardly stops me from leaving town." Gilbert sneered. The anger and fear surrounding him was almost palpable.

"You all but gave me to him." Sarah's mouth thinned into a straight, determined line. "You think I didn't See your mistake outside Old Colony before it even happened?"

"So what if you did?" Gilbert put his hands on his hips. Bill watched and listened with a sense of surreality. "I bet dollars to donuts that you got yours from Mullins before you put out. What'd he give up, a way into Radcliffe?"

"Gil, stop this!" Bill rallied his outrage, fashioned it into a bulwark, then pushed against Gilbert's feelings with all his mental strength. Had Gilbert been like this all along and Bill only missed it because love blinded him?

"Ow!" Gilbert stepped back as though he'd been slapped.

"You think you can take off to Boston without consequences?" Bill felt his upper lip curl. He had to use his anger effectively, leverage it to scare Gilbert into sticking around for the final act. "If Finn wins here, it's just a matter of time before he controls that city and forces you to work for him. How do you feel about using your plants to murder his enemies?"

"That's right, we're in this together." Sarah gave one last sniffle and stood without leaning on her brother. "We always have been even if none of you Saw it like I did."

"If you want me to accept that, you have to tell me what happens." Gilbert's head tilted, his spectacles catching the light so that the glare off the glass hid his eyes. But Bill felt the cold frost of fear overtake him. "Do I ever get out?"

"Yes." Sarah's one-word answer sounded like the cork in a bottle of effervescent complications.

Bill knew that Sight Wise, even the partials, risked changing the outcomes they'd Seen if they said too much. He kept his mouth shut, content to let Sarah handle this crisis. He could read her feelings and knew she wanted to help them.

"Sarah, you can come with us if you want but like you

said, you've done your share."

"I think I'll go home." She folded her coat together, hiding the ostentatious dress. "This isn't what I'd wear to battle anyway. I'll, um, change. Maybe I'll see you later."

"So, where are we going?" Theo helped Sarah get her arms in her coat sleeves. He smoothed her hair, then patted her head. "And when?"

"The Supper Club." Bill grabbed his hat and put it on, reading himself to venture out into the half-dark of winter's early nightfall. He had no time to retrieve and load his father's gun. The Tuccis probably had one for him, anyway. "Right now. We'll meet the Tuccis and their friends from Fall River and hole up. We want the Irish to come to us."

On the way down the street, Bill looked over his shoulder at the house. Up in the Study window, the last light of the sun bounced off his father's bald pate. Had he listened in, either with ears or mind? Bill hoped for the latter. Since Dad was downstairs, there was no way he'd slept through the argument between Sarah and Gilbert, especially with Rachel boosting his Wisdom like that.

Bill tipped his hat at his father, hoping he'd understand and stay clear of the business they had to do. Man enough to marry off had to equate to man enough to handle a threat like this, didn't it?

They never made it to the Club. After it all went down, Bill realized that Sarah must have known.

Millie crouched beside the man formerly known as her canine companion. She'd heard the whole bit about Changed, how Mr. Fallon called them monsters. Millie could never think of Bersi or the others she'd read about as monsters. Sure, they were frightening, but so was just about anything unexpected. She'd always believed that the scariest people, places, and deeds taught the best lessons.

"You'll want to move over, give me some room." Salvatore Tucci stood with one hand on the wall above the hammock's foot.

"So, what exactly do you have to do to Bersi?" Millie stood, using the pins and needles in her legs as an excuse to hesitate before stepping away.

"Just switch bodies." Shifting his weight from one foot to the other, Tucci's eyes searched the floor. She had trouble getting a read on his thoughts, of course. "You're reading his mind. He's paralyzed by something?"

"Yeah." Millie nodded, unwilling to share any descriptions of how Bersi felt, caged in his own body yet aware of everything going on around him. "How do you know you won't just be trapping yourself in there?"

"Because when I switch places with someone, we

share some things physically." He took a deep breath. "Okay. Here goes part one."

Navigating the limited space with his bulk must have been a challenge for Sal Tucci but if it was Millie couldn't tell. Apparently, "part one" consisted of the big guy sitting himself down. He wedged himself into a space against the wall and under the tie-off for the hammock but still in reach of Bersi's head.

"So, um." Millie reached out and took her friend's hand. She picked it up and turned it over, examining the calluses and lines on the palm. "When you switch, you're just going to leave your body there on the floor?"

"Yeah, something like that."

"What do you mean, something?" Millie looked up, meeting Tucci's eyes. Why did she think they didn't belong in that doughy face?

"I mean, once I'm out of this body it's gonna start changing back."

"Back?"

"I'm not really a big Italian fellow." Sal cut his eyes away. "I mean, I'm Italian and Tucci is my real name. But that's all I have in common with this, um, version."

"Okay, I understand." Millie got a glimpse at the picture of Tucci's old physique. "So, you're already in a swapped body. And you're going to lose it, doing this."

Sal Tucci said nothing, just nodded. After that, he hung his head. A week ago, Millie wouldn't have known whether he felt shame or grief. From him she felt both but the grief dwarfed the shame. Emotions were more complicated than she'd imagined, a vast land of unexplored combination and potential.

"Look, it'll be okay." Millie reached out with her free hand, put it against Tucci's sweaty brow as though he had a fever. "You're doing this to save Plymouth from a crime war with the Irish Mob. Everyone will understand."

"You're just a kid. What do you know about it?"

"I'm a mind-reading kid." Millie gave him a lopsided grin. "You should have heard what your wife thought of you as she left. She'll forgive you."

"You'll get it after the swap." Tucci sighed, reaching out for Bersi. "I'm out of time for explaining."

Burying his fingers in Bersi's bushy red hair, Sal closed his eyes. Millie watched his face, waiting for something to happen. Nothing did. It'd figure that their best hope would turn out to be a dud. Millie let go of Bersi's hand but it didn't drop from hers.

With their hands firmly clasped, Millie noticed how much colder his was than hers. She turned her head to see his face. A second later, his eyes blinked, then flew open. Bluer than the crisp winter sky they were. Millie had to remind herself that Bersi didn't live behind those eyes now. Tucci did.

Reaching out with her mind, she tried skimming his surface thoughts. Nothing. Feelings were another matter entirely. Sensing Tucci's focus and concentration was like standing between two mirrors and looking into infinity. She had to stop, close off her mind. He had to be grappling with the paralysis.

Finally, the broad chest rose and fell. Even though Changed didn't need to breathe, Tucci probably had to send air back to the other body. Sure enough, it took a ragged breath. Millie tried not to shudder. She failed. Bersi—no, Tucci, laughed.

"These Changed are powerful for sure. A bit slow, but I expect that to improve when it's full dark." Tucci let go of Millie's hand and then sat up, nearly toppling the hammock. "I've got to go and take care of something down at the warehouse."

"When?"

"Now." He stood, strode toward the cabin door.

"The other guy is in the warehouse?" Millie trotted after, following him out on to The Oguina's deck.

"Yeah." Tucci held one big hand out, steadying Bersi's body as he bridged the gap between the boat and its dock slip. "It's gonna be dangerous. You should probably stay here."

"No way."

"But I need someone to guard my actual body."

"Excuses." Millie shook her head and fluttered one hand, dismissing Tucci's warning. "I'm going."

""That's right, you are." Esmeralda paced down the dock toward them. "You've got powers. All I have are two revolvers and a holdout pistol. You go and fight. I'll guard my husband's body, thank you very much."

Millie blinked. The speakeasy's proprietress carried a paisley handbag, bulging with what could only be the firearms she'd mentioned, probably some ammo too. Her mind lay open to Millie. Was that jealousy? Yes. The green-eyed monster twined itself around a fierce sort of territorial protectiveness.

"Esmeralda, you don't want to go in there." Tucci's words came out on what Millie imagined must be Bersi's original lilt. The body swap had deepened, then.

"Why not?" Esmeralda stood with one foot on the boat and the other on the dock.

"Um." Tucci twiddled Bersi's thumbs. Of course. He wouldn't want to reveal a secret like that out here in the salty open air.

"Here, allow me." Millie focused, aiming her gaze at the side of Esmeralda's head.

Her own mind brought back a memory from the diner, the first time she'd met Tucci. Had her Wisdom tried to assert itself all those weeks ago and failed because it had encountered another Wise mind? She didn't have time for that kind of woolgathering.

Pressing her consciousness forward, Millie slipped just under the surface of Esmeralda's thoughts. The woman's mind raced, running along lines that led to right and wrong conclusions. All Millie did was light a beacon at the end of the correct idea's track.

Salvatore Tucci isn't what he appears led to *his true form will surprise you.* After that, it was all downhill from there to *his body doesn't match his heart and soul.* Millie watched Esmeralda's opinions process and develop like film in a darkroom. It felt like hours but happened in seconds. And Millie got something back for her trouble. A warning.

"I get it, Chiavo. Now take your meddling out of my head." Esmeralda gazed across the span of weathered wooden planks and into Tucci's borrowed eyes. "We'll figure this out later, husband. Together."

Tucci nodded, then turned to hurry down the dock. Millie jogged to keep up with his long stride. As her foot touched land, she glanced over her shoulder, trying to sense anything from Esmeralda even though she'd gone into the boat's cabin already.

Millie would have to wait to find out. Tucci needed to hear the information his wife had conveyed silently to her, after all.

In the cabin of Jimmy's boat, Esmeralda squinted. They'd shut the lights off so she fumbled around in a drawer to the right of the door until she found a flashlight. Once on, she swept the room with the dim beam. Nothing in there matched her husband's bulk. It'd been foolish to assume it would, so Esmeralda got down to the more difficult business of finding an unconscious person she had never seen.

She found Tucci's body after checking the hammocks, nearly mistaking it for a pile of laundry. Esmeralda put down the flashlight and scooped the slumped form off the floor to set it gently in the lower hammock. Then, she got her light back and contemplated examining the true face of the man she'd married that morning.

Did it matter what he'd looked like before they met? If that was true then old photographs wouldn't pull people in like magnets with their mystery and charm. Curiosity killed the cat, though. Marrying Sal Tucci might well prove as lucky as finding the goose who laid golden eggs. Esmeralda's childhood mind always used to boggle at the foolish human characters in that story.

But she'd left the old adage about the cat incomplete. Curiosity might have killed him but satisfaction brought him back. Marital satisfaction in a business sense was all but guaranteed. What harm, then, in having a look?

"Are you really about to ruin your life, Esme?" She spoke aloud, asking the question Liam O'Connell would have if he'd been there. Those exact words had fallen from his lips like pearls before swine.

"It's the lady or the tiger again, Lee." She sighed, shaking her head. Except she knew it wasn't this time, not really. Opening the door to a life with Liam instead of one with Raul all those years ago might have put her in a worse position on the board than the one she stood in now. She'd never know which of the men she'd chosen between had been the lady and which the tiger. Stories worked that way. Life did not.

"I gotta decide one way or the other." Hand hovering over the barrel of the flashlight, Esmeralda aimed and fired.

The light revealed smooth olive skin stretched over angular cheekbones, a full mouth. Black curls framed that face like tendrils, light catching the curves until they lit up like a hundred crescent moons. Esmeralda had never been considered a beauty, at best she'd peaked at handsome a handful of years ago. The person in the hammock rivaled the Howe girl's looks. But regardless of physique, Esme knew that the sleeping beauty she beheld was no woman.

Sal Tucci was a man. Esmeralda dealt with them nearly exclusively, had to pretend at acting like one. She knew male when she saw it. The Chiavo girl had warned her and still she didn't listen. Against her own advice, she'd raised a hatchet to the golden goose, flung open that semi-barbaric king's test of doors.

Both the lady and the tiger lay behind the portal she'd chosen.

"Enough. It's fine." Esmeralda's words hovered around her like gnats, muffled in the enclosed cabin.

Instead of letting the hatchet cleave the goose's neck, she shut the flashlight off and set it down. She did not run away from the tiger or toward the lady. Instead, she closed the door on them and sat at the table facing the door with loaded firearms, prepared to defend her spouse.

Esmeralda Tucci knew a golden goose when she saw one and she was nobody's fool. She'd keep her husband and his secrets.

"Mr. Tucci—"

The girl's breathless voice told Sal more about his enhanced speed than anything he saw with his own eyes. He minced steps, letting her catch up.

"What is it?"

"Your wife." The Chiavo girl took a deep breath, then continued. "She gave a warning. About. The fuzz."

"Fuzz?" Sal blinked, then snorted. "Worst part of this job is all the slang. So, what about the fuzz?"

"They're at," she took a breath, "the Club. Don't go there."

"Makes sense why she showed up at the boat, then." Tucci grinned despite the bad news.

Walking at a brisk pace without gasping for air was the bee's knees. He could get used to this Changed thing. Tucci tried a smile on with Bersi's mouth. A kid on a bike coming down the road toward them nearly fell off when he turned around and high-tailed it back in the direction he'd come from. Sal's expression fell.

"Mr. Tucci." The Chiavo girl tugged his sleeve. "Scary teeth. No smiling."

"Yeah, okey doke." Sal kept his pace up even though it taxed the girl.

He had to get to the warehouse fast, do something about his guests before he lost them both. His feet beat along the pavement on his previously intended route through town. Changing course because of the police wasn't an option.

Whatever or whoever had protected the drinking establishment apparently wasn't immune to a simple phone call. Two squad cars sat outside the front of the Plymouth Supper Club like panthers, engines purring as they idled. All the cops stayed in their vehicles, the building locked and empty.

Bersi's Changed ears and nose told him that even Chef Etta Franklin was missing from her kitchen. Something wasn't right, but there wasn't time to check it out even though the red-haired body he inhabited provided a nearly perfect disguise.

Sal passed the diner, the aromas within failing to make this stomach growl. Hungry didn't make the list of things Bersi was. He had the idea that would change.

What had Fallon said they ate? Flesh and blood? He hoped any future hunger pangs coincided with a butcher's shop.

The main warehouse door stood crooked, wood around the lock bent and splintered from the inside out. He pulled and the hinges sagged away from the frame as the way opened. Sal headed in, lengthening his stride down the hall and to the door of room 131.

The knob hung like a head on a broken neck in the hangman's noose. The stench of death met his nose and this time, his Changed stomach growled.

"Kid, you don't wanna look at this."

"I know about Changed, their urges and their diet."

"You got all that just with your Mind tricks?"

"Yeah." The girl didn't look at him so he thought she must be lying. He didn't care.

"Well I'm the adult here." Sal shook his head. "You ain't coming in. I gotta clean up and need you to keep watch in case the survivor comes back."

"Survivor?"

"Yeah, I had two um, guests in here. One got out and the other didn't make it."

"Fine, I'll go back to the main entrance once you're in there."

"I don't even know what we'll see when I open this but it's either a hit man or a kid like you, dead." His nostrils flared and he bared his teeth. "And this body is starving. Are you sure?"

"I'm positive, yeah." The girl stared up at him. "I know what Changed eat."

Sal nodded and pulled on the door. The lifeless body

of Eric Kovach lay sideways across both cots. The girl gasped then stifled a sob but he wouldn't have heard it without the Changed ears. Stoic, more so than her brother. He didn't share her sadness for Esmeralda's late head waiter, all he felt was hunger.

Salvatore Tucci crossed the threshold and the distance to the corpse in two steps. Forgetting the door, he bent his head and sank his borrowed teeth into the soft flesh of the poor kid's belly. The last thing he heard before tuning out to let the Changed instincts take over completely was that door behind him closing gently.

After he finished, Sal left the empty room behind. Not even a strand of hair or fragment of bone remained as proof of Eric Kovach's existence. When he emerged from room 131, the Chiavo girl wouldn't so much as look at him but he noted her puffy and downcast eyes. Something had its hooks in her, knowledge that disturbed her far more than his last meal.

"It's going down at Saint John's, in the cemetery." The girl pointed, then started walking. "Everyone's already there. Hurry, or we'll be too late."

He had no idea how his memory of an incident at Saint John's cleared brighter than the moon emerging from behind clouds. A middle-aged man stood there, index finger to his temple, his face a combination of Bill's and his sister's. Shaking his head didn't banish the memories and more came back to distract him. At least his feet kept moving.

Sal let the Chiavo girl lead the way.

When Bill saw the police outside the Supper club, he led the others around the block and decided to head for the diner. He figured Tucci would set himself up someplace familiar and that's where he'd always found the man before.

Plymouth's streets, even the main ones, had barely any foot traffic. The diner stood dark and empty, the closed sign hanging crooked as an old man in the window. Nothing opened on Christmas Day, except the churches and, of course, the Supper Club which stayed closed until well after dark anyway.

"Why are we going to the diner, Bill?"

Bill waited until they got into the alley next to the diner before answering.

"It's just a place to get our bearings."

"Yours, you mean." Gilbert leaned against the wall by the diner's door. "My bearings say we ought to go home. Let the Irish have their way."

"How can you say that after how Finn used my sister?" Theo's hands clenched and the air around them got a few degrees warmer.

"Save it for later, Theo." Bill shook his head. "Gil, that was low. Quit it."

"Oh yeah, I'm supposed to rein my personality in because you say so, clueless leader." Gil rolled his eyes.

"Can you two just shut your mouths so I can get a read on where these Boston guys are already?" Bill closed his eyes, casting his mind's ears out around him like a fishing net.

In an apartment across the street, a woman's mind prayed a silent litany of hopes for the coming year. Bill moved on. Behind the library, a man walked, out on a smoking break from his extended family's holiday visit. Muffled minds congregated inside the Old Colony Club, all male and all expressing holiday cheer as comforting as mother's milk.

"You find them yet?"

"Shh, Gilbert."

Casting his mind toward Saint John's caught Bill the right fish. He opened his eyes and started walking, waving a hand to beckon his allies. If he spoke now he might lose his tenuous connection to the mind of a man named O'Connell and his fear for Ms. Cavalcante's safety. His memories of her whirled in a kaleidoscope of delicate friendship, bittersweet love, and finally brittle enmity.

Bill would have drank to that.

"Stop," Theo's arm blocked him at chest level.

In Bill's mind-reading reverie, he'd nearly walked straight into Finn and friends' line of sight. The Irish held a position at the center of the cemetery in a complex of mausoleums, facing the gate at the street side. Blinking, Bill broke his connection with O'Connell. He searched the wrought-iron fencing for the section he'd hopped over the summer, when he'd sneak out of the house at night to think.

The dead's minds lay silent after all, unable to disturb Bill's own thoughts. Because of this, the cluster of consciousness made by Finn and his men shone out like the beacon at the top of a lighthouse, a warning to stay away. But Bill would do no such thing.

"Over there." Bill pointed, then led his allies along until they reached the right spot. "Don't go over yet. Gil, get a read on the plants and find us a spot with cover in relation to the crypts in the middle."

"Yeah, okay." Gilbert reached out, taking one leaf from a vast network of ivy between his fingers like other men might take a lady's hand. He bent over it, murmuring.

Bill used to watch his friend's vegetative communion with rapt attention but all of his interest had dried up since that afternoon. Gilbert's treatment of Sarah had blown open a door, revealing aspects of his personality that Bill could no longer abide. He left the shattered pieces of his heart alone when Gil pointed to a section of tall monuments. The trio hopped the fence and made for the limited shelter the monoliths provided, crouching as they went. He checked Irish heads and found that his guys hadn't been detected. So far so good.

He had more work to do because they couldn't fight Finn's men alone. He cast his thoughts out like fishing lines, managing to hook Fallon and Delaqua. Their mundane minds revealed flashes of the heat they'd managed to pack. He beckoned Howard Fallon to the cemetery, giving him pictures of the fence and the monolithic cover.

Contact with Jimmy reminded him about the broken ankle so he directed the rumrunner to wait in a car nearby in case they needed a getaway. He knew it'd take Jimmy a while to get to the Supper Club's delivery truck but once he did the drive was short.

When Bill reached Esmeralda, he got an image of her aboard The Oguina. She'd taken up a defensive position and her thoughts and feelings reminded him of a she-wolf defending its den. He let her be, leaving behind a flash of gratitude for her decision to guard her husband's body.

Bill walled the trio of mundanes out and searched for his remaining allies in the other direction. He sensed Millie, wearing herself out as she followed Tucci toward the warehouse. Except he wasn't as Bill remembered him. Salvatore walked along in a tall, solid body which wasn't quite human. Changed was what Fallon called them, the monsters with teeth like spikes.

He felt the alarm in Sal's borrowed head when he saw the damaged door outside and then in the hall. Millie's mind reached grief like a pinnacle, revealing a brief flash of Eric's lifeless body before plunging to the depths of horror.

Grasping at the straws of Tucci's consciousness, Bill understood that he'd done something to insulate his psyche from Bersi's changed instincts compelling him to devour the body. But when Sal came back from that, he brought something new with him.

Howard Fallon and Jimmy Delaqua might have fought, fraternized, and otherwise dealt with Changed before. Millie might have read a book penned by one of them. But none of them understood what Bill had just discovered. The Changed mind held memories like the pages of books held ink. Indelible, eternal, and complete only just barely described how their capacity for recall worked.

Tucci had stepped into one of their bodies, expecting strength and invulnerability. He'd bitten off more than he could chew, unable to see the present clearly with his history's specters playing out like newsreels in his mind. The Changed physiology went to work inscribing Sal's past. He'd be stuck in a reverie for hours if someone didn't stop it. He had to act fast.

They needed Tucci sharp, armed for battle. He was supposed to be the bomb they'd brought to the gun fight, not a knife at same. Bill meddled, ignoring the details in Salvatore's memories, walling them off as he did inside his own head. The barriers were straw houses, built temporary on purpose so Bill wouldn't have to pay for them with years of his life. Any wolf could come and blow them down, so Bill would have to devote some of his attention to keeping Tucci functional for the entire battle. He'd need help.

"Millie, I need you to run communication once you get here," Bill pitched the thought directly at his sister's mind. He felt her catch it.

"You're letting a little old me run your battle tactics?"

"Not letting. And you're not little, Mil. You're bold and fierce and not afraid to risk it all." Bill let pride for the young woman his sister had become bloom in his heart, showed it to her. "You can do this."

"Whether I want to or not." Millie's thought came with the image of wide planed under open sky. "I'm an explorer, not a fighter. But no expedition can go boldly into the unknown until everyone at home is safe. I'll help you with this Mafia stuff, just this once."

Bill waited, ready to confront Uncle Finn and his upstarts as soon as his forces assembled. But Finn's preparations were decades in the making. What chance did Bill and his group have against that?

Finn Mullins already knew the kids hid on the other side of the graveyard from him. He didn't have Donahue open fire because he hated all that noise. Jack Houlihan's way was silent as the grave. Literally.

Mounds of earth and splintered boards made too big a mess back in 1922. Finn smiled at the recently opened chambers in the mausoleum complex. The benefit of preparation pleased him.

"Cat got your tongue, O'Connell?"

"This ain't natural, Mullins."

"Neither are those dago lovers out there."

"One of them's your nephew." O'Connell held a hankie to his nose. Finn knew from experience that wouldn't block the stench.

"You got a problem with that?"

"You know I don't."

"Good."

A rustle like autumn leaves came from the narrow

slots in the walls. Houlihan's chuckle burbled like an ice-choked creek.

"They're here." Houlihan stepped out of the archway between the living and the dead.

He held his hands out at waist height, fingers poised like a puppeteer about to put on a marionette show. Finn narrowed his eyes when he noticed the rivulets of sweat on Jack's brow. Out of practice didn't begin to describe the state of his powers. Finn had warned him this day would come, recently, too. Of course, being stuck in a rest home probably hadn't afforded him much opportunity to exert his Necromantic Wisdom. Finn supposed he couldn't fault his associate for that, but Fallon would pay for putting a talent like Jack's in harm's way.

"Don't worry, Miss Franklin." Finn smiled at the Plymouth Supper Club's head chef. "Your long-lost lover will come to rescue you, though of course he'll fail.

The ebony-skinned woman emitted a string of muffled responses from behind the rag in her mouth. Etta Franklin's chin jutted forward in the only act of defiance she could muster with her hands and feet bound. Finn admired her spirit as well as her culinary talents and he regretted her imminent demise.

"Curse me as much as you like, it will all be over soon."

Houlihan's undead minions stepped forward, hair unkempt as underbrush. Eyes stared like blank slates and mouths hung open, askew where worms had eaten away at tendons. All twelve of them ambled along until they reached the edge of the paving stones that marked the edge of their family's plot.

After that, Houlihan dropped his hands, turning them and all Hell loose on the kids across the lawn.

Bill Chiavo listened for minds, trying to anticipate an attack. At first, he though he heard nothing because building straw walls in Tucci's mind distracted him. But he was wrong.

A stream of curses, harsh with unshed tears, assaulted his head like a hailstorm. They dried up, replaced by a maelstrom of dread. Images of walking corpses flashed through Bill's mind in a panicked slideshow. The woman who'd sent them mourned, for herself and for a man he immediately recognized as a younger version of Jimmy's friend, Howard Fallon.

"Theo, I need you."

"I'm sure he's flattered, Bill, but—"

"Where?" Theo's staid tone cut through Gilbert's attempted barb like a hot knife through butter.

"You need to burn the walking dead."

"Um." Theo blinked. "What?"

"Finn has some kind of necromancer over there."

"I guess he knows how to put the fun in funeral." Gilbert winked. "The Finn, too."

"Eww." Theo waved his hand. Bill felt the temperature rise. "On it."

Peeking out from around his monolith, Theodore Webster pointed a finger then withdrew it.

"They're running, Bill." He shuddered. "How are they running?"

Bill had no idea. He didn't bother having a look for himself, either. Mind Wisdom gave him an unadulterated view of Theo's terror.

"Gil, trip them up."

"Roger Dodger." Gilbert curled his fingers into a tangle of ivy at the foot of his monolith and winked. When his eye opened again, it gave Bill a window into the section of Gilbert's mind that communed with the plants.

Bill saw human figures, scuttling across the lawn and over graves. They came in a noiseless headlong rush, like an angry mob in a silent film with no soundtrack. Bill wasn't sure how many of the unliving threatened them, only that they were grossly outnumbered.

Growth surged through the ivy as though days of midsummer light and rain nourished it. The vines surged forward, casting swift roots beneath them like a centipede's legs. They wrapped around ankles to trip and wrists to hinder, finding purchase in decayed flesh that had been denied them behind marble walls.

"Any time, Theo."

"Right."

The Fire Wise stood and turned to step out from behind the obelisk. His arms stretched out as though in mockery of the oncoming undead. He held matches, struck one against the box to bring forth a baby flame. Bill knew Theo only felt grim determination as he stoked pent-up rage. Gilbert Edgewood was the fuel on his fire, though he directed all the fury he could muster at the little flame.

Well-fed, the tiny light rolled like thunder, roaring through the night air until it struck the first dead thing in the face. It went down without a sound and Bill shuddered. He couldn't sense these attackers at all and it unnerved him. Even after just a few weeks, he'd come to rely on his Wisdom for warnings but his power meant nothing against these creatures.

Theo lit another match, prepared for a second blast but he had to step back before it burst forth.

Donahue had opened fire.

Salvatore Tucci wasn't sure what stopped the onslaught of memories but he thanked God for the relief. He ran, putting on as much speed as his borrowed Changed body would allow, leaving the Chiavo girl in the dust. He'd caught the scent of long-decayed flesh and thanks to that trip down memory lane, he understood what that meant.

The dead walked in Plymouth once again.

By the time he reached the wrought-iron fence, Sal heard rustling leaves and shortly after, the heat of a controlled inferno. Munitions oil was the next thing he scented, along with the ratchet and clank of a deadly mechanism about to trigger a deadly rain of gunfire.

But bullets couldn't pierce a Changed hide.

Salvatore leapt out into the space between the dead and the living. If he hadn't, Theodore Webster would have been blown to crispy bits. He let rage take him, magnified by the fact that the commander behind the attack on these good kids was one of their own.

Pushing past the dead walkers, Tucci knocked a few down in the process. They paid him no mind in any event and Sal thought he knew why. Their faces and reaching hands spoke of a hunger he'd come to know recently, one that his Changed flesh wouldn't sate.

Someone had to stop the damned Necromantic Wise who'd killed his dad or none of the kids would make it to the mausoleum. It was no man's land out in the cemetery. But Tucci in Bersi's body wasn't a mere man anymore.

"I'm coming for you, Houlihan!"

His voice drowned in another hail of bullets. They buzzed past him, the muzzle flash from the tommy gun dazzling his eyes just enough to annoy him. Salvatore Tucci threw his head back and laughed. Somewhere at the border between land and sea, shrouded in the body of a comatose girl, Bersi Olafsson approved.

Gilbert hadn't met the graveyard ivy before but he had plenty of experience with *Hedera helix* in his own yard and greenhouse. Encouraging the plants toward their invasive tendencies sent little thrills of potential through his body and mind. Usually, his work with the evergreen plant involved hindering its progress instead of advancing it.

Once unleashed, the ivy's momentum grew like any other object in motion. The best part of this was, it cost Gil nothing in terms of his Wisdom's drawback. Only making growth from dead plants cost him memories and that was impossible here in the well-tended graveyard.

Gilbert Edgewood hadn't been more wrong in his short life.

Theo's fire was no threat to the ivy. Gilbert's skill and alacrity commanding the vines meant he had no trouble keeping them out of harm's way. His communion with the plants let him see and feel the fire in time. So when they started shriveling from the root up, he had no idea why or what to do about it.

Each time a root died, Gilbert had to pull his control from it and search for another. This served until the red-haired giant showed up, rampaging through the tommy gun's deadly rain. What was his name again? Gilbert couldn't recall and he didn't think it mattered at that point anyway.

The bullet rain turned away and Gilbert counted four screams that choked off one by one. The open-fire stopped, the gun's mechanism silenced in a death-cry of metal that groaned as it twisted in the inexplicably strong hands of the ginger monster. The firearm's operator fled through the cemetery and the monster pursued. Gilbert took the chance to focus his perspective through the vines on top of the mausoleum and felt a hand, cold and deadly.

The man it belonged to chuckled as the ivy tendril Gilbert controlled withered and died. He stayed with it through its death throes, forgetting why he shouldn't.

That lopsided man was sucking the life-force from his plants. No Wood Wise could abide such harm coming to their charges. He'd kill to stop the assault on the plants and his own connected mind. Gilbert had one shot to end the man sending power to the undead attackers and he took it.

A strangling cry flew from Gil's mouth as he forced the dead vine to surge forward like a striking snake, piercing the man's left leg at the femoral artery. But something was wrong. That leg had no life in it, no blood either. It was as dead as the wood.

And then, Gilbert stopped, his hands dropping from the arrow-shaped leaves he'd held between his thumbs and forefingers.

"What am I doing here?" Gil shook his head.

He'd just put on his coat and hat to tend the root cellar at the Howe farm on Thanksgiving morning. So why was he out with Bill and Theodore in the cemetery after dark?

Gilbert Edgewood couldn't remember a damn thing.

Bill Chiavo watched through Liam O'Connell's eyes as Tucci bent the tommy gun with Bersi's bare hands and sideswiped Donahue across the chest with it. The gun's former operator toppled with a strangled shriek. Tucci leaned over him and the screams cut off.

Finn Mullins sneered at a dark skinned woman who sat bound and gagged across the marble from the lopsided man by the crypts. When Gilbert's dead vines pierced that man's leg, Bill expected him to topple.

Instead, Bill watched the man laugh through O'Connell's eyes and felt Gilbert let go of the plants beside him. The ivy dropped, crunching under dead and silent feet. Theo lit more matches and called more flames but Bill felt the Fire Wise's fatigue setting in.

His center let go, failing to hold. The Yeats poem haunted Bill as all of his plans fell apart. Even with Tucci in the borrowed juggernaut's body, they were going to lose this battle and the war, exactly as Uncle Finn had intended.

And then he felt three minds, their arrival inspiring hope in his mind like a sunrise. Millie, Rachel, and Fallon hopped the fence behind him. His cavalry had arrived. Now he just had to direct them.

But Bill Chiavo sagged with exhaustion. He couldn't issue orders and shield Tucci's memory from that borrowed body's total recall at the same time. He'd have to let the blood-dimmed tide take Salvatore for a few moments. He could only hope he hadn't doomed them all with that decision.

"Kid." A hefty hand shook Bill's right shoulder. "Snap out of it."

Bill stared at the scarred and callused hand, trying to remember where he'd seen it before. But not enough of his mental capacity remained to sort it out and he couldn't. He blinked up into the weathered face of a man with salt and pepper hair and a map of frowns across his forehead and along his cheeks.

"Hallon?"

"Name's Howard Fallon, but you call me whatever you want as long as you're giving me directions on what to do out there." He waved one hand at the graveyard where the shambling horde appeared to be winning.

"Fire." Bill thought he'd spoken aloud instead of just in his head at Theo.

"Jeez Bill, I'm out of matches." Theo leaned against a gravestone.

"Here, take this." Howard tossed him a small leather case.

Theodore opened it and removed a metal instant lighter with a can of Thorens Fluid.

"You're a life saver, you know that?" Theo hefted the lighter and put the fluid in his back pocket, then went back to work shooting fire at the walking corpses. Too bad about his lousy aim.

"Anything else I can do for you?"

"Tucci," Bill managed.

"Oh yeah." Howard rubbed the back of his head with one hand. "It's the memory fugue. All the Changed have to deal with it."

"Ugh."

"Yeah. Needs something to bust through it." Howard tapped Bill's foot with the toe of one scuffed gumshoe. "You're at the end of your rope, huh?"

Bill could only nod and mop at his brow with one sleeve.

Don't worry, Bill. You big sister's here to pick up your slack.

"Mil—" Bill blinked and rubbed his eyes. "Mill—"

"Million!" Gilbert lifted his head up off the grass

where he'd fallen when the ivy died. He looked right at Bill. "And Billion!" He reached toward Bill, nearly falling on his face but ending up on his elbows instead. "I haven't seen you in a brace of weeks."

"Oh Gil." Millie reached down and righted Gilbert. Then, she hunkered down beside Bill. "I told you both not to get mixed up in all of this business."

"Stop rubbing their noses in it and help." Howard Fallon put his hands on his hips, looking down his nose at Millie.

"Already on it, Mr. F."

"Oh no. You don't call me Mr. F. like I'm a—"

But Bill couldn't make out the rest of Howard's words. He was too focused on the conversation going on inside his own head.

35

You're a mess, Bill.

I know. So help, already.

What do you need?

A boost from Rachel. Tell Theo to keep firing. Tell Fallon to flank them and do a sneak attack. I'll get Tucci back in play.

What about Gil?

I don't care.

Bill's weariness threatened to crush Millie like a ten ton weight. She coaxed him like she used to do when he wouldn't come out of his room as a tiny tot. Her brother didn't answer with words, spoken or otherwise. Instead, he showed her how Gilbert had acted earlier, with Sarah. Millie recoiled, sending an image of herself shaking with her fists clenched.

When this is over, he's getting a piece of my mind.

Okay, Mil. But for now let's get to work.

Millie sent Bill's strategic decisions to the right people. She relayed the message to Rachel without really knowing what Bill meant by a boost. But after she sat at his side, Millie got the picture. Literally. Rachel had partial Wisdom, some way to amplify for others, like the microphone sang into at the Supper Club. Bill stopped all the sagging and flagging.

Tucci roared and sprang back into action, tearing limbs and heads from the undead advancing on his allies' position. Fallon snuck well for such a large fellow but Millie supposed that if he hadn't mastered that skill, some monster would have killed him ages ago and he wouldn't be here to help them.

Theo ducked back behind the monolith, then refilled his lighter with the can of fluid from his pocket. His face looked drawn, dark hollows under his eyes. He stepped back out from his cover but came back almost immediately, hissing with one hand over his leg.

"Shot," he growled. But inside his head, Theodore screamed like a banshee. The hand with the lighter shook like a tambourine.

Millie let her hands work, unwinding her scarf to tie it around Theo's leg. Pulling tightly made him stagger, lose balance.

You're not walking out there, Theo. Only as far as you have something to lean on. And stay low. You're taller than the dead folk.

Theo sent her an affirmative. She turned her mind to the areas outside the graveyard, casting out a net to sense other minds, people who shouldn't get too close to a dangerous conflict like this.

She counted two.

The first didn't trouble or surprise Millie. Giuseppe Chiavo had heard all of the Mind Wise commotion. With both of his children involved, of course he'd come to see what transpired. But Millie assured herself that he'd only get here after all the gunfire and zombies had ceased. Old men, even the ones who'd only lived for thirty some odd years, moved much slower than this fight.

The second might prove to be a problem. Father John watched the whole messy battle from his window at the Rectory. All of the noise must have woken him and of course he'd want to get a peek. What surprised Millie was the fact that the Father watched without even a thought to lift the phone and call the police.

She wanted to try sifting through his mind but had to save that for later. If he wasn't reporting or interfering, Millie would leave Father John alone. He'd know exactly what all of the cryptic references in their next confessions meant, though.

That left her with one other task. Jimmy Delaqua sat in Esmeralda Cavalcante's delivery truck, keys in the ignition, revolver under a hat on the seat beside him. She gave him directions to park on the other side of the cemetery along with an order to stop any of Finn's guys leaving the scene. She gave him a clear picture of aiming for the knees, then had to withdraw from his mind as he began the excruciating process of engaging the vehicle's clutch with a broken ankle.

Millie Chiavo didn't have time for other people's damage. She had her own to make and manage.

Howard Fallon didn't have time to wait for Tucci to snap out of the Changed fugue. Instead, he clung to the shadows at the edges of the cemetery, skirting the lantern-lit central mausoleum cluster without worrying about the zombies set loose on the grounds.

He'd done this sort of thing in graveyards before but not with such a blatant distraction or against human opponents. Maybe human was too soft a term to apply to people who desecrated graves and raised the dead as a battle tactic. Howard shook off the impulse to label his enemies in favor of continuing to move against them instead.

Making his way to the furthest-flung tomb, Howard sighted along its rear wall, then decided to advance his position. A bushy cypress tree provided cover and a partial view of the enemy camp. After he'd spotted his opponents, Howard froze. One of Finn's allies was his old pal, Jack.

His jaw dropped as he stared at the big man with his hands in an open crypt. He and Jack Houlihan went way back. Once upon a time, Jack wanted to marry Howard's sister Pearl, even though she didn't believe that institution was her thing. She'd parted ways with the family and when Jack pursued her years later, she'd parted him from his legs.

All the same, there Jack stood. On feet with mismatched shoes attached to legs of different lengths. Howard's brain made connections he'd never considered possible before. But he'd recently been reminded that one of his greatest strengths was mental flexibility. His thoughts did gymnastics, flipping over implausibilities until it landed on the truth.

Jack Houlihan had Wisdom that let him reanimate the dead and, according to Esmeralda's stories, was involved in both the conflict that had established the

Plymouth Supper Club and the one where Raul Cavalcante met his demise.

Being a quick study, Howard remembered Bill mentioning how each type of Wisdom had a cost or drawback. He'd seen the state Gilbert, Bill, and Theo were in when he arrived with Millie. But Jack seemed to suffer no such affliction though his undead minions still rampaged through the other side of the graveyard. So what was his weakness?

Howard didn't have to wait long for the answer to this mystery. Jack reached out with one hand, directing it at something or someone on the other side of the cypress tree. The whimper that followed sounded unquestionably human. Jack stood straighter after he withdrew his hand, leaning against the open crypt like a man who'd just finished a satisfying meal.

Peering through the branches, Howard caught a glimpse of a floral dress with a Peter Pan collar and the neck strap from a white apron. Dark skin emerged from that collar, compelling him to move more fronds for a better view. What he saw inspired a growl in his throat that would have put an alpha wolf's to shame. Jack was using a living person to fuel his zombies, someone both of them had known since their school days.

He hadn't seen Etta Franklin since he'd left to find Pearl when they were seventeen. Fifteen years hadn't diminished her beauty one bit, or his affection for her.

"Check out that noise, O'Connell." Finn Mullins' voice cut the growl off. His hand hovered near the switch on what could only be an explosive device.

Howard waited, ready to pull out all the stops. The

old monster hunter had never killed a human before but he'd start with Finn Mullins' crew. They'd crossed the one line in the sand Howard would defend to his last breath; hurting someone he loved.

All bets were off.

Rachel's arrival felt like a sunrise, lifting the dark exhaustion that had nearly run Bill into the ground. With her help, he went to work on Tucci's mind, this time applying houses of sticks around his invading memories. Once their juggernaut had his senses back, Bill tagged Millie in to watch and maintain the structures as needed, then turned his attention to the minds behind enemy lines.

Two of those psyches stayed closed to him, assured satisfaction and grim glee the main distinction between Uncle Finn and whatever twisted Wise talent he'd enlisted to raise the dead. Three other minds lay like open landscapes before him. He identified Howard by his furtive curiosity and O'Connell by his righteous reluctance. The third mind belonged to a woman he'd met before.

Rosetta Franklin's terror lay as silent and buried as the corpses on the other side of the graveyard. It was pain and anger that thrust up from her mind's surface, nearly palpable from Bill's perspective. Stretching his thoughts toward her, Bill focused on countering it. The most comforting image he found in her mind was of her at a lakeside picnic with a youthful version of Howard Fallon.

When he touched her pain, he sent it back below the level of consciousness. Her anger surged forward and it had a direction which she named; Jack Houlihan. The man had been draining her life force to fuel his necromancy, a talent he'd managed to hide all the years she'd known him back west in Worcester. She couldn't act against him, of course, but Bill comforted himself with the knowledge that she wouldn't feel physical pain for a while.

He couldn't break into Jack's head to stop him, or Uncle Finn's either. So it was up to O'Connell. When he homed in on the reluctant Mobster, Bill found a treasure-trove of information. Liam O'Connell's fate was in Bill Chiavo's hands, weighed and measured without the Irishman's knowledge or consent.

He'd gotten wind of Finn's plan months ago, tipped Esmeralda off. It was because of O'Connell downplaying Plymouth's value that the guys in Boston only sent six of their least adept men. Liam also had three young kids at home, his wife a good Catholic girl fresh off the boat five years ago. He didn't love the woman he'd married but he loved his kids more than anything in the world. Bill understood that. One other thing, Liam thought this entire operation was nuttier than a year-old fruitcake and twice as unwanted.

Wouldn't you like to stop all this madness, Liam?

Who are you and how do you know my name?

It doesn't matter. Just let me help you put an end to this.

It matters. You got two choices. Tell me or I conk myself in the noggin so you have to get out of my head.

I work for Esmeralda Cavalcante and all we want to do is keep the status quo here. I can get you out of this mess.

You're the Chiavo kid then. This situation's impossible. Let me show you the lay of the land and then if you can work this, I'll owe you twenty greenbacks.

The entire area at the center of the cemetery revealed itself to Bill. He saw through Liam's eyes but also picked up on his hearing. Houlihan had just finished reanimating another corpse. But that wasn't the real threat.

Finn shouted out insults in the general direction of Bill's friends. They'd think that was the last trick he had up his sleeve, to try and get them to hurl back an insult so he could See something. It was a ruse. His hand rested on a switch box, connected to a wire at the bottom. Liam let a final piece of information drop. That wire went all the way across the graveyard, to the position Bill himself had chosen for his friends earlier. Three bundles of dynamite, one for each obelisk, sat hidden in the floral arrangements at their bases.

You see what I mean, kid. Ain't time to go after Houlihan. If I go after Mullins, Houlihan hits me with his dead things. That wire's already hot so cutting or shooting it's likely to blow your guys to Kingdom Come. It's impossible.

No, it's not. You've been a Godsend, Mr. O'Connell. I won't forget it.

Bill sent a message to Theo, hoping the Fire Wise still had the strength to put a big chill on Finn's fireworks.

Just before leaving Liam's mind, Bill heard him answer an order from Finn with a definitive no. He gave the Irishman a mental thumbs-up, then skipped back to check on Tucci's head.

Theodore Webster got Bill's message. Gritting his teeth at the sickening throb in his thigh, he looked around. With Rachel and Bill occupied, he turned to Millie. She met his eyes for a moment, then turned away, staring out across the graveyard at the burly red-haired monster.

He hadn't expected love from his fiancee but a little support, moral or otherwise, would have been nice. Sarah's unconditional affection had spoiled him, though it was sisterly. Right then. Theo was on his own.

Finding the first dynamite bundle was easy. Once he touched the wire, he followed the potential heat energy along that until he located the other two and the switch box. Theo wouldn't have to get to all three explosive devices, at least. The hard part was going to be conjuring up cold.

Back in his practice sessions with Mom and Mr. Chiavo, he'd tried thinking cold thoughts. But with the low ambient temperature, that wasn't going to cut it. Theodore knew a mere degree or two below freezing wouldn't break a hot wire safely. He might need permafrost, iceberg, or possibly Antarctic levels of cold. But he'd never touched that before.

Hoping this attempt wouldn't backfire and blow them up, Theo honed his concentration to an edge keen enough to make his blacksmithing forefathers proud. With the wire between his thumb and forefinger, he let a trickle of all the cold he could muster through from his imagination to his hand.

It wasn't enough. He'd doom them all if he couldn't deliver, but Theo wasn't sure how a guy like him who ran so hot could call up ice. Closing his eyes, he thought of all the people he'd miss after being blown to bits. Mom and Dad. Gram Howe. Most of all, Sarah. What would she say right now? He imagined her face and voice.

"If the problem won't work, try the inverse." It was Millie speaking, not Sarah, but the words could only have come from his sister, the math whiz.

"Thanks. I know what to do now."

Theodore Webster reversed his process. Instead of projecting cold, he stole heat. The wires went brittle, breaking on their own under the stress of the icy snap.

Another thread finished joining the tapestry.

"No." O'Connell put his hands on his hips, defying Finn's order. Howard still gripped the revolver in one hand and his dagger in the other, waiting to see if this conflict would result in enough infighting to cause a distraction big enough to save Etta. Even with decades dividing them, he felt more sure of his lost love than ever. Finding his sister Pearl had done that much for him, at least.

"When I give an order, you do it."

"You ain't my Boss, Mullins."

"I will be when this is done."

"When this is done, you'll be fodder in Houlihan's special ops unit."

"Hmm." Finn Mullins took a step back. "I don't like what I'm Seeing here."

Howard watched Finn's face go so pale it was almost blue, his gaze on the crypt where Houlihan stood, coaxing out another corpse. This one was different from the others. It was a lady, expensively dressed and with obvious care.

"How dare you raise my Cloris!" Two spots of red lit Finn's cheeks. He pushed down on the switch.

Houlihan covered his ears. Etta closed her eyes. O'Connell smiled.

Nothing happened.

Howard looked across the graveyard, at the obelisks that marked his allies' position.

Bersi's eyes met his. No, Howard told himself, Bersi was out to lunch. That was Salvatore Tucci.

Tucci had cut through almost all of the walking corpses out on the field, including the guy with the tommy gun and his four buddies. His borrowed teeth glistened red with blood in the mingled lantern and moonlight.

Howard nodded, his gut telling him he could count on Tucci in battle as much as he'd trusted Bersi before. Had it really only been twenty-four hours since that last one? Howard would be lucky to escape his second fight in as many days unscathed.

Tucci jerked Bersi's chin at Finn. Howard shook his head and designated Jack as Tucci's target instead.

After that, they set out to meet in the middle.

Tucci advanced, tearing the arm off one of the undead to use as a club. Silent and inevitable, Jack's minions had a weakness; imbalance. The last three fell like dominoes, getting back up for one last round. They couldn't take more than two hits and Tucci in the Changed body made short work of them.

Howard moved as quickly as he could for a scarred and battered man pushing forty. He skirted O'Connell, sparing him because he'd stood up to Finn. Howard admired that. After all, he'd recently been there and done that with Bianco.

When he reached the Wise ringleader, Howard raised his dagger, prepared to take a human life for the first time. He'd started hunting to put down masterminds whose agendas called for high body counts. What's one more?

The similarity to the newly Feral Oguina's last coherent words haunted him and he hesitated, pushing another question to take its place. How was it possible to get one over on a man who'd plotted and planned this day for as long as Howard had been hunting monsters?

It wasn't.

Howard Fallon's gut churned out a warning not to engage Finn Mullins only seconds before the sawed-off hit him with both barrels. The kick sent him hurtling back across almost all the ground he'd covered. Howard came to rest beside the cypress tree that had so lately given him shelter.

He went down but before going out he watched as O'Connell fled, leaving down the path that led to the main gate. After that, Howard saw his Etta with a little old man at her side, cutting the ropes from her wrists. She reached for him, pulled his head into her lap, and sat with her hands cooling his brow and cheeks as she used to in their stolen moments years ago. He gazed at her until he knew no more.

"You know what they say about the best laid plans, Finnegan." Giuseppe Chiavo brushed strands of cut threads off his hands. He'd taken the time to read all the minds in the cemetery, Wise, human, and Changed. Living, unconscious, and undead. For once, he had some idea of what Seeing future events was like. It gave Finn no reasonable excuse for his behavior.

"You got me. This time." Finn Mullins turned the empty sawed-off shotgun, brandishing its butt at his old enemy. "But there's no next time for you, filthy dago."

"Oh, Finnegan. If only you'd made your true feelings known years ago, perhaps we could have avoided this whole mess." Giuseppe stood where he was, prepared to take the blow if his unlikely ally changed her mind at the last minute.

She didn't.

"I died for you, Finn, and this is how you repay me?" Cloris Mullins' wormy arms snaked around her husband's waist, her hands clamping around his wrists in a vise grip.

"What? Cloris, I can explain." Finn struggled in his dead wife's grasp but it was no use.

"You'll do no explaining, only joining. With me in death, that is. Maybe then we can finally have peace." Cloris's rotting mouth made her words less than coherent but Giuseppe's pathway into her mind meant he understood every word.

"No way." Jack Houlihan backed away from his Boss, directly into the Changed body inhabited by Salvatore Tucci.

"Way," said Tucci. He put his hands on Jack's shoulders.

"Heh." Jack shrugged, knocking Tucci's borrowed hands off. "Never bring a monster to a Wise fight."

Tucci dropped to one knee as though commanded by some unseen force. Jack whipped out a revolver and fired two rounds which rattled that big, red head, then took off. Jack Houlihan had gotten what he wanted. Escape.

"Hold him for me, Cloris." Giuseppe took a few shuffling steps forward, hoping he'd saved enough energy for this last task. Raising his arm, he cupped Finn Mullins' face in his hands. Unless he did this, Bill would end up like him. If only he could manage, Giuseppe could save his son fifty years. Sixty if he was lucky.

Dad, no! Wait and I'll do it!

Father! You can't!

Giuseppe knew that Cloris couldn't hold her husband for long. Even if the Necromantic Wise hadn't fled, tendons and ligaments that long dead had to let go sometime. Last time, Giuseppe hadn't acted fast enough but he had learned much since then. Finn might have prepared for the dark heat of battle, but Giuseppe made his elsewhere; with learning, light, and love.

Bill, don't let your heart go cold. You are capable of joy and you will find it someday. Remember that, when we mend ourselves, we're stronger at the broken places. Millie, no knight worth her salt has shining armor. Fighting blurs lines and warriors risk falling on the wrong side from time to time. Never let that make you give up. I love you both.

This time, Giuseppe would stop Finn Mullins for good, even if it meant his own demise. When he kissed his brother-in-law on both cheeks it was in parting as decades of memory starting at childhood vanished out of Finn's head. His children called out for him with their throats, bright, high pitches reminding him of the years before they went to school.

Their mingled voices were the last thing he heard in this world.

Bill got to the mausoleum first, dropping Theo's arm to race past Millie. He couldn't let her take this one on the chin, wouldn't risk losing her right after Dad. He barely even bothered taking in the mess around him, didn't have to. He'd do damage control later, for now he had to fix this mess he'd made by thinking he could take on his uncle with a band of inexperienced Wise.

Finn pushed Giuseppe toward Bill, the old man's body dropping like a cicada's husk falling off a tree. Bill ignored it and went straight for his uncle, tackling him like this was a football game and not a battle to the death.

"Nice trick, little shaver, sending that guy I'd never met at me. What was he, some greasy dago hitman?"

"Irish, actually. His name was Fallon."

"Well, it worked. I wasted both the barrels with your dad's name on them for your guy. But I got the dried up old fool in the end, didn't I?"

"Shut up, Uncle."

"Make me."

Of course, that was the idea. Now that Finn knew he was beaten, he'd take anyone he could with him.

Bill didn't care. He understood his father's sacrifice

now and years ago. His son would follow that example. He leaned down and gave his uncle a kiss on each cheek just like Giuseppe had, pulling Finn's memories out until the Sight Wise forgot everything including how to speak. The process reminded Bill of how a wolf might unspool intestines from a goat. The ancient Romans had used those as signs of portent, things to come. And for just a moment, like his early forbears, Bill Saw everything.

His parents had all this in mind all along. They'd known what actions to take in order to get this outcome and it was the only one in which both twins survived. His own mother had called the police to the Supper Club, just to make them too busy to investigate the graveyard. Katherine had even Seen Sarah's part in this and let her perform her own shepherding of destiny.

Bill shook the Sight off early even though he knew it was only temporary. The police wouldn't stay away forever and there were things he needed to do. He got up, knees popping to remind him that he'd lost years of his life to putting Finn down.

Looking around, Bill saw Jimmy Delaqua hobbling up on a set of crutches.

"Howard, oh geez. What am I gonna tell your sister?"

"Tell her to visit him in the hospital." Etta Franklin blinked up at Jimmy, her face ashy and running with sweat despite the chill January evening. Tears, too. "If you can get him there in the next five minutes. I stopped some of the bleeding but this is a big wound and my Wisdom's only partial."

"Wait a minute. Everyone here has a super power but me?" Jimmy scratched his head. "Guess I should get used to it," he grumbled. "Anyway, Tucci can fix him up."

"Huh?" Bill blinked. "And here I thought we'd have to wake Father John for some Last Rites."

"Yeah, no. Fallon's a tough old bird. With a little Changed blood, he'll make it just fine."

Tucci stood there holding the knife Howard dropped earlier. He held the blade up in front of his face, marveling at how it had bent back when he pressed against his borrowed skin.

"How does Bersi bleed anyway?"

"You gotta use his teeth." Jimmy made a biting motion in the air.

"Oh, okay." Sal hunkered down next to Mr. Fallon. "So I just drip it in his mouth?"

"Or on the gut wound." Jimmy adjusted his weight on the crutches, wincing a little. "It works in the blood. But you have to think about him getting better, too or it'll make him crazy go nuts."

"Good to know." Tucci bit his arm and let the blood run over Howard's stomach, which had started to resemble a mound of hamburger.

Everyone watched as flesh knit together, leaving uncannily bloody holes in Howard's clothes. He moaned, turning his head from side to side in an attempt to roll over.

"Hush now, you're only healing." Etta held him close and he stilled at the sound of her voice.

Bill wondered if he'd ever cared that much someone. But even if that person existed, Bill wasn't ready. His father's last words to him had been as much warning as inspiration. He needed to get stronger at the broken places and he had to mend himself before that could happen.

"Did you stop him, Mr. Delaqua?" Millie walked around the perimeter of what had been Finn's base in the battle.

"Stop who?"

"Houlihan, the guy controlling the zombies. He ran off."

"He didn't pass by my way or I would have."

"Hmm. O'Connell's not here, so that leaves just the tommy gun guys to worry about."

"You don't have to worry about them." Sal looked everywhere but at Millie. "He's all gone."

"You gave him the Kovach treatment?"

"Yeah." Sal bowed his head. "Sorry." Millie gave him a shrug.

Bill had no idea what they'd meant but guessed it had something to do with Esmeralda's Head Waiter.

"Listen, here's our story." Bill told them all a police-friendly version of events. "We're sticking to it. Dad and Uncle Finn came here to visit some old graves and the vandalism they saw gave them both massive coronaries…"

They all heeded Bill Chiavo's advice, except Gilbert, who couldn't remember a thing since Thanksgiving.

The last light of New Year's Day vanished from the

sky and Salvatore Tucci woke up for what he hoped was the last time in another body he didn't want. He'd have to decide who to inhabit after Bersi Olafsson but it wouldn't be any Changed. The things he'd done had been powerful for sure, but Tucci always intended to be a hero. The life of a nearly invulnerable flesh-eating person carried too much temptation for someone with as much of a tendency toward gluttony as Sal possessed.

Also, Bersi wasn't Italian and couldn't pass for it in a rainstorm. In order to take up his new place as Boss of Fall River and Plymouth in person instead of on the phone, he needed to be full blood Italian. His Capo, Bill Chiavo, was a half-and-halfer, though with the forgery job Esmeralda did on church and state records, there wasn't any paper evidence of it. And Bill looked Tucci's actual age now, another obfuscation on his heritage. No one would find out.

His wife would keep her club, of course. She knew the place like the back of her hand and had such a knack for that kind of business, Sal wanted her to train all the up-and-comers he'd have running the juice joints in Fall River. Etta Franklin stayed on as Head Chef, though they needed a new Head Waiter. Tucci thought he'd never have another bite at the diner if he could help it. Etta's cooking literally had magic in the recipe.

Howard Fallon stayed on the payroll, on account of Daniel Denton's leftovers still at large. He kept Jimmy too. The man's instinct was uncanny and he had a good rapport with the Changed who used to be the Fall River Gang's enemies. He could hardly wait to meet Leo Riley and Pearl Fallon, ask them to tell him everything they knew about Bersi. Millie Chiavo wouldn't.

He'd asked her to at least visit Fall River as she began her travels but she'd declined. Providence would be her first stop and he didn't blame her. Out of all the kids, she'd lost the most and gained the least. Sarah Webster was her opposite.

The whiz kid was set up with an apartment and four years paid in full at Radcliffe, in addition to holding Mullins' Plymouth holdings in trust. She'd pulled strings better than Pietro Radillo, the man who revolutionized marionettes in Italy. Sal had an agreement to send any books that needed cooking up to her.

The Edgewood kid stayed on in his job at Cordage, coming into the Supper Club every payday to blow his cash on cigars and hooch. He sat at the bar and listened to the music but never danced.

Esmeralda kept Sal's secret. It didn't seem to bother her, though she had reminded him the night before that he had to make himself Italian again before wiseguys from Providence decided to check on the new Boss in Fall River, who was Wiser than them. But first he needed a body fitting that description in the right shape. Fortunately, the latter part was flexible thanks to Bersi's blood.

He headed out the warehouse door where the delivery truck waited with Esmeralda in the driver's seat and his original body in the back. Yesterday, they'd gone to Worcester. Today, they'd try Brockton. He'd avoid Providence and Boston unless he couldn't find a full-blood Italian anywhere else.

But Sal knew that something would fall into his lap. It

always did.

Dear Reverend Father Francis Bonaventura,

I write this today to deliver more information and advice on the curious subject of monsters and magic in our midst. I know that our Lord God put such things in His world to test us but I fear they may be reaching a dire and unstoppable limit.

It seems the Changed and the Wise have joined forces in no small way in my little Parish. Further, they've taken up the reins of power that Giacomo Bianco dropped upon his death. This alliance is both formidable and troubling. Together, they have managed to hoodwink both the lawful authorities and the rest of the criminal element.

As you know, such a merger has not occurred at any time in recorded history since the Crusades, when the Changed Orders did more than shut themselves up on a mountain with moldy tomes. If you have not read the texts detailing the Church's experience with that union, I urge you to try. It would mean a voyage to Rome, which is risky for a man at your time of life.

As an alternative, I recommend you write to Brother Sebastian. He's a man whose vigor and zeal for travel are matched only by his devotion to Mother Church. He has served as a courier for texts of this sensitive a nature before and will do so again should you mention my name in your request.

Again, I must urge you not to set aside your concerns or otherwise neglect this letter and its advice for too long. I've enclosed the best course of contact for Brother Sebastian. I pray you use it promptly.

D.R. Perry

*Respectfully Yours in Christ on this First day of January,
1930,*

368

*Father John Smith
Saint Peter's, Plymouth Massachusetts*

Thanks for reading! If you're looking to explore other worlds created by D.R. Perry, you can find them at: **www.DRPerryAuthor.com**

www.ingramcontent.com/pod-product-compliance
Lightning Source LLC
Chambersburg PA
CBHW050615170726
48283CB00001B/252